READ WHAT THE CRITICS SAY ABOUT
CHRIS MCKINNEY

The Tattoo
"...This is a book about 'the sins of the fathers', how anger and pain and patterns of destructive behavior get passed from one generation to another... McKinney has written a gritty, troubling book and he's done it well. The issues he raises are key to Hawai'i today, and for future generations.
— *The Honolulu Advertiser*

"McKinney's very first novel is thought provoking and revealing to say the least. The way this first-time novelist keeps the story moving is a credit to his skill as a writer... We highly recommend this book to those who enjoy contemporary fiction, readers who can't get enough of Hawai'i and those who just plain want stories with good character development."
— *The Dispatch*

The Queen of Tears
Renewing and revitalizing the genre of Hawai'i noir fiction, Chris McKinney tells his tales of Honolulu's lower depths with an insider's authority and the zeal of a real writer. Beyond all that rings true in McKinney's fiction, what elevates it most is the author's unexpected compassion for those at the bottom or in emotional jeopardy.
— Tom Farber, author of *A Lover's Question*

This novel begins with a memorable story of a Korean girl's achievement of self salvation in a journey on foot into a new world, which, she discovers as an adult, is confused by a series of failures in the family of her own making. *The Queen of Tears* has a fascinating lineup of characters, all presented with a brutal honesty, in a story that is rich in description and in the complexity of its plot. Great storytelling from cover to cover.

—Ian MacMillan, author of *Village of a Million Spirits* (winner of the PEN USA – WEST Fiction Award) and *The Red Wind*

What amazes me about Chris McKinney's new novel *The Queen of Tears* are the intricate psychological profiles the author paints of each of his characters; McKinney knows these people, their histories, yearnings, failures, machination and ultimately their acts of heroism both of the small and of the essential. What amazes me is McKinney's gift: his deep understanding of our cultures and subcultures, the nuances of relationships that coexist therein, his excellent prose that tells an intensely felt story with a stunning fictive music, his unflinching look at ourselves in a way that is recognizably disconcerting. What amazes me is McKinney's generosity as a writer; he allows his readers to know the characters who people *The Queen of Tears* as real. He allows us to see our families and friends both the estranged and the beloved. McKinney focuses his writer's lens on the consistencies, allegiances, pretenses, and the betrayals of the most intimate relationships in our lives, showing us how to understand and know them often in spite of themselves. Fans of *The Tattoo* will surely revel in Chris McKinney's new novel, *The Queen of Tears*.

—Lois Ann Yamanaka, author of *Father of Four Passages*

LIST OF CHARACTERS:

Charlie Keaweaimoku: A Hawaiian in his early 30's who does not surf, eat poi, dance hula, or speak a word of the language. He grew up in Honolulu, raised by a Japanese step-mother, and is an assistant manager at ABC Store #64 in Waikiki. His marriage has just ended, and he has agreed to house his step-sister who is coming out of prison. Housing drug addicts is often a bad idea . . .

Winnie: Charlie's step-sister who lives by the phrase "No worry, beef curry." Fresh out of prison, Winnie has great ambition to do what she has always done—whatever she wants to. Her drug of choice is crystal methamphetamine. She also likes to burn things.

B: Bully Ching, or "B" to those who know him, another ex-con who is Winnie's friend. He works at a lunch wagon stirring curry for a living. Though he is physically fit and has cool tattoos, he is a glaring example of why not to get into drugs and crime.

Mom: The mother of Charlie, Winnie, and Mark. Married three times and owner of a dive bar in "Bolohead Row," Mom, though a raving alcoholic, and a horrible example for her children, is really a caring mother.

Mark: Charlie and Winnie's step-brother. An ex-high school wrestler and a Kapiolani Community College dropout, Mark's drug of choice is an online computer game called "Everquest." He finds living life as Bolo Badcow in Norrath, a virtual world, with dragons, wizards, and other dorky stuff, is a far more satisfying existence than anything RL (real-life) has to offer.

Taks: Charlie's friend from high school, Jon "Taks" Takahashi, does not work. He owns a really old orange Porsche, and has spent the majority of his adulthood in bars. Walk into any bar in Honolulu and chances are he's there with his gelled hair and designer clothes hitting on girls.

Ollie: Robert "Ollie" Olivera, another of Charlie's friends from high school. He made a lot of money as a pager and cellphone salesman, being in the right industry at the right time, and retired at thirty and moved to Bangkok. He is back for vacation. There is nothing more relaxing than visiting with friends over cocktails and watching them ruin their lives.

Preschool and the Rapozo Twins: They are looking for Winnie. When guys like these are looking for you, you do not want to be found. Even though they are brutal thugs, they are nice guys once you get to know them.

The Game of Life: A board game by Milton-Bradley

BOLOHEAD ROW

OTHER BOOKS BY CHRIS MCKINNEY

The Tattoo

The Queen of Tears

BOLOHEAD ROW

CHRIS MCKINNEY

Mutual Publishing

ISBN-10: 1-56647-722-0
ISBN-13: 978-1-56647-722-2

Library of Congress Catalog Card Number: 2005921844

Design by Wanni Cheung and Emily R. Lee
Cover Design by Sachi Goodwin
Cover photograph by Ian Gillespie

First Printing, May 2005
Second Printing, June 2007

Mutual Publishing, LLC
1215 Center Street, Suite 210
Honolulu, Hawaii 96816
Ph: (808) 732-1709
Fax: (808) 734-4094
email: info@mutualpublishing.com
www.mutualpublishing.com

Printed in Australia

TABLE OF CONTENTS

The Game of "Life"

1

LIFE IS SO cherry, I tell you. Sheila, my soon-to-be ex-wife, was staying over at her parents' house, and I was in the garage packing up my stuff, when I ran across an old Makaha Sons tape under my class-of-'89-yearbook. It reminded me of the time I'd pawned my ukulele. Knowing that I was not the Hawaiian who would blow the lid off contemporary Hawaiian music—my playing was just as suspect as the music itself—I'd taken my songbook and tossed it in the trash, then gone to a pawn shop and sold my four string. I'd been teaching myself Prince's "Raspberry Beret" by ear when I quit, so it was definitely time.

The songbook was a brown three-ringed binder filled with pages of lyrics. The chords were written above words like surf, beach, lei, country, words travel agents used to describe Hawai'i to customers looking for a slice of paradise served up on the firm white flesh of a cracked coconut. It took me four years to realize I was looking at lyrics from older pop songs from the seventies, remade to include supersonic ukulele-picking solos. The funny thing was that this music was for people like me, people born and raised in Hawai'i, but the marketing of the state had gone overboard. They now seemed to be trying to sell it to those who'd lived here all their lives. These songs, they were all about longing for a return to the good old days when you surfed as a kid or fished with your dad out in the country. You know, the country, where you'd grab your board in between skipping school, smoking cigarettes, and getting your ass beat by your alcoholic father—real Huck Finn shit. "Take me back to da kine." I'll pass.

I might be generalizing; it wasn't all shit. There was Iz and Makaha Sons. But I never saw friends bust out the Jawaiian— that style that seemed to take the worst from Reggae and Hawaiian and meld them together—when they'd just had their heart broken; And when they wanted to be alone and drive around the island to think about life, they wouldn't bust out the tapes of bands that seemed to make music just to show how fast the ukulele guy could pick the four string. How many versions of "Ulupalakua" or the yodel song did one need to hear? It occurred to me that I only pulled out the Hawaiian when I was drinking beers or smoking weed. Realizing this made me sad because I knew that there was certainly room for sad or meaningful songs in Hawaiian music. Most top-forty music has about as much depth.

The callus on my fingertips took a couple of months to disappear, and I spent some of those healing days wondering if this was what life was all about. You embrace something for a few years, then you see it's a sham, so you toss it out, try to get a good resale on it, and then rinse and repeat . . . Now that I was thirty-two, with about four serious relationships, one marriage, three jobs, four hobbies, four substance-abuse problems, three cars, among other things under my belt, I was beginning to see that life is not one long road. Life is lived in increments. Three years here, four years there. Life is like an album of songs written independently of each other but all recorded by the same artist, hopefully not by NWA. And maybe a good album is about a real life, but probably a life shorter than forty years. Hell, with most people, the album starts skipping at about thirty. Marriage, kids, pressure to buy some new, fee-simple house in Kunia for $300,000 to $400,000 just to learn what "accrued depreciation" means, the bills, the job, the middle-class angst. Welcome to the scratch in the recording, that one groove dug so deep that it makes the needle or laser skip and skip. And no matter how much you try to rub away that scratch with the bottom of your T-shirt, it won't disappear. Some people keep that album, and some people throw it away.

It was time to toss that scratched recording so I took my box of nostalgia out of the garage and threw it in the trash. The rubber mouth of the trash bin gaped. I shrugged and jumped into my red Dodge truck. I was running late for my marriage pauhana, suck-um-up session, so I went to the nearest Kaneʻohe gas station, picked up a pack of cigarettes for five bucks, and went to go get drunk at my stepmother's bar. Throwing that last box out was the final part of my smashing my marriage Pete Townsend style, and I felt I deserved a reward. I drove up the Pali, where the smoked-colored clouds capped the green mountains. It looked like someone had lit a bonfire up there, but as I got closer and closer to them, the clouds faded in the dark.

2

Mom loved the board game "Life." When I was a kid, she, Winnie, and I would sometimes play at the bar until two in the morning. The pink twenty-thousand-dollar bills, the rainbow-colored spinning wheel that went from one to ten, and the old cardboard that smelled like packaged vomit. The goal was simple: whoever had the most money at the end of the game won.

It was a kid's game, in which a seven-year-old could beat a thirty-year-old on any given day. The game started by deciding whether or not you would go to college, and Mom had always forced Winnie and me to go. "Betta chance win," she'd say. Winnie always wanted to be the Superstar, which required no degree, but we'd go to college, get a job and earn a salary, get married, buy a house, possibly have kids, pay huge bills for vacations, operations, or the kids' educations, possibly win the lottery or the Nobel Prize, and then retire, we hoped at Millionaire Estates.

Winnie, my stepsister and Mom's real daughter, had been the best at the game. It wasn't that she'd won more than anyone else, but she had a way of making it more fun than Milton Bradley ever intended. She'd yell out the number she wanted with each spin like she was playing craps for real money. "C'mon, Nancy! I love you, Nancy! Mama needs a new pair of shoes!" When we got to our early teens, she'd fill her little red car with baby-blue pegs when she landed on the "Get married" square, nod and say, "That's right. Man harem incoming." When she'd fill her car with kids, she'd say, "Uterus power!" Even when she had to pay taxes or her house flooded—Winnie never bought home insurance—she would say, "Pfft. Forty grand? A drop in the well!" Then she would lick her thumb and dole out the cash from her wad of yellow ten-thousand-dollar bills.

But one night when Winnie was about fourteen, she came to the bar drunk, poured some Bacardi 151 on Millionaire Estates, and lit a match, singing "The Roof Is on Fire." Mom tried to snuff out the flames with her hand, but her hand got booze on it and caught on fire. She dunked it in a sink full of water, ice, and beer, then told Winnie she had about ten seconds to run before she kicked her ass. It was a mistake, the ten seconds I mean, because Winnie was out the door and didn't come back for two days. She never got an ass-kicking anyway, which wasn't surprising because aside from the occasional hard slap on the ass as a kid, Mom never touched us. Mom salvaged the game board. I suspected that she thought the game held some sort of life lesson for us kids, but we rarely played after that night—all of us together anyway.

So I was surprised to see the game out at the bar when I walked in at eleven. The creases where the board folded were ripped. Some of the white plastic houses were missing, and the once-bright colors on the board and the wheel were dull. There was a burn mark where Millionaire Estates should have been, and it sort of looked like a crater, as if a smart bomb had found it. Mom and her boyfriend, Mario, were playing quietly. The only other people there were the usual customers, and the employees, who could grab their own booze from the back. I looked at Mom, who was playing the game for the first time in years, and I knew that Winnie must have called her, too. Two weeks ago, right when my marriage was coming to an end, Winnie had phoned to say she was getting out of prison and needed a place to stay. "That makes two of us," I'd told her.

I walked up to the bar. "Hey, Mom."

She looked up and smiled, her eyes streaked with red lightning. "I thought you quit drinking?"

I raised both my arms, signaling a touchdown. "I'm getting a divorce."

She sighed. "Shitty, yeah?" She had been married three times herself: once to Winnie's dad, a mystery haole guy who was supposedly some white-collar big shot living on the mainland, somewhere on the east coast; my dad, a half-Chinese, half-Hawaiian homeless beach bum–turned janitor who drank himself to death a year after he and Mom married; and Mark's dad, a Korean who owned a small limo company and who, the last time I'd seen him, seemed one step away from also drinking himself to death. I was the only one who wasn't her own kid, but she'd raised all three of us, and before we became teenagers, we'd split our time among school, a two-bedroom apartment in Makiki, and the bar.

Mom opened a beer and put it on the cocktail napkin already in front of me. It felt like I'd come home for dinner or something.

I put my hand around the Bud Light bottle and squeezed it hard. It was a habit left over from when I wondered if one day I'd be able to put enough pressure on the neck to break it. "Yep," I said and I took a long swig. The enzymes were popping in my mouth like crazy. After two years of hardly drinking, I knew I'd be back sometime, but I'd waited until the last of my stuff was out of Sheila's house in Kaneʻohe. "So I'm gonna pick up Winnie Monday," I said. It was Friday night. There were five people in the bar besides me, Mom, and Mario: a waitress sitting in a booth talking to a couple of Japanese guys; the bartender, a skinny, sixty-something Japanese alcoholic; and some little guy wearing a sweater hood over his head and sitting by himself in the booth closest to the door. The place was like a living room–turned bar: so small that all of the booths were close to the door. It was the only bar that I knew of where there was dart traffic because you were in the line-of-fire every time you went to the bathroom. The clientele was mostly local Japanese, like Mom, who was born and raised in Hilo, and was one of the few non-immigrant bar owners in what was the bar-central district of Honolulu: roughly, the square mile surrounding Keeaumoku and Kapiolani Boulevard. What me and my friends called Bolohead Row was where Keeaumoku ended at Kapiolani, right in front of Ala Moana Shopping Center. Mom's bar, Lynn's Place, was one of many here whose name had the word place or club in it. With a parking lot in front of it, it was a pretty good bar even if it was small. I'd take a parking lot over interior bar space any day.

"So where you going live now?" she asked.

"I found an apartment in Makiki last week, finished moving my stuff in today. You know, the one by Punahou, the high rise? I think Winnie is going to stay with me for a while." Punahou was the private school that Mom had dreams of sending us to when we were kids. In the ninth grade, Winnie had scored so high on the entrance test that she got a scholarship. At the end of tenth grade, she was kicked out. It was a very bitter memory for Mom, but then again bitter memories and Winnie went together like punch and pie.

Mom spun the wheel. It ticked against a sliver of white plastic, making the same sound as the big wheel on The Price Is Right. Mario winked at me, then made his way to the bathroom, pausing in front of the dart line-of-fire while the bartender made his third throw. "Ah, fuck this," Mom said. She put the game back in the box, then turned up the stereo, which was permanently set to some pop-music station. Apparently, Britney

Spears had done it again. After swig three, my bottle was empty. Mom opened another one and put it in front of me. "Smoking again, too?" she asked. I nodded and pulled out two cigarettes, lit them both, and handed her one. I had never really quit. I would just sneak a smoke here and there, hiding it from my wife. The idea of myself sneaking a smoke in the bathroom at home and creeping around in the dark like a burglar at three a.m. triggered one of those rock-bottom moments of clarity.

"Yeah, fuck this," I said, not really knowing what particular thing I was cursing. "Wanna take a shot?" I asked.

"Yeah, on me tonight, though."

"I'll pay. It's Friday, and there's like eight people here."

"I got it." She paused, probably wondering if what she wanted to say next would be smart. "Just stay away from that drug shit. Tell Winnie, too." Mom had always believed that alcohol kept you away from hard drugs. She had a point: most of the people I'd known who were into ice rarely drank; the ones who did both alcohol and hard drugs were retards, rock stars—and Winnie.

The waitress got up to grab drinks for herself and the two Japanese guys she'd been sitting with. They looked like younger guys, maybe just out of college, guys who would be my friends if I were their age. I grew up in town, and most of my friends from high school were Japanese, though I was almost a foot taller than some of them. The waitress was new; then again, I hadn't been there in ages.

"New girl?" I said.

"Momo? Maybe two months."

I laughed. "Her name is Momo?"

"Yeah, 'peach' in Japanese."

Momo asked for two Bud Lights, the local Japanese beer of choice, and a chilled Crown Royal for herself.

"Momo, dis my son, Charlie."

I shook her hand. She smiled and took the drinks back to the table. She was wearing black "pleather" pants and a lavender spaghetti-strapped top. She was tanned and wore a lot of makeup, which seemed odd on a tanned girl. She was the kind of girl who'd shot me down constantly in high school because, compared to most of the townie Japanese crew, I was built Frankenstein-style. It wasn't until the girls were a few years out of high school that they began to like me. They started looking at their Japanese boys—boys who looked exactly like they had in high school, except that some of them could grow goatees now—and decided they wanted boyfriends who looked more like men. I overheard Momo talking to the two guys in the booth and caught the barrage of "and he has like" and "she was all" dialogue tags. Her voice was squeaky with excitement.

I toasted Mom and drank the shot of chilled Crown she had poured me. The coldness of the shot dulled the taste and the sharp warmth that would have normally filled my chest. It has been said many times that it takes a bit of time for fads from the mainland to hit Hawai'i, but that was changing with every new satellite shot into space. Now we're maybe only six hours behind, at the most, when it comes to watching TV shows. Chilled Crown was all the rage, just as Bud Light was. Bolohead Row was about as anti-microbrewery as you could get. The hangover beers were for the haoles. "So Mom, where's the karaoke book?"

"Don't you dare, Charlie."

"What? Can't a guy sing?"

She heaved a sigh and gave me the book from behind the bar. It was a binder filled with just about every imaginable top-twenty hit in the last thirty years. "If you back, stop messing with my girls. Remember what happened to da last one?"

"Yeah, I married her." I looked for Marvin Gaye's "Let's Get It On," thankful that those ukulele, Hawaiian-music days showed me one thing: I could sing. From memory, I wrote the song number on a small slip of paper, thinking how funny it was that I didn't need the book at all. I wondered if I'd always been an asshole, or if it was something that started in my twenties. On slow nights, this was pretty much a self-service bar, so I loaded the song in and came back to the bar. I was no Marvin Gaye, but most of these tone-deaf girls thought I was his second coming.

"Mom, was I always an asshole?"

She smiled. "Yeah, but you da only one of my kids who got a college degree, so I neva said nothing."

I had been the only one who took the game of Life to heart. Toss one pink peg out of the car, fill it with another. The old song was about to begin. I took out the board from the box and spun the wheel, playing with the idea that my fortune was about to be told. The only problem was that I didn't have a car on the board, so it was impossible to tell which square I'd landed on.

It was a good night, considering. I liked talking to Momo, though it all ended with Mom screaming at Mario at two a.m., drunk off her ass, and complaining about something he'd done, something small and dumb. When she was drunk, she could turn not hearing her from behind a closed bathroom door into your never loving her ever at all. It was good to be home.

3

I'd once had this book filled with famous quotes. When I'd bought it, I thought that it would be filled with stuff on love and life that I could plagiarize for love letters, or smart stuff that I could throw in the front of essays I wrote for school. Professors dug that shit. But when I'd gotten home and started to flip through it, I was surprised to see how so many of the quotes were cynical. There was nothing really love-letter worthy, but it was a good read anyway because a lot of the stuff in the book was funny. One on the subject of home went something like, "Everybody is always talking about people breaking into houses, but there are more people in the world who want to break out of houses." When I'd read it back in my freshman year in college, I'd instantly thought of Winnie, who had spent much of her teens doing both: breaking into other people's homes while trying to break out of her own.

I'd been happy living with Mom while I was growing up; it was a much better scene than living on the beach with my dad when I was a little kid. For about a year, I'd actually been homeless with my father, living under a blue tarp on the beach and getting chased away by the "popo," the police, every once in a while. The old man could never hold a job, and it wasn't until he'd gotten one as an Ala Moana Shopping Center janitor that we'd left the beach. I was about eight years old when he and Mom hooked up at her bar, which was right across the street from Ala Moana. Why she married him, I'd never figured out. Her ex, Winnie's dad, supposedly was a straightlaced haole guy with a stick up his ass, so maybe she'd needed a change of pace. Well, marrying a homeless Hawaiian degenerate alcoholic was more than a change of pace; it was like going from a coma to a heart attack. I'd known even as a kid that the marriage wouldn't last. As the love quote goes, "Love never dies of starvation, but often of indigestion." My father was serving her up some nasty-ass Hawaiian chili peppers right off the vine, and as sick as it sounds, I'd been relieved when he'd dropped dead while scraping gum off the sidewalks at Ala Moana. I imagined his wild, long white hair sprawled out on the sidewalk like a broken geisha fan, his gray beard speckled with spit. I don't know why I added the spit to the picture. Spit and death just seemed like they'd go together.

I'd been so scared by the beach that I've only gone a few times since then. When you've lived on an island your entire life, it's quite a feat to avoid the beach. I didn't mind driving past it, but whenever you step on that sand, it has a funny way of sticking to you.

So I'd pretty much kept my feet on good old manmade asphalt. I'd grown up in Makiki, which was less than a mile mauka of Ala Moana and Mom's bar. I went to high school at McKinley, less than a mile west of the bar. As for anything recreational, there was Hawaiian Brian's for pool and all around me, bars galore. Bolohead Row had it all. Sure, I got out of this square mile once in a while, but it was home for me, and returning to it after the end of my marriage made sense. I guess both me and Winnie were coming home.

I was thinking about all this cornball family stuff—about the return of Charlie and Winnie to Makiki—while following Momo to her Makiki studio apartment. We'd decided to hook up there since my new place was pretty much just the few boxes that I'd decided not to throw out. Momo lived in one of those three-story buildings in Makiki with a name that had one of the following words: tropical, oasis, vista, estate, heights. Of course the building wasn't tropical or vista-like at all. Instead it was just an ordinary one occupied by service-industry tenants who appreciated the closeness of Makiki to Waikīkī. The area was filled with these places: apartments perfect for waiters, waitresses, valets, security guards, maids, and so forth, most of whom seemed twentyish going on forty. Some had college degrees that served no practical purpose, and some, after one of countless nights drinking after work, woke up to find themselves with the worst kind of hangover: the spouse-and-kids type. These were the independent types, the ones who left the rent-free environment of their parents' middle-class homes to pay eight hundred dollars a month for sticky, un-carpeted floors and quarter-devouring washers and dryers. Parking was especially unpleasant here. If you didn't spend fifty a month for a parking space, you were reduced to waking up at six in the morning to move your car from one side of the street to the other to be in compliance with no-parking hours. Competition for spaces was fierce; I'd seen fistfights break out over the tiny slots left by graveyard-shift workers the night before.

Momo pulled into her parking space. I parked right behind her. The wind blew against the bushes, the leaves sounding like waves crashing on sand. After we got out, I asked her if she was sure that I wouldn't be towed. She shrugged. "You aren't blocking any other spaces, and the security guard is cool with me."

Her studio reminded me a lot of Sheila's old place when she'd worked at Mom's bar. Actually, they had all been the same, I guess, even the ones before Sheila. There was the ton of shoes by the door: platforms, sneakers, slippers, heels. Then there was the music. These girls liked their music, and evidently they had a wide range of tastes. There was always contemporary top-forty stuff, some old best-of albums, and some Hawaiian. The CDs would be in a tower case from Wal-Mart, and the tower would be right next to the stereo: usually one of those small ones with the amp, tuner, cassette and CD player squeezed between two speaker boxes of equal height, making it look not so much like a mini-stereo but an oversized boom box. TV, VCR, desk with a computer on it, usually an older computer that some well-meaning mother or father had given them for school years before; the computer would have a plastic cover on it, and the cover would have a thin film of dust. Stuffed animals: some liked the Flintstones, some Winnie the Pooh; others collected one type of animal—horsies, duckies, and bunnies being very popular. Then there were the photographs: framed pictures of family and friends on the desk, on the walls, on anything with shelves; unframed pictures taped to the refrigerator. The poses were always the same: family with their arms around each other at some restaurant; friends with a ton of leis around their necks after high-school graduation; and girls with guys wearing T-shirts, and baseball caps, either holding up a can of Bud Light or giving the shaka sign.

Momo had a cordless phone with neon lights right by a Headshots picture of herself: powdered white face, heavy makeup, permed hair. Her image was in soft focus, sort of like the dream sequences you see sometimes on daytime soaps.

These single-women studios in Makiki always seemed clean, too. They might be messy, with clothes draped over chairs and stuff, but they were always clean. Momo's apartment was very much like Sheila's had been; she even had a copy of the movie Dirty Dancing, which had been Sheila's favorite. I was smart enough to know that there might have been a woman walking into a guy's studio at that exact moment and thinking the same thing, so it wasn't a "guys are better than girls" thing, but more of an "I am over thirty now and life is completely unable to show me anything new and exciting" thing. So why did I squash my marriage? Sheila was the one who'd officially squashed it, but I didn't really give her a choice. By the end of our relationship, I treated her like a ghost haunting her own house. I'd leave food out for the ghost and try not to anger it—like not smoke cigarettes around it—but other than that, I pretended it wasn't even there. Finally, she'd asked, "This isn't going to work, is it?" Nope.

Momo and I had left the bar talking and laughing, despite Mom's tirade, but things had gotten quiet once we stepped out of our cars at her building. I couldn't keep up with the fun tempo anymore, and the sight of her apartment depressed the hell out of me. I don't think it was because I missed Sheila, which I did; I guess I was disgusted by the apartments all looking the same. "Boy, you aren't any fun anymore," Momo said.

"Yeah, it's the first time I drank in a while; starting to hang, I think."

"Well, why don't you sleep over? You told me you don't even have a bed at your place, and you don't want to get a DUI. I guess I'm going to take a quick shower and change. Want a soda? There is stuff to drink in the fridge."

I opened the fridge, and it was as spartan as I'd suspected. Three Bud Lights, half a bottle of chardonnay, half a loaf of bread, some sliced cheese, and chunky peanut butter. There was also a liter of Diet Coke. I grabbed a beer and plopped down on her loveseat. The squeaking sound of shower knobs being turned came from behind the bathroom door. There was no way I was going to be able to sleep on this loveseat unless I got really drunk. I lit a cigarette and carefully used the bottle top as an ashtray. It was past three in the morning. I had to be at work in two hours. Just like the old days, I thought, as I drifted to sleep, probably almost igniting my shirt with the cigarette. Wouldn't have been the first time.

I woke up in Momo's bed, under a sheet with white rabbits on it. The sheet was stiff and felt brand new. Momo was sleeping on the loveseat. I had thirty minutes to get to work. I slipped out of bed and cleared my dry throat. I felt the familiar dehydration after a night of drinking, but the cigarette hangover was worse, as it often was. I coughed, and that one cough released a flutter of coughs that brought bile up my throat. I closed my eyes and breathed slowly. One always had to be careful of what one released from the mouth when drinking was involved, both during and after. I knew smoking a cigarette would give me a headache, but I lit one anyway and made my way out of the apartment. Momo looked sweet crashed out in a tight little ball on the loveseat, like a napping cat. I wondered if she hated her parents for naming her "peach." Normally, I would have been all for getting to the bottom of that question, but I didn't want to be there. The muffled sound of passing cars reminded me that I didn't want to be at work either. In fact, I didn't want to be anywhere. I wasn't feeling suicidal or anything stupid like that; I just didn't crave a particular place or activity. Some might call that contentment, but it was more like a strong desire for nothing.

4

Work was really cherry. I was an assistant manager for ABC Store in Waikīkī, which did not narrow it down, considering that there were like seventy ABC stores in Waikīkī alone. I was an assistant manager at ABC Store #64, which was on Lewers Street, half a block away from ABC Store #63. ABC combined the inventory of 7-Eleven with cheap tourist trinkets and T-shirts. During the recession of the nineties in Hawaiʻi—then again, Hawaiʻi always seemed to be in recession no matter how the rest of the country was doing—the ABC Stores were the only shops in Waikīkī consistently making money. I made a whopping ten dollars an hour as ABC Store #64 assistant manager. It was nice, at age thirty-two, to see the benefit of a business degree from the University of Hawaiʻi at Manoa kicking in. Granted, it had taken me nine years to get my bachelor's, and the 2.5 GPA didn't help, but I had friends without college degrees making more than twice as much as I was. They weren't even game-of-Life Superstars; I'm talking cell-phone and auto-parts salesmen. Mom brought home more than I did with that tiny bar. For all the good it did me, my degree might as well have been printed out of the same cardboard as the game.

The air was cold and the sun wasn't out yet when I dragged my ass to work and went through my chores zombie-style. I turned off the alarm at 5:20 a.m., slid the steel curtain open, and unlocked the store. I turned on the fluorescent lights, which sometimes aggravated a hangover more than sunlight did, and clocked in. I kept a few shirts, ties, and pairs of slacks at work. Slacks, a collared shirt, and tie—your basic church attire—formed the get-up for an assistant manager at ABC from Monday through Thursday. From Friday to Sunday, we got to wear aloha shirts—joy. After putting on my flower-printed Reyn Spooner shirt and my slacks, I got started on my routine.

The typical day at ABC went like this: make the cash cans for the cashiers, check inventory, make orders, price stuff that vendors brought in, do time sheets, monitor sales, stock the shelves, and sweep the front sidewalk. By nine a.m., I was convinced that time moved slower at ABC than anywhere else in the world. Every day at work, I stepped into an anomaly of the space-time continuum, and this stretch paid ten dollars per real hour. This job had to go, but I could only handle Pete Townsend-ing things one at a time.

I had to deal with customers, too, most of them tourists from Japan. They walked the aisles slowly, not sure what they were looking for, but eager to find something. Sooner or later, they settled on a T-shirt, or a can of chilled coffee, anything to not walk out empty-handed. Anything cheap was worth having no matter how worthless. It was a good thing that they rarely asked me to find something specific. I'd never had an ear for language; in fact, my long-term memory was suspect. I'd taken two years of Japanese in high school and two years of Latin in college— the latter because Latin was a dead language and there was no language lab. I played the ukulele and sang some songs in Hawaiian while not knowing what the words meant. I had been exposed to both Koreans and Japanese for most of my adult life, but all I could really say was Makudonarudo e ikimasu, Japanese for "I go to McDonald's." I was a retard when it came to foreign languages, but when I'd applied for the ABC job, I built up my two years of high-school Japanese as if I had been in the country in a monastery and pouring over ancient texts. The truth was that the only thing I remembered about Japanese class, other than the McDonald's thing, was when me and Jon Takahashi, "Taks" for short, took out one of the teacher's Japanese-language records and tried to scratch with it. We'd been good friends ever since.

At about noon, while I was sweeping cigarette butts into the gutter, Taks pulled up to the store in his orange slant-nosed Porsche. It was an older car—he'd bought it used and repainted it—but it was still a nice car. Him being a high-school friend meant I'd known him for about half my life, but for some reason, it didn't feel that long. He'd never had a "real" job, so the sight of him was just rubbing salt in the wound. He killed the engine right in front of the no-parking sign and got out. "Charlie's back, yo!" His mouth grinned under his three-hundred-dollar sunglasses. He was the kind of guy who'd have a lifetime subscription to Maxim magazine.

"Wow, you're awake," I said, lighting a cigarette. "How'd you hear?"

"Grapevine, brotha, grapevine." He pulled out a cigarette from his shorts pocket. He was tall for a Japanese guy, but so skinny that back when we smoked ice, I swear he didn't lose a pound, or gain one when he stopped. Nothing short of death could touch his metabolism. "So what, beers tonight?"

"I only had about two hours of sleep, plus I might pull overtime here." I wasn't tired, though, which was pretty much the only benefit of getting a sharp left hook from life. It woke you up, but didn't knock you out.

"You get a new place yet?"

"Yep, one bedroom, eight hundred dollars a month. Back in town. First month and deposit really smashed me." Sheila and I had been living in a townhouse in Kaneʻohe. Her parents bought it for her. It amazed me how people like Sheila, her parents, and Taks could throw down a wad of cash for nice, big things. With overtime, I pulled in about thirty grand a year and never had more than three thousand dollars in my checking account, even when I didn't pay rent, drink, or do drugs. I could sit perfectly still and sweat money—no problem.

Taks eyed the store. "No honeys work here still?"

"Nope."

"Shit, no reason to work here then. You should come in with us," he said, referring to the money scheme he had going.

"What, betting?" I asked.

"No, playing lacrosse. Of course betting."

"What the fuck is lacrosse anyway?"

"Beats the shit out of me. What's curling?"

"Beats me."

Taks had had his hands in a bunch of illegal stuff over the years, but it was always small, manini stuff. Back in my first year of college, he'd sold stolen-car CD players, slim-jimming his way all over Bolohead Row. He never came up with these hustling schemes on his own; it was always a friend's idea, and he knew everyone in town it seemed. So he'd just hitch his little wagon to one thing after another until it got blown apart. His current money-making scheme was sports betting. He had hooked up with this guy who studied sports and could break houses by betting. For every grand he'd throw in, Taks would throw in a hundred dollars. Because he'd lived with his parents all of his life, the five hundred dollars he averaged a week was big bucks. He was the only guy my age whom I still talked to who had a smaller bank account than I did. But he didn't sweat money. He spent it straight-up.

"Fuck that. One bad week, and I'm fucked. Where you going anyway?" I asked.

"Beach, man. Gonna do some girl-watching—some curling. Let's call it curling. We on tonight then, yo?"

"Yeah, pick me up then. I'm at that tall building across Punahou."

He nodded. "By the way, we ain't going to your mom's bar. I gotta hide out for a bit."

"Haha, what now?" Taks was the only one who'd screwed more of Mom's waitresses than I had.

"Same old shit. Pissed off some chick I was fucking. Your mom said she had it with me."

"Peach girl?"

"Momo? Nope, not her. This one actually tried to OD. Otherwise, your Mom wouldn't have aggroed. Can you imagine? Tried to OD. Blamed me, of course." He shook his head.

"What'd she OD on?"

"Aspirin."

"Can you even OD on Bayer's?"

"No clue. Brain lacrosse."

"OK, well, pick me up later."

Taks threw his cigarette on the ground and stepped on it, almost tripping a Japanese tourist walking by. "Sweep that up, boy!" he said and jumped in his car. I left the butt there for a second, staring at the gray smoke coughing from his muffler, then swept to the gutter once the car was out of sight. When I walked back in the store, I was feeling pretty good about the fact that Taks hadn't slept with Momo. I don't know why I was happy, but now that I was single, it was good to know there were girls around that he hadn't fucked yet. The only girl who'd ever given Taks the boot was Winnie, twelve years before, and he'd been on a revenge trip ever since. He'd once told me, "No offense, but I fuckin' hate your sister." You had to love her. I went back inside to do more inventory and kept my eye on the clock. I swore that the minute hand moved counterclockwise for a moment. Fuck overtime.

5

As I got dressed for the night out, I gave myself the honest single-guy once-over, which I hadn't done in years. I'd never looked better naked than clothed, a dream of mine that I'd never labored toward, like my dream of being a millionaire. However, my body was even worse now, ravaged by marriage, meaning the arms were smaller and the stomach bigger. Was I a good-looking guy? I was decent looking. My height was my biggest selling point. Sometimes, though, I thought I looked like a big, clumsy retard, like I should have been wearing clown shoes or something. I was a big guy, but not Lennox Lewis big. I was more of an old Larry Holmes big. My face was more cute than handsome, or so I'd been told. My hair was curly as hell, and when I started balding, I thanked God for the whole Michael Jordan, shave-your-head fad of the nineties. I would never be People magazine's sexiest man alive, but I'd learned about girls over the years, leading me to a few general conclusions about them and how to get them. I could make them laugh, and I could sing. I was like a fifth-rate Dean Martin.

One of my selling points, and I had always been embarrassed by it, was that I was Hawaiian. I wasn't embarrassed about being Hawaiian, but because I'd always felt like an illegitimate Hawaiian, considering my general ineptness at language and a general disinterest in all salt-water sports. The language was as foreign to me as Japanese was, and I'd never had any interest in learning it. I knew as much about Hawaiian history and culture as your typical townie did, which was next to nothing. I could name some fish and some foods, like poi and laulau, and I could say mahalo instead of "thank you" or aloha instead of goodbye, which nearly anyone who had lived in Hawai'i for a number of months, maybe even days, could do. I knew jack-shit about Hawaiian issues, except that Kamehameha Schools was willing to cut me a check for college, so I forgave them the whole corrupt-trustees thing. I also knew that a professor at UH thought that

Hawaiians should be able to establish their own government and kick anyone non-Hawaiian off the islands, but I figured it would never happen and was a waste of time thinking about.

I was raised by a local Japanese lady who owned a bar in town; the closest to my heritage I got was when I'd been recruited to wear a malo for the May Day program during my senior year in high school, and that took some convincing. Some would blame the schools, my parenting, or whatever for the fact that I would rather eat rice than poi with my laulau plate, but I just was never into all that roots stuff. Other people around me were, though, and girls liked it that I was Hawaiian. Even though they would never admit it, they'd either taken some class in high school or college that showed them something they appreciated about the culture, or they had aspirations of having kids and being able to send them to the private, Hawaiian-only, school, Kamehameha, for chump-change tuition, forgetting that there was a tough entrance exam. There wasn't any of that deep-seated desire to be ravaged by a savage or anything like that; at least I don't think so. It was just sort of cool being Hawaiian, hence all the Japanese and haole boys and girls walking around with Hawaiian names. The worst was when they actually tattooed themselves with these names.

I had other selling points, I suppose. I worked. I was decent at sports. I had a decent-looking truck. My papers were in order, I guess. I wasn't handsome in the male-model, washboard-stomach sense, I was what I liked to call boyfriend handsome.

So after I finished getting ready, after Taks and I made the hostess-bar run, where we went for the cheap, two-dollar beers—not to blow twenty dollars a drink on a hostess in exchange for a leg rub, but just to get a cheap drunk on and harass Korean hostesses wearing pancake makeup—I do not know why my singing, Hawaiian, boyfriend-handsome ass was at the massage parlor. But there I was with Taks, looking through beer goggles at the line-up of hookers at Rest and Relaxation of the Orient. Except for the first hour or two, the whole night had seemed stale to me.

It had started out typically enough at Club New Office, perhaps the hostess bar with the greatest name ever. We sat at the bar and were fed for free—rice, roast pork, taegu, kimchee, the works—and we each put twenty on the counter, so the beers kept coming. It had been the first time in ages that I was in a hostess bar, and I had that nice feeling you have when you've been away from home for a while and just come back. I'd never even been a big fan of hostess bars, but understood their utility: free pupus and two-dollar beers. Hostesses, mostly Korean immigrants, walked under a pink neon glow, buying drinks for customers. These hostesses were for the most part different from the waitresses who worked in bars like Mom's place; they tried to dress with more class, wearing Italian labels and high heels. I guess this was ironic, but I wasn't quite sure what the definition of irony was. I just knew it when I saw it.

Taks and I met Joe Yoshimura there, the gambling expert who had taken Taks under his wing. It was easy to see why. Joe was a dumpy-looking guy who dressed like Taks but was about four inches shorter and fifty pounds heavier. He wore a DKNY collared shirt spun from some shiny material that wasn't crazy-shiny, but just shiny enough so that you knew it cost money. He also seemed to have adopted Taks's shiny-hair look. The main difference between them was that he was wearing a gold Rolex; Taks wasn't into the bling-bling.

"Ace, ready for a shot?" Taks asked, nicknaming Joe after Ace Rothstein in Casino. It was so very gay.

"Shoots, I got it though," Joe said. His voice was deep, almost James Earl Jones deep, and I thought how funny it was that voices often didn't match people. He leaned over the counter. There was a big mirror behind the shelves of liquor. With the light at that angle, it looked like a shrine.

"I'm good. Don't get me one. I work tomorrow," I said.

"Fuck that. Order brotha one, yo," Taks said.

"Fuck you, get a job."

"Yeah, mean your job."

The three shots came. The hostess who'd been sitting next to Joe slapped him on the shoulder and pouted. "You buy me drink too!"

Her hair reminded me of my senior prom. It was in frosted, hair-sprayed ringlets, but she was about ten years too late. Joe sighed and looked at the bartender. "And one for her."

"Fuck that," Taks said. "What you gonna do for us?"

"I no ask you, I ask him," she responded, then mumbled something in Korean under her breath. She had on a tight pink blazer that pushed up her breasts and showed off her cleavage. Taks ripped off the corner of a cocktail napkin, wadded it up in a ball, and tried to throw it down her top. He hit her on her bottom lip, and she involuntarily spit, as if a bug had flown into her mouth. The wad landed in front of me, untouched.

Taks smiled. "Then you betta love him long time or something! Twenty dollars expensive you know. You probably make more money than us."

"I poor, you know!"

"Yeah, yeah." Taks raised his shot. "To brotha Charlie. Welcome back to Bolohead Row!"

"Welcome back!" the hostess said.

"You don't even know him, yo!" Taks yelled at her.

"I know him," she said, looking at me.

We toasted. I looked around at the booths where forty- to sixty-year-old men drank with women young enough to be their daughters. When I stood up to go to the bathroom, I caught sight of their bald spots. The pink neon reflected off the shine of skin and whatever it was they used to slick what remained of their hair. I wondered when the whole greasy, flat, side-comb look had been in, but then JC Penny aloha shirts and slacks had never been all the rage either.

When I got back, Taks was still insulting the hostess. Probably craving something a bit more wholesome, I wondered if Momo might be working at Mom's. It was weird how Taks spent money on hostesses to get insults off instead of leg rubs. Joe was quiet, grinning at Taks like he was the greatest thing since sliced bread. "We need to get a maintenance check," Taks said.

I paid my fifty at the door, expecting to haggle for sex after my thorough shower and brief rubdown. Taks grinned at the line-up as if it was his first time there. He had a way of experiencing things for the first time again and again. I used to call him Peter Pan. Well, Pan was about to pay some Korean woman roughly $150 to $200 to take care of his Tinkerbell, his Captain Hook, depending on how good he was at haggling tonight. Korean music was pling-plinging in the reception room. He pointed to the platinum blonde sitting on the couch. Since she was the only blonde there, I wondered how hard she had to work. To people in Bolohead Row, she was exotic. I picked the youngest-looking Korean, probably the second-hardest-working woman in the place. She grabbed my hand and led me from the reception area to a private room. Then she sat me on the bed and handed me a white towel. "You take off clothes now," she said as she walked out of the room and closed the door. On the stand by the bed was a little clock radio set to adult contemporary music. How romantic.

I took a quick peek at my nakedness in the mirror before wrapping the towel around my waist. I probably resembled a stretched-out version of Joe Yoshimura. I'd always envied those little Japanese guys in high school: the skinny ones who walked around with washboard abs despite what seemed like every effort to lose them through beer and greasy food. When I used to smoke ice, I'd thought—or hoped, I guess—that weight loss would be a side effect, but the drug seemed to just freeze my weight. I was a fat, frozen, spongy wedding cake. Marriage had put another twenty pounds on me, but maybe that had nothing do with it. I didn't ever remember getting skinnier in my entire life, just fatter and fatter.

The door opened, and the girl, now wearing a silk robe with tigers on it, grabbed my hand and led me to the shower. My towel, stretching at the waist, almost fell off. I was getting cold from the air conditioning, and my buzz was wearing off. When we got to the bathroom, which was a dimly lit room walled with pink tiles, the girl removed the portable showerhead and turned the water on, adjusting the temperature. She told me to take off my towel and lie on the long vinyl bench, which looked like the ones in doctors' offices. She scrubbed soap on me as I imagined what had brought this poor girl to this point in her life: scrubbing down a flabby, two-hundred-and-fifty-pound Hawaiian at two in the morning and rubbing soap on his dick for money. Spin the colored wheel of Life, ding, ding, ding, and you landed on "Fuck drunks, ugly guys, and ugly drunks during the best years of your life." It had to be a square you landed on because there was no career card for a hooker pimped out through a massage parlor. I didn't want to be there, but Taks's greatest skill was getting people to willingly do what they didn't want to do. It was probably why he was so good at getting laid—and was why he never had to get a real job. His was another career card Milton Bradley forgot to include.

After the shower, I was led back to the room. I took $150 out of my jeans pocket, handed it to the girl, and told her, "Just a massage." I ended up fucking her anyway, but I wasn't into it. I couldn't help wondering why Sheila ever left me.

Taks was eating rice and kimchee with a couple of the girls. His hands fluttering, he was trying to beat back the steam rising from the rice bowl. The girls ate, blank expressions sagging from their eyes. He stabbed his chopsticks in the rice and left them there. As we walked out, he slapped me on the back and said, "Good to have you back, yo."

The mama-san smiled and said, "Come again," as if we'd just picked up a bucket of chicken from KFC.

All of this was old hat. I'd heard this song before. My marriage ended because I was tired of that song and wanted to hear a new one, but here I was pressing "rewind" and not "play." For the first time in my life, I'd traded in something old for something older. It was like I'd decided to listen to Hawaiian music and play the ukulele again. It was like I was spinning the wheel of Life but moving my car backward instead of forward after I'd thrown my pink peg out. All of this would have depressed the hell out of anyone who did not understand what my lawyer friend, Lance whom I'd taken History 151 with in college, had called "The Power of Indifference." He'd once wanted to write a book on it, the first nihilistic self-help book in history. He'd said that there is great power in not giving a shit about anyone or anything, because it all didn't mean shit in the long run anyway. Who the fuck are you? Live, have fun, do what you want, then die. That was all there was to it. He joked about making a set of tapes and an infomercial and hosting seminars. The idea spoke to me despite the fact that the last time I'd seen lawyer Lance, he was at a birthday party for one of his kids and complaining about the long hours, the wife, and family. The kids were running around the swimming pool like they were on crack. He told them to stop running around the deck, then sighed when they didn't listen.

But the concept was still in my head, and I thought, Yeah, fuck Sheila, fuck Taks, fuck it all. The only thing that lay ahead was the hardest one of all—finding something that floated my boat. This rewind to my twenties wasn't cutting it. It was time to cut a new live production, spin the wheel of Life, move forward, and get out of the Bolohead Row. I thought about all of this before I took my nap: two hours of sleep, just like the night before. At least I didn't have to take a bath before work in the morning.

Winnie

1

I'D SCHEDULED MONDAY and Tuesday off, knowing I had to pick up Winnie from WCCC, the Women's Community Correctional Center. After work on Sunday was supposed to be my sleep time, but thinking about sleep all day sort of wore out its appeal. I spent Sunday night watching TV in my new apartment. The cable wasn't installed yet, so NBC, ABC, CBS, and Fox had to battle for me while I battled with reception. By midnight, wire hangers and tin foil drooped off the antennae, making it look like a Christmas tree for the homeless. Fighting with static kept me awake until I finally realized that I was fighting to see midgets who married hookers who slept with their albino sisters. That was when I stopped, crawled in my sleeping bag, and snuggled up against my unpacked boxes. The heat and motionless air of the high rise kept me up, and I remembered enviously how easily Sheila had conked out at night, as if losing consciousness was as simple as brushing her teeth.

WCCC was in Kailua, on the other side of the mountains from Makiki. Unlike the men's prison in Halawa, which was surrounded by industrial buildings and warehouses, WCCC was in the country farmland. I'd been there four times in the three years that Winnie was in jail, and the last time it wasn't even her I was visiting.

Except for the coiled razor wire running across the high fence, WCCC looked more like an intermediate school than a prison. In the front, it even had a nice, brown wooden sign with "Women's Community Correctional Center" in yellow letters. It reminded me of the sign in front of the old sugar mill on the North Shore, which was a tourist attraction. As I pulled in, a woman wearing the standard-issue red T-shirt and blue canvas pants was hosing down the cement under the picnic benches outside the gate. She was dark and had a Hawaiian mullet: a puff of kinky hair in the back and at the forehead. As I pulled into a parking spot, I wondered if she was my aunt, a long-lost relative whom I'd visited one day after Winnie told me her new friend had the same last name as me—Keaweaimoku, a standardized-test nightmare. "Small island," I'd said.

I was disappointed when I got closer and saw that it wasn't my aunt. She'd seemed like a really nice lady. When I told her that I'd completely forgotten what my father, her brother, sounded like until hearing Ozzy on The Osbournes, she'd laughed and said, "Yeah, you could understand him betta when he sang."

Winnie was knocking on my window, smiling, actually, more than smiling, simply beaming, probably as only a person just getting out of prison could. Her skin was as white as ever, like the color of cooked fish.

"Charlie!" she screamed.

I unlocked the passenger door. She jumped in, leaned over, and squeezed the hell out of me. "Free at last, free at last, thank God almighty, I'm free at last! Let's blow this joint!" The way she said it made me think we were pulling a prison break.

"Sounds good." She looked older to me. I hadn't seen her in over a year, and she was sliding into her midthirties. The last ounces of baby fat that were holding on to her face for dear life in her twenties were completely gone, but when she smiled, her cheeks still bunched up into tight little balls under her eyes, making her face look girlish. "Good ol' Charlie," she said.

"That lady over there shooting down the benches—no one is even watching her, huh?"

"She's just working."

I reversed out and pulled on to Kalanianaole Highway. "Wanna go Pali or Waimanalo way back to town?"

"What am I, a tourist? Who gives a shit?" She laughed. "Where we living?"

"Back at Makiki."

"What we doing tonight?" She squeezed my arm.

"Mom wanted me to bring you over to the bar later. Mark is coming, too."

"Those two asses never visited or called me. You're the only one who ever came."

"Only three times."

"Believe me, three times is a lot when you're in this place."

"That bad?"

"Nah, it's just that hardly anyone ever comes when you're here. It's prison, you know? They think they're gonna get strip-searched by some big lezbo ACO and sodomized with a baton. Or they think that the stink of prison won't wash off. Well, it's that or the alternative."

"Alternative?"

"The Power of Indifference."

With the fervor of an apostle, I'd tried to pass the phrase around after I'd heard Lance's theory. Winnie had been one of the first I'd told. "Haha," I said. "you remembered."

"Good ol' Charlie, it's like I wasn't even here."

"Yeah."

I took the Waimanalo way around the southeast side of the island instead of going over the mountains, figuring Winnie would get a big kick out of driving past Sandy Beach, which had been her second home in high school. She'd loved body boarding and the lifestyle that went with it: listening to Bob Marley in a parked van at the beach, thinking his music was only about smoking weed, then being out there in the harsh shore break, sometimes getting lifted and slammed on to the sand by a swirling tube of white water. Like most kids, she'd much preferred it to class. She'd taken me with her a couple of times, the tag-along little brother, but I'd just sat in the van and smoked her weed while she was in the water. I wasn't sure what I hated more: the sand and salt water or being out there shirtless. The guy body boarders walking to and from the shore break would flaunt brown, chiseled muscles as they crossed the hot asphalt of the parking lot and bounced on their heels to avoid burning their feet. Some of them had such a coolness about them that even their duck dance across the asphalt had a style to it.

The rain started as we got closer to the beach. The water slammed my windshield like little fists. Even with my wipers on max, I was having a hard time seeing out. The windward side was all green and pretty, but the rain was frequent, hard, and sloppy. As we got out of Waimanalo, the greenness faded, and rocks and dry weeds surrounded us as we were coming around to the southeast corner of the island. That was one thing about this island that I really liked. The terrain could change on you very suddenly, unlike what I'd seen in the mainland, where hundreds of miles of landscape looked the same. We were coming upon the cliffs hanging over the ocean—rockslide country.

As we drove, I told Winnie what everyone was up to, which was a damn short tale because everyone was up to what they'd always been up to, and she told me about prison, about working for twenty-five cents an hour, taking classes, and living in a dorm with other girls and women, who called their quad "home." It was probably a lot more boring in there over the last three years than it had been outside; then again, I'd been married and Winnie didn't have to sneak smokes like I did. "I refused to call my bunk 'home,'" she said.

"You know, I'm not even sure what landed you there. You were doing a lot of crazy shit last I heard."

"Yeah. Drugs—it always pretty much comes to that. That and my daddy left me when I was a baby, or so they say. Did you know like over one-third of felonies committed in Hawai'i are ice related? My counselor told me." She said it as if proud to be able to bust out some kind of statistic. People love numbers.

"I felt bad about the jail thing," I said.

"Like you have that power. Don't, it was my fault. Good ol' Charlie. Let's not talk about it."

"Yeah. So any topless pillow-fight, lezbo scenes in jail?"

She laughed. "Oh yeah, then we'd get hosed down. We'd have to soap each other up first, of course. Get ourselves in a lather."

"That's what I thought."

I was trying to lighten things up. I didn't want to talk about the one thing that scared me about seeing her again, thinking that we'd have to rehash what happened, during our bouncing-off-the-walls, four-day ice binge. In a nutshell, on the most demented, drugged-out night of my life, Winnie and I had a one-night thing. All people have skeletons in their closets, but there was a big-ass brontosaurus leg bone in mine, smashing the other bones so that they didn't even matter. That was the last night I'd smoked ice—and last time I'd spoken to Winnie until the day I visited her in prison to tell her I was getting married.

Both of us had been sitting cross-legged on the bed, passing the pipe back and forth. I was telling her that ice always tasted like apple Jolly Rancher to me. She had her Magic Eight Ball on her lap and shook it, reading out answers without asking questions. In those days, she pretty much lived by those answers, not because she thought the ball was magic, but because she figured its answers were as good as any. With the sweet taste of apple Jolly Roger burning on our lips, we did, what was for me at least, the most fucked-up thing ever. It started as she leaned over and gave me a kiss. Agreeing that we weren't really brother and sister, we both laughed shyly, feeling naughty, I guess, but so charged up on ice that we just launched into it. We pressed against each other hard, violently.

I can't say that I really thought about it until the high came crashing down hours later. We were both in bed, and when I got up to turn off the fan, the oscillation sounding unbearably loud, I swore I saw a single eye peeking out of a crack in the closet door. Instead of getting up and opening the door, I went back to bed and shrunk under the covers. I woke up hours later, and Winnie and her Magic Eight Ball were gone. I would find out that she'd left with the contents of my wallet: a whopping thirty dollars and a few credit cards I raced to cancel.

Rock bottom drove me to marry the first girl who would have me; it drove Winnie to perform a vanishing act, which made me feel relieved, but then she followed that up with jail. After going off-board to land on the "I-fucked-my-stepsister" square in the game of Life, I got back on quick, promising I'd stick to the board like glue, get my pink peg, pass every pay day without incident, and play by straight-up rules.

We were driving through Hawai'i Kai, some of it Hawai'i's version of Millionaire Estates. The rain let up, and I smiled, thinking that maybe the rich could even control the weather.

"Marriage didn't take, huh?" Winnie asked.

"Well, we only had a fifty-fifty chance, I guess. Seems it's all fifty-fifty."

"Nah, it's all six-five. You always gotta pay the house."

I smiled. "I like that: six-five. Sad, but true."

She nodded. "Sad, but true." She clasped her hands together and shook them, the split a small hole by her thumbs and looked in. "Magic Eight Ball says, 'You may rely on it.' Good ol' Charlie. Can we make a stop before we hit the apartment?"

"Yeah, if it doesn't involve picking up any illegal substances."

"What if it's plutonium?"

"Plutonium would be fine. Seriously, though, don't mess with that shit anymore."

"What is plutonium anyway?"

"It's the substance used to turn a Delorean into a time machine."

"Haha, seriously, oh wise college one."

I didn't understand how it worked, but had to try to explain, being the only one in the family with a college degree. "I think it's the stuff you need to start the chain reaction of splitting the atoms in the air."

"So it makes the air dangerous, huh?"

"More like the air is already dangerous. No drugs, Winnie."

"It's all about chemicals, huh?"

"Well, it's all about something."

We were officially in town. Kalanianaole Highway led to the freeway, and we took it. We rolled down the windows and smoked cigarettes. The sky was an anemic light blue. Sunlight reflected off the white clouds and onto my left arm, which was more tanned than the right. We'd just been in heavy rain about fifteen minutes before, and as we passed an apartment building pressing against the freeway, I wondered how there could be so much weather going on at the same time in such a small place smack dab in the middle of the largest ocean on earth.

2

To my relief, the stop we had to make was Mom's apartment in Makiki. I wasn't the kid who'd stolen from her, so I still had a key. Mark, our little brother, was home as usual. Mark was a celebrity, the genuine article in a day and age of classified ads claiming you could make big bucks working from the comfort of your home. He proved them right.

The game of Everquest was what was called a massive multi-player online role-playing game, the most popular at that time. You paid $12.95 a month to play this game, which was set in Dungeons and Dragons fantasyland. You created a character and played with other computer geeks across the globe, killing dragons and shit. For some of its four hundred thousand subscribers, it was just an after-work or after-school diversion, a game like any other game, but for those who called it Evercrack, it was a forty- to eighty-hour-a-week addiction. For them, it was about building guilds with other players, building web sites, competing with other guilds to see who could kill what first, and selling the weapons for real money through Ebay and other sites. Mark was a celebrity because most of the four hundred thousand players knew who he was: his guild's web site had the hits to prove it. I'd played for about two years myself, and it was probably the most enjoyable part of my marriage, but Sheila had gotten fed up with it. What she had not seen coming was that when I gave it up, it just left empty air between us. Everquest wasn't replaced by quality time, just time. Either way, I'd never been able to put in the time it took to succeed like Mark did. I had a job. But he'd taken care of me.

Mark's room looked like Sanford and Son meets Star Trek: a computer graveyard of fifteen- and seventeen-inch monitors and gorged laptops and motherboards spilling their guts in the form of frayed wires, in the middle of which was a big L-shaped desk with two twenty-one-inch monitors and a laptop. Mark was sitting at the desk as always, playing three different characters at the same time. He didn't even hear us walk in. Winnie put her hands over his eyes. He blindly finished typing out a chat message on computer two, then swiveled his chair around and smiled. "Hey, Win."

"Jesus Christ," Winnie said. "Last time I was here, it was one computer, the one I gave you."

"The one you stole for me," he said with a grin. Then he swiveled back around, looking like a piano player. He pointed to a small refrigerator under his desk. "Want a Diet Coke?"

The desk was covered with empty Diet Coke cans and a big glass ashtray with a mountain of cigarette butts rising from it.

"Where's Mom?" I asked.

"She went to open up early, I think. Probably putting up balloons and shit for Winnie. I dunno."

Winnie grabbed a can of soda and took a cigarette from Mark's pack. Her eyes bounced from screen to screen.

"What you doing?" I asked.

"Nothing much, man. Just power-leveling another guy, getting ready to Ebay him. Here, take a seat," he said as if about to explain the merits of life insurance. He took a stack of papers and calculator off the chair next to him and put them on a stack sitting on one of his monitors. Of the hundreds of thousands of people who played this game worldwide, Mark was one of the few who looked at the screen and saw math. He was like a character in the movie, The Matrix. He had always been good at math.

"Check this out," he said, pointing at one of the monitors. "See this club? It's called a Septre of Destruction. I have like three, being guild leader and all. It's damn old and gimpish, but it doesn't drop anymore. Someone bid five hundred bucks on it. Once I get the cash, all I do is give it to his character when he logs on. See this cleric?" He pointed at another monitor. "It took me maybe a few days to get her to level sixty. I'm selling her for around five hundred bucks, too. It takes the average player like a year to get to level sixty. Fucktards. But the real cash is in buying up plat and selling it at my own price. I'm thinking about buying some web sites, too."

Mark made more money than I did last year, and his was tax-free and the result of doing what he liked. He had no college degree, but probably had more money in the bank than most people I knew. He lived rent-free with Mom, and his only expenses were Diet Coke and Marlboro Lights, and the cigarettes he bought for $14.95 a carton from Russia through the Internet. I envied the hell out of him.

"Mark, you got my package for me?" Winnie asked.

"Yep, hold on, need to put up AFK." Away from keyboard.

He stood up and grabbed a Phillips-head screwdriver from the top of computer one, then he pulled out a tower from a corner of the room and began to unscrew its back. He slid off the cover and removed a folded manila envelope. "Here you go." He sat back down, turned off AFK, and resumed playing. "I'll be there tonight. Cleared my schedule."

Winnie looked at me. She asked Mark, "You got a schedule?"

"Yeah, but I'm the boss, so I make it."

I was scared to find out what was in the envelope. Winnie kissed Mark on the cheek. He was already back to piano playing, calling someone an ass hat.

"See you later then, bro," she said. "Thanks for taking care of this for me."

He didn't look up. "NP," he said. No problem.

As we were going down the elevator, Winnie said, "It's money. Let's go shopping."

"How much?"

"Hmm,'bout twenty thousand?"

"Oh man, where the fuck did you get that?"

"No worry, beef curry," she said. It was one of her sayings— maybe even a philosophy. It was usually followed by bad shit going down.

"I heard that one before," I said.

"Stop being such an old man. Good ol' Charlie."

"So where to now?"

"Ala Moana, babe. I need some clothes and makeup and shit. This is all the clothes I got ATM." At the moment. She was talking like Mark. She smiled, pointing to her pink Roxy T-shirt, her denim shorts, and slippers. It was probably the clothes she'd gotten arrested in.

"That brother of ours is a trip," she said.

"He got on me for quitting."

"You played that? That's unlike you, getting caught up in some geek-fest game."

"I wanted a place in geekdom. I was moving too fast in RL." Real life.

She laughed as we got out of the elevator and started walking toward my truck. "He pulls in money off of that for real?"

"Yep, people pay him for bytes."

"It's amazing what you can sell nowadays."

"Yep. So when I told him I was quitting and he put up a fight, I asked him, 'What about real life?' He said, 'RL is overrated.'"

"Ain't that the truth."

"Yeah, he might be the wisest of us all."

"I need new clothes. My stomach is busting the button on these jeans. The one good side effect of ice is that it keeps the pounds off."

"So what you gonna do now?"

She smiled. "No worry, beef curry."

I lit a cigarette and got in the truck. She would spend about four thousand dollars at Ala Moana on her Bolohead Row survival kit: several pairs of platform shoes and tight-fitting long, black designer pants that flared out at the bottom; tops; a lot of bras and underwear, all thongs; makeup from Neiman Marcus; and a bag and wallet from Louis Vuitton. She'd borrow T-shirts from me for sleepwear, she said. I was the one who had to suggest we go to Longs for a toothbrush and other stuff for the survival kit. She was glad I suggested it. She needed a lighter, tweezers, cotton balls, and eyebrow gel. Her skin was so white that I could see faint lines of blue through the skin on her legs. If the sun was bright enough, I wouldn't have been surprised to see some organs. There were scars, too. Winnie had the kind of skin that could scar just from scratching a mosquito bite too hard.

When we got to my apartment, pushing through the elevator door with a ton of shopping bags that wrenched our fingers white, Winnie dropped the bags on the kitchen floor, which was just a corner of the living room, and smiled. "Looks like both of us are starting from scratch, huh?"

"Yeah, I threw most of my old stuff out, didn't unpack yet. There's no phone or cable either."

Little feet were pounding on the ceiling. My upstairs neighbor probably had kids. "Jesus, what happened to your TV?"

I looked at the mess of hangers and tin foil sprouting out of the antennae. "No cable."

"Haha, we got cable in prison even."

There was no furniture either. Just a television, three cardboard boxes, two laundry baskets full of clothes, both clean and dirty, a white plastic trash bag full of hangers and sheets, and a sleeping bag. I'd managed to unpack my toothbrush, toothpaste, razor, shaving gel, deodorant, soap, shampoo, toilet paper, and towel. The place was clean and empty, like a one-star hotel room, except that the last guests stuffed the furniture into their suitcases along with the towels and miniature bars of soap. "Yeah, sorry you don't have a bed or anything. I figured we could get around to that stuff this week."

She lit a cigarette. "No biggie. Do you at least have an ashtray?"

"Yeah, that empty Diet Coke can by the sleeping bag." She grabbed the can and put it on the kitchen counter.

Besides laziness, I didn't know why I hadn't bought any furniture. I'd known for a couple weeks that Winnie was going to stay with me. I guess her not liking the place was making me happy. Housing an ex-addict with sixteen thousand dollars cash was not something I was crazy about.

"Jesus, let me set up in the bathroom, get ready, and let's get outta here. I don't even know where to sit or anything. It's like we should just stand here."

"Yeah, I pretty much only come here to shower, change, and sleep. So where we off to?"

"Let's go to the bar. I gotta make myself presentable first. God, look at these clothes. Inside, I spent all my money on cigarettes. I should've bought a shirt and pants at least."

"You can buy shit in prison?"

"Yep, there's a two-page list of stuff. Most people get their money from relatives. Twenty-five cents an hour don't cut it. None of you bastards visited or gave me money, so . . ."

"I didn't even know you could have money in prison."

"Well, there's a debit card and account."

"Is a quarter an hour even enough for smokes?"

"Nope. A friend used to visit and help out, though."

"Who?"

"A guy I met in a counseling program a couple years ago. He got out of jail before me, and we wrote and stuff. I'm supposed to check him out later."

She dropped her cigarette in the can, grabbed a couple of her shopping bags, and headed toward the bathroom. Once she left the room, the lack of sleep from the last few days hit me hard. I knocked on the door and told her I was going to take a nap, but I had a hard time falling asleep while thinking about her bag of money and this friend who'd been taking care of her. She'd walked out of jail with nothing but the shirt on her back, but she was bringing a lot more than that with her. I tried to sleep on my sleeping bag, but it was hotter than hell, even with the windows open. I looked out. The white and gray clouds were motionless and the leaves on the trees below were frozen in the hot air. I was taught between naps in high school that motion created heat, but it was never hotter than when the air was not moving. I'd missed that meteorological lesson.

I managed to get a couple hours of sleep after all. When I woke up, Winnie had the TV on and was toying around with my homeless Christmas tree. Behind the black-and-white fuzz was a commercial about the next episode of American Idol. The sun had begun to set, so the air was a bit cooler. Still, I felt the sweat on the back of my neck and woke up feeling tired and sick, like I did after just about every nap. I grabbed a cigarette and lit it.

"Man, I heard about this American Idol," Winnie said. "You watch this show?"

"Yeah, sometimes. It's better than all that other shit on TV. At least they can do something, not just act like dumb asses. Though they do some of that, too."

Network news was on. Winnie sat on the floor and leaned against the boxes. She was wearing makeup and her new designer clothes and looked like she hadn't spent a single day in jail. The only thing missing was jewelry. In the day, her wrists and forearms had been shackled with gold bracelets of every shape and size, making her look Egyptian or tacky, I wasn't sure which. All pawned for ice, I suspected. "You should've tried out," she said.

"I'm too old. They're looking for the next Britney or Justin, not a fat-ass Hawaiian in his thirties."

"That's right, you're Hawaiian. I forget sometimes."

"Haha, bitch."

She laughed. "There were some real Hawaiians in jail, like your long-lost aunty. She ate up all that Hawaiian-studies stuff they offered. Roots, baby."

"Man, was that jail or camp? Cable TV, school, cigarettes."

"Yeah it wasn't like the stuff you see on TV, not like a men's prison. Much better than O-triple-C." OCCC was the prison in Kalihi with the guard towers. "But I'll say this. You don't know how shitty not doing whatever you want to do is until you can't."

"Tongue twister."

"Asshole. Get up and get ready. Let's get out of here."

"Shit, I'm good to go."

"Good ol' Charlie."

We got to Mom's a little before seven. There were only a couple of customers there. One was an old haole man, a regular who for years had been coming to the bar right after work. He was a painter, or so I thought, because he was always in worn blue jeans with white paint stains on them. The seams of his jeans were frayed, and the knees were worn down to white string but there were no holes . His T-shirt was also faded and stained. His tanned, jerkied face had white stubble on it, but it probably wasn't a look for him; there wasn't that Don Johnson thing going on. He probably only shaved once a week. He'd been there just about every time I'd ever come to the bar early, with his Marlboro reds and Coors Light, watching his CNN. He rarely stayed past eight o' clock, and he always drank alone.

The other customer was like Mario, an old client of Mom's from her hostessing days. He was an older Japanese man, a carbon copy of the ten or so I saw at Club New Office. These were the guys in their fifties, married with kids, who worked white-collar jobs and never kicked the habit of hitting the bar after work. They all wore casual business attire from Sears or JC Penny, and they always made me wonder at what age a person completely loses his fashion sense. During my marriage, I was pretty much dressed by my wife, so I figured it wasn't that the husbands could no longer find the pulse of fashion, but that their wives had become practical and cheap. Not even looking for a pulse anymore, they'd pull a white sheet over fashion and let it rest in peace. These guys were old-school Bolohead Rowers. Most of them spoke with heavy pidgin accents, having grown up before TV became the national pastime—the babysitter—while Mom and Dad were at work. These guys grew up in the Stone Age, before you could buy SUVs with TVs in the backseats.

This guy, Eddie, was sitting at the bar and talking to Mom. Mario came out from the storage room—or the beer closet, as we used to call it as kids—bringing in a box of Bud Light to throw in the sink full of ice. "Early, ah?" Mom said.

Winnie walked behind the bar, hugged Mom, and kissed her on the cheek. It was a careful peck, both of them making sure that no makeup was smudged. For a moment it looked like someone was holding a mirror between them. "You rememba Uncle Eddie, Winnie?"

"Yeah, hi."

"Long time no see, eh?" Eddie said. "Ho you kids, grow up so fast. I rememba when you and Charlie running around dis place when you wuz dis high." He lifted his hand, carefully trying to estimate three feet. "Mark was one baby. How tings been?"

I remembered how in college there'd been this big thing on pidgin. It was scary the kind of shit eggheads had the time to think about. Pidgin was one of the many things I didn't have an opinion about, didn't give a shit about; to me, you either used it or you didn't. You were either old school or you weren't. The only thing that bugged me was when people who didn't come by it naturally tried to speak it, tried to be old school, like the haoles and Japanese guys running around with self-given Hawaiian names tattooed on their arms or shoulders. Eddie was old school, and even when he tried to speak plain English, he couldn't shake the pidgin. That was old-school country shit. It was real. People around my age learned to talk from the TV, radio, magazines, and movies, witnessing just about every situation imaginable. We had a line for everything and would bust out the mental Rolodex for gems like "Bitches ain't shit but hoes and tricks." These days, Clueless talk and Ebonics were bypassing pidgin in schools across the island.

Winnie talked to Eddie, showing a surprising amount of patience. Several years ago, she would have walked away without excuse or apology, leaving jaws floored. The one thing about Winnie I'd always been awed by was that she did whatever the fuck she wanted to do. She was like a basketball player who just refused one day to dribble the ball.

But she was smiling and listening to Eddie. Mom gave me a Bud Light. "Dis not da warm ones, eh?" I asked. The pidgin was contagious.

"No, I had um in da fridge since last night, dodo." Mom was old school.

Eddie was chatting away. A lot of these old drunks were motor-mouths, always asking the same questions and always pushing the two end-all-be-all issues on younger people: marriage and school. For them, if you went to college and then got married, your life would be candy. Eddie was talking to a thirty-four-year-old woman fresh out of jail, and it was like he was talking to Winnie at sixteen. Listening to him reminded me of being in ABC, the time warp and all, so I looked at the clock, waiting for Taks and Mark to show up. Winnie and Taks had had a three-week relationship over a decade ago, but he'd come, wanting to confirm that he got off light when she dumped him. With Taks, anything that happened years ago was still fresh. Two nights ago he'd asked, "Remember when we went to those two chicks' apartment and got stoned as hell, and they had that dick-sucking contest to see who could make one of us come the fastest?" I'd told him, that it'd been too many years to remember. Taks loved to talk about the good old days, though, and sometimes it was like listening to bad Hawaiian music.

Winnie politely excused herself to use the phone, which was within arm's length of her, like everything else in the bar, and Eddie said to Mom, "Good girl."

Then Eddie set his sights set on me. When I'd told him I was getting a divorce, he looked at me sort of puzzled. I had the degree and the wife, but my life wasn't candy. The marriage thing had turned me from a twenty-something into old man Charlie in a year. I'd wake up when it was still dark, turn on the Mr. Coffee for Sheila, buy my forty-four-ounce fountain Diet Coke from 7-Eleven on the way to work, read the sports page before I had to clock in, drive in traffic back home to Kaneʻohe, log on to Everquest for like five hours, take a break for dinner in between, brush my teeth after EQ, look at the stack of newspapers by the can, read the labels of shampoos, conditioners, and body soaps in the shower, seeing words like renewal, revitalize, enriched, and replenish, and then fall asleep to an old Seinfeld episode. It was the life that millions of parents dream of for their kids. But one day, I'd been pushing the lawnmower past my truck when I caught sight of my reflection: white T-shirt, khaki shorts, sandals over black socks. The image was made wide and short by the bend of the metal, and it looked like a big hand was pushing on my head, smashing me towards the ground. Eddie didn't say anything because Mom, the Yoda of divorce, was standing behind the bar. She didn't have a college degree, though, so Eddie, probably thought it was due to that. He was the kind of guy who told new parents to make sure they made their babies sleep on their stomachs.

Mom poured some Crown into a stainless-steel shaker and began to pour us chilled shots. Winnie was standing in the corner under the '84 Budweiser Los Angeles Olympics neon light, fighting for privacy while jammed up against Mom. Mom tapped her on the shoulder and handed her a shot, then gave ones to Eddie, Mario, and me. "Hey, Rudy, you like one shot? My daughter just came back home."

Addressing the old haole man sitting by himself in a booth, she was talking as if Winnie had been backpacking in Europe these last couple of years. When he joined us at the bar, we raised our glasses. "To me!" Winnie said. We all laughed.

It wasn't until about ten that the others started showing up. As with most bars, there were shifts. The geriatric squad, Eddie and Rudy, clocked out, and the younger guys began to trickle in to start the second watch. A few Japanese guys came in together, probably fans of Momo, who'd started her shift at eight. Mark showed up and then Taks. We were sitting in a booth by then. Taks shook hands with me and Mark and kissed Winnie on the cheek.

"Damn, Jon, you look exactly the same," Winnie said.

"Peter Pan," I said, smiling.

Momo came to the table, and Taks kissed her on the cheek and ordered a Bud Light. I hadn't talked to Momo yet. Winnie was cracking us up with her prison stories. There weren't any sordid tales of cat fights or strip searches gone bad—jail seemed more mundane than anything else—but she had a way of making things seem funny. She told us about a woman who'd spent five years inside, serving all of her time, and then was back one week later. Every time that happened, the other women would sneer or shake their heads, tripping on how someone could be so stupid. It was like going back to a Jerry Springer audience even more fucked up, Winnie said. But even if they all said, "No way, not them," everyone knew that the numbers didn't lie. When they got out, some would be coming back. It was probably like being a newlywed, Winnie said: you get married, going in knowing that there's a greater-than-fifty-percent chance the marriage will end in divorce, but never thinking it's going to be you. "Like you, fool." She looked at me.

"Yeah, only now it's your turn to face the statistics," I said.

"Pfft, bring on the six-five. Magic Eight Ball says, 'Outlook good.'"

"Damn, I get that at home whenever Jake comes out for vacation," Taks said.

"Nah, the women's prison sounds tame compared to what Jake said about Halawa," I said.

"You know why that is?" Winnie asked. "Men. I swear most of the chicks were there because of some man—or what some man got them into."

Taks had two brothers and one sister. All of their names started with "J." I knew at least four sets of families who were into that. In his, they had Jason, Jon, Jacob, and Jamie. There was always a Jason in a "J" sibling set, and a John, but the John was rarely the oldest. Folks seemed to be holding out before they hit the most common "J" name in the book. In Taks's family, Jason was the golden child: an engineer living with his wife and kids in Northern California. Jamie was the other college graduate; she had majored in something useless like political science; and now she worked as a waitress in Waikīkī. John and Jake were the pair of black sheep. Jake was in and out of prison because mixing grand theft and ice made people really stupid car thieves. Jake had one of the best arrest stories ever. He'd been on the freeway, cruising at about ninety and wearing an ear piece tuned to the police scanner. When it picked up some news about the pursuit of a stolen motorcycle, it took him a few to realize that they were talking about him. There were so many blue strobe lights, he said, he felt like a nightclub was chasing him. He tried to get away but crashed; no broken bones, no nothing but scrapes and bruises. It was funny how it was always the semi-cleancuts who bit it on motorcycles; the criminals seemed to walk away from what should've killed them. In a nuclear war, roaches and guys like Jake would crawl away from the mushroom cloud.

Mark was daydreaming as usual, probably thinking about his computer game. When I'd been playing, we used to talk on the phone every day, but that had stopped when I quit. "EQ jonesing?" I asked.

"Yeah, sort of. I left a raid. Hope it's going OK."

Taks shook his head. The Japanese guys Momo was sitting by were singing Prince's "Seven" on karaoke. It was right up there with "Mandy" as one of my least favorite karaoke songs. I wanted to say they sounded like cats fucking, but it was worse than that because it was much louder and lacked the romance. But I'd been coming to bars at Bolohead Row for so many years, it was like I lived by the freeway. I got used to the noise and pollution.

"You still messing with that stupid game?" Taks said.

Mark was half-Japanese and half-Korean, so , he was short, but he didn't look like your typical computer nerd. He'd been

McKinley's best wrestler, and he power-lifted after that, getting his bench up to four hundred. Though he hadn't touched a weight in three years, you could imagine it'd take him about three seconds to smoke Taks. It'd be like watching a bullet go through a matchstick.

"Yep, still playing. You still get drunk every night?"

"Yeah, but I get laid."

"Big man," Mark said. His voice was getting high, which it tended to do when he got excited.

Winnie put her hands up. "This is what I mean. Men. Just let me know when either of you move out of your parents' house. That guy is the winner."

We all laughed. "Seriously, though," Mark said, "I get heat for playing EQ, and you know what? I like doing it, and it pays the bills. People ask, 'But what about real life?'" He raised his hands and looked around the bar. "You mean I'm missing all this?"

Mom came over with a tray of shots for us, then squeezed into the side of the booth with Mark and Winnie. She was drunk. It was the only time she got close to people, even her kids. "Jon, you shithead, I thought I banned you," Mom said. "And Winnie—so what, you going work?"

She'd always been this kind of drunk: circling her turf, looking for blood. She drank every night, but she only got drunk about three times a week. She was slowing down. "Take it easy, Mom," Mark said.

Winnie ignored her. "Charlie, sing a song!"

"Yeah!" Taks said.

This sort of thing happened whenever I went to a bar with a karaoke machine. It got old fast, and it was most often the people who had to be the sickest of hearing my voice who asked me to sing the same three or four songs. Sitting, talking, and drinking weren't enough. A successful bar needed a large inventory of blinking distractions.

While I launched into my rendition of "Me and Mrs. Jones" for the bazillionth time—not even following the words—Winnie's friend came walking in. It had to be her friend because this guy had tattoos that went up each arm and anti-Bolohead Row written all over his face. Plus, he was Winnie's type.

For some reason, seeing him made me remember going to the doctor's office when I was a kid. The waiting area used to have this small, wooden table with shapes cut out of its surface—squares, rectangles, circles, triangles, and stars—and a lot of blocks in different shapes painted crayon colors. The idea was for kids to match up the blocks with the holes, keeping them occupied, stimulating their minds, whatever. I'd never stopped doing this, only it was with people now. I'd look at someone and try to figure out where he or she belonged.

Winnie's friend looked like he belonged in a cage. He had an over-the-top prison look: his head was shaved; he had tattoos running from his wrists up, blotches of black I couldn't make out in the dim lights; and he was veiny and tanned. But it was his face that most made him cage material. He looked like he was waiting for something bad to happen—not in a paranoid way, but in a relaxed way—like something bad happened every time he stepped into a room.

He came to the booth. He was about Taks's height and Asian to boot, but Taks looked like a Japanese, wigged-out-on-heroin male model compared to this guy. Plus, Taks had big eyes that seemed un-Asian, while this guy had little slits below his veiny forehead. The wooden blocks at the booth fit at this bar, even me. Me and Winnie, the two who weren't trapped in the look, used clothes like chameleons. I liked to think we could probably fit into most places without raising eyebrows, at least at first.

As soon as Winnie saw the guy, she jumped out of the booth and gave him a hug. One of his forearms had a big koi on it, I saw now, the other a dragon. Original, I thought. It was a hard hug. Soft hugs were like shaking hands.

The song ended, and Winnie said, "Hey everyone, this is my friend, B."

He shook hands with everyone. Mom smiled, then went back to the bar. "B"? People wanted to be black so bad it was funny. At least it wasn't Grandmaster B. "Holy shit," Taks said. "You used to do security at the derbies, yeah? Long time ago?"

"Yeah, that was a while back."

"Charlie, you don't remember him? Fuckin' small island. I used to always go. You had my dream job." The image of Taks working security for anywhere made me laugh. If anything, the sight of him would egg criminals on.

"Yeah, any job that you would have would have to be in a dream," Mark said.

"Look who's talking."

"I made four thousand dollars last week, bitch. What about you?"

"You need to get laid, man."

Mark was drunk. He'd been in front of a computer for the last three years, so what little alcohol tolerance he had was gone. He'd always had something against Taks, but then, a lot of people did. Taks was one of those guys whom everyone liked at first, but started hating soon after they got to know him. Taks would say, "They just jealous," and he would be partially right. Taks never sweated anything. Peter Pan is all right unless that little bastard is flying around you constantly, rubbing that never-never land shit in your face.

"Maintenance check, no problem, 'cause I got the money," Mark said.

"Shut the fuck up," Winnie said. Her alcohol tolerance had always been high, but we'd started drinking earlier than everyone else and it'd been a while for her.

"What's 'maintenance check'?" B asked. He was grinding out pretend curiosity for Winnie's sake.

"Massage parlor." Taks smiled. "It's what we call it."

Winnie got up and went to the bar. I turned to B, trying to be friendly. "So what do you do now?"

"I stir curry."

"You stir curry?"

"Yeah, at a lunch wagon in Kalihi."

"No offense," Taks said, "but how the hell do you go from running derbies to stirring curry?"

We all knew the answer right after he asked, even Taks, who had a tendency to ask questions that he would know the answer to if he'd just shut his mouth and think about it.

"I was incarcerated," B said. He sounded professorly, but his voice also had a note of melodrama, like one telling ghost stories.

Momo came by and asked if we needed any drinks. We ordered a round of Bud Lights. Winnie was at the bar, talking to Mario.

"Hey, you ever met a guy named Jake Takahashi there?" Taks asked. "My brother is in Halawa."

"Nope. I was in federal. Terminal Island. Sounds bad, but better than Halawa. I do federal time standing on my head."

It seemed impolite to ask what he'd done to land himself in jail and how long he'd been there, so I knew that Taks was about to ask. I was curious, too. This guy was mixed up with Winnie somehow, and besides that, townies like me had a thing for ex-con stories. It was like we had two superstars in the bar.

"So what'd you do?" Taks asked.

"Jesus, man. It's none of your business," Mark said.

B put his hands on his head, fingers locked. "Take a wild guess."

Despite hopes of presidential assassination attempts or the robbery of the U.S. Mint, we all knew, of course: drugs.

"Damn, that sucks," Taks said. "My brother is in for a hot cold twenty and petty drug shit." He was trying to speak the lingo. Mark looked at me and shook his head.

"I just got one thing to say," I interrupted. "You need to make a curry-stirring exercise video or something, because it must be one hell of a workout. Look at those arms."

We all laughed. Momo returned with the beers. I felt like I should talk with her or something, but the only thing that had happened between us was I had passed out at her place for a few hours. I figured there was no reason to sweat it.

"Hey, you remember a girl they called Wonder Woman at the derbies, with all the bracelets?" Taks asked.

B shook his head. "There was more than one."

"She was fuckin' fine, yo," Taks said.

To someone watching us, the scene would've looked pathetic. A bunch of townie guys trying to talk to B while making sure our voices didn't crack. We might as well have all had our palms up. There was no missing the look. He wasn't one of those fools you saw at bars: small-time dealers who bought fifty-thousand-dollar automobiles but still lived with their parents and never did time once. Those guys had the same looks on their faces as cops: cockiness without the pain. B had the pain, looking like it had been shoveled on him all his life.

By the end of the night, Mark was sleeping in the booth and Taks had left to meet Joe for KB—Korean bar—hopping so that Joe could pay for leg rubs while Taks insulted hostesses. Winnie, B, and I were sitting in front of warm beers while Mario swept and Mom cashed out the register. It was two thirty, and I'd gotten past the point of drunk. My head pounded as a hangover set in.

"Can we give B a ride?" Winnie asked. "He caught the bus here, and I promised him I'd find him a ride."

"No problem. Maybe we should give Mr. Computer Geek Superstar a ride, too. He can get his car tomorrow."

We woke Mark up and went back and forth with him on whether he should drive home. Deciding to drive himself, he crawled into his Lexus SUV, paid for by Everquest. Mark loved posting pictures of himself in that car on his server message boards. It was like he was trying to convince people that he wasn't your typical loser computer geek. He shrugged off snide Asian jokes and knew the message took: "I'm better at this game and RL than all you assholes." The truth of the matter was that that car saw about as much daylight as he did. But I wasn't one to criticize; my life was lived under fluorescent lights during the day and again, the dim lights of bars at night. And Mark had fun. A god in his never-never land, he even had the phone number of some of the game developers.

Mark had two names in Everquest. One was Bolo Badcow, his level-65 ogre warrior who had some of the best gear in the game. He'd named him after the Korean actor who had a monstrous chest and played bad guys in Enter the Dragon and Kickboxer. Bolo was guild leader of "Descent." His other name, his Ebay player-auctions name, was Mifune. This was the guy who drove the prices of platinum pieces up and down every time he beat the game developers and created a program that enabled his characters to manufacture platinum when he wasn't even at the keyboard. He was like a robber baron in his universe, and it left little room for the RL Mark. That Mark was just a typical Korean-Japanese townie whom you wouldn't look at twice. You wouldn't be interested in the humdrum facts: he was good at math and sports in high school, a good power lifter after high school, an ex–banquet porter at the Hilton in Waikīkī, a community-college dropout, and a guy who still lived with his mom as he approached thirty. He was no superstar in RL.

The Mifune thing reminded me of B, who was giving me directions to his place in Kalihi. He didn't look like Toshiro Mifune, but he had that same scowl: the "Life is hard, but I'm harder" look. I wondered what it looked like when he got mad and whether he really stirred curry for a living. I stopped wondering when we got to his place and saw the sign in front that said in red, "Studios for rent: $300 a month." There was a little counter window by the glass double-door entrance that had another sign: "Cigeretts $3.00." The counter looked shady, like more than smokes were sold there. The place was the kind you'd imagine an ex-con curry-stirrer lived in: like a three-story building held up by a million cockroaches. When I was a kid, I'd lived in a place just like it after me and my dad got evicted from the beach and moved to town so that he could scrape gum off sidewalks.

"Charlie," Winnie said, "I'm gonna stay with B tonight. He has furniture."

I smiled. I'd often dropped her off at guys' houses before, after nights of drinking or two-day binges of smoking rocks all over Makiki and Bolohead Row: at the apartment, in the parking lot of Hawaiian Brian's, in bathroom stalls at bars. I wasn't thinking that B was a druggie. He looked too healthy, too tanned, too buff.

I wasn't thinking he was a dealer either; living in a shit-hole like that would defeat the whole purpose of dealing drugs. He was a curry-stirrer, like my dad was a sidewalk-gum-remover. I was beginning to fantasize that Milton Bradley would hire me to make a new-and-improved version of Life. The possibilities were endless. Then again, anyone who drew the career cards for curry-stirrer or sidewalk-gum-remover probably would quit right then and there and not touch the color wheel. These job cards would have to be ones you brought out in the middle of the game, maybe when a player landed on a jail square and had to draw a new career card. He'd also have to draw a new house card: projects, roach motel, tent on the beach, cardboard box on the street with a pillow of cigarette butts and a mattress of broken glass.

B shook my hand and thanked me for the ride. Winnie gave me a kiss on the cheek and said, "Good ol' Charlie. Pick me up tomorrow? You're off, right?"

"Yeah, call me on my cell. Maybe we can go get some furniture."

The desire to buy furniture reminded me of Sheila. After I pulled away, I decided to drive through downtown instead of taking the freeway back home. There was no such thing as three-a.m. traffic. I drove through Chinatown, through bum-and-crack-ho central. Me and Taks used to come here and hit the "casino" back in the day. It was a far cry from Vegas: big, metal door with stairs behind it leading to a small room with stained blackjack and craps tables, old mamas bringing you drinks in one hand and taking drags from lit cigarettes in the other. Sometimes we'd come out of the door at six a.m. and watch downtown turn. The bums, prostitutes, and down-and-out hustlers were slowly replaced by men in aloha shirts and women in smart business suits. I suppose every city has a downtown like this.

I passed a couple of hookers a block past a police station. One of them might have been a man—maybe both. This wasn't like Waikīkī or the massage parlors in Bolohead Row. Some of these hookers wore jeans and looked like they did their makeup with finger paint. Most of them were druggies. I passed a dealer; I knew he was a dealer because he had nice clothes on. I grabbed a bottle of aspirin from the glove compartment and took four for the hangover; if a hundred-pound girl could take two, a two-hundred-and-fifty-pound man could take four. I didn't have anything to drink, so I chewed the tablets. My mouth was so dry that the chalk stuck to my tongue and the roof of my mouth. I lit a cigarette, thinking how funny it was that rock bottom was right in between a police station and the state capitol.

I decided to call Momo. She answered and told me that she had class in the morning. I apologized for not talking to her, saying I had to entertain my sister and all. I asked her what she was majoring in, but she didn't want to talk, so I let her go. I called Taks; no answer. I called Sheila; no answer. I regretted calling her. She'd see my number on caller ID. I was driving down King Street and going through the numbers on my cell. Some of these people I hadn't talked to in years.

I slipped in my Mary J. Blige CD. A six-foot-four Hawaiian singing "Sweet Thing" at the top of his lungs, spitting out aspirin dust on the steering wheel of his Dodge 4x4, driving down King Street, hanging a left on Keeaumoku to head into Makiki to sleep by his cardboard boxes. The night was cool, probably its normal low seventies, the stars were out, the music was cherry, the wind was blowing on my bolohead, and I wanted to drive into a telephone pole and didn't know why. If it was Kaau Crater Boy's "Surf" playing on my stereo, I would've rammed the Dodge right through the lobby of my building.

3

Crystal meth, like just about any other street drug, has a bunch of aliases. The most popular is "ice," but people also call it "batu," which means "rock" in Filipino or Malaysian or whatever. There are other names, like "Hawaiian salt" and "ma'a," which means "rock" in Samoan. I've never heard it called "pohaku," Hawaiian for "rock," but I figure someone probably has.

My story was typical I guess. I'd tried it for free in high school, thought it tasted like apple Jolly Rancher, then started buying quarters once in a while because I felt bad about people turning me on and my not returning the favor. I didn't get carried away until my late teens. I was buying quarters for a hundred bucks from one of Winnie's friends, who basically lived at Hawaiian Brian's and played pool the way Mark played EQ. The quarter thing soon wasn't economically viable, though, so we'd buy grams for about two-twenty-five, getting more bang for the buck. It was like smoking cigarettes: a pack-a-day smoker buys a pack every day. A pack-a-day smoker turns into a two-pack-a-day smoker, and thinks, damn, I should just buy cartons, turning that fool into a three-pack-a-day smoker. Drug dealers and tobacco companies knew what they were doing.

I was more of a drinker than a druggie in high school, but in college, I'd found a pretty study partner for chemistry class, and we were in Hamilton Library one night, tired as hell and studying for the final. She led me to the bathroom and we took a few hits. We then studied our asses off, and I felt like I was retaining the information better because of the ice. I swore I could see the periodic table when I closed my eyes. We joked around, breaking down the word methamphetamine, moving our books to her dorm room. She told me how nervous she was about asking me if I wanted her to turn me on, then she described her boyfriend, and explained how their relationship sucked. We went into the final with zero sleep and aced it.

Her name was Lynette, and I'd been grateful to her; she was my first pretty little Japanese girlfriend, the type of girl who hadn't given me the time of day in high school. We'd hang out in the pool halls, at her dorm room, and drive up to Tantalus at night, smoking ice while looking out at the "Honolulu City Lights"; I'd play the song on my ukulele even. We'd get high and horny, telling each other sex was a bazillion times better on ice, but the A I got on my chemistry final was the last A of that year.

We all smoked, even Taks, but he never got caught up in it. He was like I was in high school; he'd buy once in a while just to not feel bad, but he never got hooked. He liked drinking better; he liked crowds, not sitting in a car with a couple of friends and sneaking hits while everyone anxiously kept an eye out for cops.

Winnie had been hooked since high school, and when Lynette left me for her ex-boyfriend, the dealer, the one whom she'd claimed beat her and threatened to kill her, I was left without a partner, so me and Winnie hooked up. By that time, I was twenty-one, and it'd been two years since I'd been kicked out of college. I was waiting tables at a four-star steakhouse, making enough money to not have to steal shit to buy ice.

Winnie, on the other hand, didn't have a job, so she stole. She broke into cars, stole cars, stole motorcycles, and broke into houses. She stole from Mom and was out of the house after that. Her thieving went from snatching purses through open windows of parked cars at graveyards to breaking into houses randomly at night, thinking that just because the lights were off, no one was home. She sometimes got chased out by people wielding things like kitchen knives and three-pronged spears. She even had a can of roach spray thrown at her once.

It was at about this time that I dumped the ukulele and songbook. After work, I started hitting karaoke bars with Taks and when the bars closed at two, hooking up with Winnie if I didn't hook up with a girl at the bar. Smoking with Winnie till the sun came up, I would drop her off at this guy's house or that guy's house afterwards.

Then came Rhonda. Rhonda was the new hostess at the steakhouse. She was a haole girl from California, some town with "Santa" in front of it, who was working part-time while majoring in marine biology at UH. I cleaned up my act. She was the microbrewery type, so I found myself in bars that I'd never stepped in before. Some of these bars were in Waikīkī, some in downtown. Her crowd all seemed to play in the ocean on weekends; they all surfed, sailed, kayaked, or paddled. Rhonda loved to kayak and was sorely disappointed every time I told her I didn't want to go, lying that I'd gotten my fill of that stuff when I was a teenager.

To her credit, she'd come out with me and Taks and sit in the karaoke bars, sometimes even drinking Bud Lights. I liked her a lot. She was the one who'd gotten me back into school and helped me decide my major. "What are you interested in?" she'd asked, and I'd said, "I wouldn't mind making money." So I busted my ass at Kapiolani Community College, returned to UH, and majored in marketing. Living with Rhonda was easy because she was so active; on the weekends, she'd go to the beach with her kayak strapped to her '83 Ford station wagon, which had the fake wood paneling, while I'd stay home and watch sports. I was so far gone on ESPN that even stuff like women's pool would keep me indoors.

"Sorry, babe, women's pool is on. I was waiting for this one."

She dumped me, of course, for a haole surfer guy who was in med school. So I ran back to Bolohead Row and Winnie. Winnie was dealing at this point, but she fixed me up and begged me to get out of my funk and finish college because I only had one semester left. I used the ice to get out of bed, and just like during the Lynette days, it worked great at first. If I hadn't graduated, I would've still been at the steakhouse, making twice as much as I did at ABC. That would have been tragic.

Then, one day, me and Winnie were on day four of Winnie and Charlie on Ice, hiding out in my Rhonda-free apartment from Winnie's boyfriend, who was accusing her of ripping him off, and we began to talk about all the bastards and bitches we'd hooked up with. In bad shape after Rhonda, I kept thanking her for saving me, and she'd said, "Good ol' Charlie, what are friends for?"

I didn't look at myself, but I imagine that I'd been leaning against the bed, sweating and bug-eyed, wearing the same T-shirt I'd had on for two days, smelling like ammonia, and being played by my sister, who was playing with her magic Eight Ball while talking to me. "You mean 'what are sisters for?'"

"Well, technically . . ."

I came down bad after that, slept for about twelve hours straight, and found myself cleaned out. Not that I had much, but the money and credit cards in my wallet were gone, my CDs too. The thing of it was that I felt so damn bad about what'd happened that I wished she'd taken everything I'd owned. I would have felt cleaner. She didn't have to sleep with me. She could've just waited till I passed out. I never knew why it'd happened, and I didn't want to think about it. It was like I was the victim of a series of piss-poor carpenters who built bad houses and then ran the hell out after the roof was done so that shit wouldn't fall on them. All three of them ran from me, Lynette, Rhonda, and Winnie, though I was glad Winnie ran. After it happened, I shrugged and told myself, I guess I was due.

Sheila called Tuesday morning, and at first I didn't understand why. Then I remembered my three-a.m. phone call and thinking that she'd see my number on caller ID. She called early, too, probably assuming that I'd be going work.

Sheila was worried, and it was sort of a high talking to her and feeling nervous about it. I told her it was just one of those nights. She knew me well enough to know that this meant I was drunk and feeling un-cherry. "Charlie," she said in her motherly tone, "you can't call me like that."

That was another thing about being married that bugged the shit out of me. It was like my wife had become my second mother. Take out the trash, pick up your laundry, I bought you clothes today because I dress you now, don't smoke, don't drink. I'd wished I could've said, "I was doing just fine before you came along," but that would've been bullshit. My choices seemed to be reduced to two things, like most choices are, because people never see door number three or four. They live on the board of Life with almost no chance of landing on the Nobel Prize square or ending the game at Millionaire Estates; or they get off the board. One of my favorite songs of all time was Springsteen's "Born to Run," but the Boss never told me to where to run to, though I was pretty sure he meant off the board. Putting the semi in reverse and rolling back to the thing I'd been running from in the first place was not it.

"Sorry, Sheila." It felt strange calling her by her name. She'd always been "babe" or "honey" to me, so I felt like I was addressing a stranger. "How you doing anyway?"

"Not bad. You?"

"Same 'ol, same' ol." The quality of the conversation hadn't changed.

"Take care then."

"You, too."

It was about seven a.m., and it was already hot. Sunlight streamed through the window, making the parts of the carpet I wasn't sleeping on hotter than what was underneath me. I'd scored three and a half hours of sleep, which was becoming standard. I felt bad that I couldn't say more to Sheila, but it didn't feel like I was holding back, which made it even worse. I thought about the one thousand origami cranes she'd made for the wedding: a thousand silver-foiled birds pressed against a frame and locked in by a plate of glass. I wondered if she'd kept that. It was probably damn hard to throw something like that away.

I went to the bathroom to brush my teeth and shave the stubble off my head. I threw on some clothes and headed for the 7-Eleven by Puck's Alley, about a mile east of Bolohead Row. I was in morning traffic, but this 7-Eleven had the best fountain Diet Coke in town—the perfect mixture of carbonated water and syrup that was never flat—so the trip was worth it. I loaded my cup up to the top with ice, filled it with soda, threw a Slurpee dome cover on it so that it wouldn't spill in the truck, and grabbed a Slurpee straw, the only straw long enough to drink from with that clear, plastic dome on top. I'd never understood how people drank coffee in the morning in Hawai'i; it was too damn hot.

The soda was going to work on my cotton mouth. I popped four aspirins and was feeling oddly cherry for some reason. I had the air conditioning on and, thinking of the Springsteen song I'd remembered earlier that morning, put in "Born to Run" and just drove. I was about a quarter into my drive around the island, which meant I'd only been on the freeway for about thirty minutes, when Winnie called me. I had a tough time figuring out which cutoff to take so that I could spin around and head back into town. The only thing I'd learned about weather in Hawai'i all these years was to be able to tell when it was going to rain. There might not even be that many clouds in the sky, but there would be no wind and the air would get sticky, as if it was made of glue. It was that kind of hot. Back in college, an English professor had asked us to write about the most important thing in our lives. I wrote about air conditioning.

Winnie was waiting outside the roach motel, wearing the same clothes she'd had on last night. The sun was beating down on her light-brown hair, and the black clothes probably weren't helping her stay cool. Her bare feet were in the gutter, her clunky shoes and purse clutched to her side, and her white skin wasn't turning pinkish, but looked even whiter than usual. She looked tired, too, which was a good thing. She got into the truck. "Thank fuckin' God: air conditioning."

"Yeah, it's fuckin' hot today. Where's B?"

"He had to go stir that curry."

I laughed. "Have a good night?"

"Yeah, it was nice."

"Damn, one day out of prison."

"That ain't a new headline."

"I drove through downtown after I dropped you guys off. Made me worry."

"No worry, beef curry. B is about as anti-drug as you can get."

"Yeah, he seems like that." Anti-drug drug dealer—that had to be a first.

"Can you take me home? I need a shower something fierce. B's place has a community shower, the kind you gotta wear slippers in."

"Yeah, so what after? Furniture shopping?"

"Sure, whatever. I got the mother of all hangovers. I need a soda."

"7-Eleven right there." Winnie had been the one who'd gotten me into fountain Diet Coke years before. She preached it good and was right; once you started on the diet, the regular stuff was way too sweet.

"So how'd you meet B again? You said some program?"

"Yeah. Can you believe that shit? Happens all the time; you know, there ain't no more romantic place than rehab."

"SWA lookin' for SWA."

"Yeah, he's on parole now, like me. Dealer, not user."

"Do those even exist?"

"Very rare. The Feds busted him at the airport. Profiled at HNL. They say that's illegal, but the Feds pretty much do whatever they want. It's a crazy story. Let me grab a soda, and I'll fill you in."

We stopped at 7-Eleven. Winnie came back with a large cherry Slurpee, which sort of disappointed me. "Mmm, you miss this kind of stuff," she said. "So anyway, B and this Mexican get off the plane from California, the Mexican following him to baggage claim, then the Mexican gets stopped. Idiot gives consent, and that's all she wrote."

"You play, you pay."

"I guess. Either way, B is arrested a month later. He's flown to Oakland a day after that—no lawyer, no nothing—and thrown in with a bunch of strangers in Humboldt County Jail. The only Hawaiian there. Land of the free and the brave."

It didn't surprise me. He looked Chinese, which meant jack in Hawai'i. If you had any Hawaiian blood, you were Hawaiian. You could have blond hair and blue eyes, but if you had the blood, that was it. "And he don't smoke?"

"That month he was waiting to get arrested, he smoked up a storm. Said it was the worst month of his life. You know how it makes you paranoid. Said he'd never smoke that shit again— was almost happy to go to jail."

"So where's his lunch wagon?" I asked.

"Just across the canal."

"Why do they call him B?"

"His real name is Bully Ching. Now, you know what kind of father someone had if his name is Bully. But 'Bully' is a bit retro, so people just started calling him B. He grew up in Kalihi. KPT."

Kalihi is about as close to a ghetto as Hawai'i can manage. It has Kuhio Park Terrace, KPT, the most notorious of the low-income housing projects, packed with Samoans and Filipinos; Pua Lane, which had been a landmark drug-dealing corner; and a couple dozen Korean Bars, KBs, that are the poor man's version of Bolohead Row. Kalihi is on the west side of town. As you move east, you have downtown, then Bolohead Row, Ala Moana, then Makiki to the north and Waikīkī to the south, Manoa and UH, then Kaimuki. I'd heard that Honolulu was one of the bigger cities in the U.S., and it surprised the hell out of me. It seems damn small to me. All of these places are squished together, but then that's what a city is.

After Winnie gave me background on B, I explained the whole Slurpee dome thing to her, which I'd considered possibly the only invention of my life. She nodded with approval, and we went back to the apartment. "I'm gonna go bocha," she said, using the same word for "bathe," probably Japanese or

Hawaiian, so she showered while I fiddled around with the TV. There was no air conditioning, and at one point I wanted to throw the TV out the window because it was so hot. A TV shattered on the sidewalk would have been a nice shake of the fist at the sun and motionless air. When Winnie got out, I decided I needed a shower, too. After I came out, I found her crashed out on my sleeping bag. As long as I'd known her, she'd slept on her back, arms across her chest, like she was in a coffin. I guessed furniture shopping would have to wait.

It was a weird feeling looking around a room and not knowing where to sit. It occurred to me that when I'd been living with Sheila, everything had been hers. The queen-sized bed—the one she used to try to inch me off of by going fetal in the middle of sleep—was hers. On some nights, I had to go fetal in a corner myself just to stay on. The sheets, pillowcases, and blankets were all hers. The furniture, the sofa, the bookcases, the dressers, the TV and stereo stand, mostly from Wal-Mart, were all hers. The computer and its desk were hers. Everything in the kitchen was hers, except for my knife set and spice rack, both of which she'd bought me as gifts; these were now in one of my boxes by the TV. Even the shirt on my back might as well have been hers; she'd bought it. I did bring a La-Z-Boy into the marriage, and I regretted not taking it with me, but I'd been too lazy to throw it in the back of my truck. Considering that just about everything was hers, the fact that nothing matched didn't make sense to me. Then I thought of something. It wasn't that everything didn't match; it was more like the old had been continually replaced by the new. If I'd held out for several more years, the pink sofa, the old white dressers, the Tweety Bird shower curtain, and even the kitchen sink, would've been replaced. But by then, the new stuff would be old. That was no way to live.

I didn't need any of that, but I would've killed for a chair. I stood over Winnie for a few minutes, not knowing what to do with myself. What a cherry day off, I thought. It was early, not even noon yet, and I knew Taks was sleeping. I figured I would check out Mark. Maybe he'd let me kill time on one of his computers. It was a toss-up for me which was the best time killer: the TV, the computer, or drinking. All I knew was that time needed to die something fierce.

When I got to Mom's apartment, she was sleeping and Mark was running the show on his computers. He was in his normal monster-raid attire: boxers—purple today—and nothing else. "Hey man, what's up?"

"Setting up for an RZ back flag raid. We got a bunch of apps that need flagging. It's early, though, so attendance is lacking. Fucking slackers."

RZ, Rallos Zek, was the god of war in Mark's world. In Mark's world, Mark conquered gods. "You got a free computer?" I asked. "I'm bored."

"Yeah. When you come here, it's gotta be desperation. Where's Winnie?"

"Sleeping."

"Hold on, let me log off my plat mule."

His plat mule's name was actually "Plaatmuule," probably because "Platmule," "Platmulle," "Plaatmule," "Plattmule," and so forth, were all taken. You couldn't have duplicate names on a server. You could always tell that someone was old school if his or her toon's name was spelled how it was meant to be spelled. Well, Plaatmuule was moving back and forth—buying supplies, making food, and selling it back to the vendor for a profit—and Mark wasn't even at the keyboard. He'd written a program or something. He ran it 24/7 and would sell the plat for real-life cash until the programmers pulled the plug on him again; then he'd have to work on making a new exploit program. You'd think he was the one with the business degree, the CEO dodging and adapting to new tax laws. He should've been working for Enron.

"You wanna say hi to the guys?" he asked.

These were my best friends for a couple of years, most of them named after a character in some fantasy novel. I only knew a few of their real names. "Nah. I'll check my e-mail or something. You sure you want to take this guy out of the sweatshop? I could use another one."

"Nah, it's cool."

I checked my e-mail. There were junk-mail solicitations saying I'd won, or that today was my lucky day, or that I could buy cures for just about every male affliction, from limp dick to sex deprivation. I logged off. "Wanna go eat lunch or something?"

"Sorry bro, can't ATM."

I wondered how much harder it was to say "at the moment." "ATM" was easier to type, but to say?

Mark's room used to be our room. The bunk beds were gone now, and the room was filled with broken computers, a futon, and the sound of tapping keyboards. "So what you gonna do after they shut down EQ?"

"They won't for a while. If you had twelve bucks a month flowing in from like half a million people, would you? Besides, Sony got SWG and EQ 2 coming out. There will always be a game. SWG is like EQ, but it's set in Star Wars land. Most noobs say stuff like they can't wait to raid Vader and own his punk ass. Idiots. You won't be able to kill Vader in-game. It would ruin the continuity of the whole storyline. It'll probably suck, but these games are being pumped out now. One will own."

I had that burning feeling in my eyes from lack of sleep. I supposed a nap would do me good. I had to be at work the next day. I flopped on Mark's futon and closed my eyes, putting out the fires with tears. "It's as hot as fuck here."

"Yeah, sec." He turned on the air conditioning with a remote control. "So, Charlie, no offense, but you got friends or what? Or a hobby or some shit? I mean, I don't mind that you're here, but why the hell would you come over on a day off? I mean, ABC sucks ass, yeah?"

"My friends are either at work or sleeping. Plus, it's Tuesday."

"Wanna play my cleric on the raid?"

"Nah, I'd probably fuck it up, rusty and all."

"So you just gonna wait here for everyone to wake up?"

"Yeah, wait just like you're waiting."

"No shit. I know the east coasters are getting off from school and work now. Fucking slackers."

I faded off and dreamt that I was sitting in a red car, and Winnie was driving. The top was down, and she kept saying, "Let's go to Countryside Acres or Sandy Beach." My other least favorite song—I had about two dozen of those—"Love and Honesty" was on the radio, only it was some awful karaoke rendition of the song, like you'd hear in a bar on Bolohead Row on any given night. Winnie kept repeating, "Countryside Acres or Sandy Beach?" Then she started yelling random things like "Visit a museum!" "Flat tire!" "Lose your job. Start a new career!" "Happy honeymoon!" "Twins!" I woke up, my neck sweaty as usual. Mark hadn't moved. "How long was I sleeping?"

"I dunno, maybe two days in game time."

"Damn." I stood up and stretched, cracking my back. Cracking bones was always a good time. Each snap convinced me that I was getting older, and it was weird, but being right about it seemed more important than wishing it wasn't happening.

I went to the living room where Mom was talking on the phone. She wore a beat-up, powder-blue bathrobe and fuzzy slippers that were so old they had bald patches. The slippers had been around since I was a kid. Her hair was short, the way most fifty-somethings cut their hair. I'd always thought they did that because they didn't care about their looks anymore, but Taks had told me one night, "Nah, they trying to look cute."

She hung up the phone. Winnie got her little-girl cheeks from Mom, and maybe the long mouth with the pouty bottom lip, but other than that, they didn't look much alike. It might have been the different expressions they wore. Mom always looked mad or worried, while Winnie could be staring down a gun and look as if the world were her oyster. Mom's furrowed brow dug so deep that it looked like the spot between her tattooed eyebrows was going to keep swelling until it split open. "That was the police, by da way."

"What's up?"

"Afta all you guys left last night, some guys came and said dey was looking for Winnie."

"What kind of guys?"

"Big guys. Dey said twins, but neva look like each other."

After shaking off the eerie feeling of déjà vu from just dreaming about Winnie saying "twins," it all made sense to me. Where did a one-hundred-twenty-pound addict get twenty grand? From big guys. Then Mom said, "I told dem she was staying wit' you, but dey said you wasn't listed."

"Yeah, I didn't get a phone or anything yet."

"So I called the police 'cause I was scared."

"Winnie is on parole, Mom. I dunno if that was a swift move."

"I dunno what she into. Dey asked, the big guys and da police. 'I don't know nothing,' I said."

"Man, it's only been one day."

She could look grumpy as hell, but for some reason, never defeated, never tired. She lit a cigarette. "Dey was scary-looking guys, like dat guy dat came last night, Winnie's friend, except dey had nicer clothes and was bigger."

"Did they threaten you?"

"Dey didn't have to. I was scared anyways. Dey was staring at your Uncle Mario when dey was asking questions."

Mark came walking out of his room. It was weird how he felt comfortable shirtless all the time with those big-ass areolas. Thirty more pounds, and he'd have full-blown titties. "What's up?"

"Sounds like drama to me," I said.

"Winnie?" he asked.

"You know it," I said.

"Cherry," he said, then walked into the kitchen, rubbing his stomach. The atrophied muscles from sitting in front of the computer were all in his gut.

"I'll talk to her, Mom," I said.

"OK, OK, you good boy, Charlie. What Winnie always say? 'Good ol' Charlie.'"

"I always hated that."

"It's true, though, not like your father. You good boy."

I'd gone to the apartment out of boredom, looking for something to do. That seemed to be the way of the world: boredom led to nothing but trouble.

I'd never broken a single bone in my body. I'd sprained my ankle a couple of times, but I wasn't even sure if they'd been sprains; I could still limp along. I'd never had an injury or been sick to the point that I felt I needed to go to emergency. Maybe it was because I'd never played organized sports as a kid, or had a tree house, or skateboarded, or surfed. I had a bicycle, but everything was so close that I never had to ride it very far or very often. I'd never gotten into a fight in my life, never punched inanimate objects in anger, never drove a car ridiculously fast, never rode a motorcycle outside a parking lot or suburban street, never felt rebellious enough to break the law just for the sake of breaking it. My childhood and adolescence were filled with TV, Nintendo, cheeseburgers, plate lunches, smoking cigarettes, beers at parties, drugs later, and I'd watch other people break bones, some of the tough ones making fist craters in car doors, the wannabes making shoe dents in them, but I never felt the urge to risk breaking bones myself. My biggest crime as an ice smoker was skipping on responsibility: I skipped school, work, paying bills, taking out the trash, dates, basically anything I was supposed to keep up with. I knew and hung out with "exciting" people, but I was as bland as poi myself. Then there was Winnie.

Winnie had broken her bones once—the whole damn set. One night she and her then boyfriend decided that it would be a good idea to swing by Kapiolani Community College and try to launch the car off the steep hills, Steve McQueen style. She was fifteen at the time, more than half her life ago, and they'd taken a hill and launched into a telephone pole. Flying through the windshield, head first, Winnie landed up in a coma for half a week. When she'd regained consciousness, all Mom could say was, "I hope she learned her lesson. I hope she slows down now." Then she'd cried. Winnie got her share of speeches on how lucky she'd been to survive and receive a second chance, but the only thing she'd told me, laid up in that hospital bed with tubes and gauze and casts and stitches—some from the crash, some from surgery—was how she was jonesing for a smoke. She came out of the experience with a lesson confirmed, not learned: life was short, and she could go at any time. Like the commercial said, play hard.

So when I got home from Mom's, thinking about the twins—not knowing them, but knowing of them and having no clue as to how Winnie had gotten money from them—and opened the door, to find Winnie sitting in front of the TV with her lips on a glass pipe, I wasn't surprised. I wasn't even surprised when she turned her head toward me and asked with a smile, "Want a hit?"

And I wanted one. Though rusty, my mental rat-wheel hit high gear: it'd be a good idea, or at least OK, if I sat my ass down with Winnie and took a couple of hits. First, there was the lack of sleep over the last half week. Smoking would recharge my batteries, and it was too damn hot to sleep anyway. Second, I was a good addict, not like Winnie. I had some control, and though I might start to slack off, I'd never become a thief or homeless guy. People tended to think that there was only one kind of drug addict: the kind who loses everything. Marion Barry ran the nation's capital on crack; I could certainly keep a crummy-ass, monkey-boy job.

But guilt and pride took control. Some people had a little angel on one shoulder and a little devil on the other; I had guilt and pride, and they didn't always argue. I'd feel guilty if I messed with drugs just because, as silly as it sounded, drugs were very, very illegal—at least jail sentences said so. It was the one obvious thing about drugs everyone seemed to miss. Everyone knew they were bad, but did them anyway because they made you feel so damn good.

Pride had a better speech for my ear. Pride told me that there was nothing more pathetic than a thirty-something drug addict. I'd look like a damn fool sneaking into bathrooms or smoking in a car in some parking lot at my age. The worst thing you could do, in my mind, was look like a fucking clown. The best anti-drug message I'd ever seen—far better than the memorable frying egg, the "this is your brain on drugs" one—was from the movie New Jack City: Pookie, Chris Rock, is sitting in a pool of pathetic sweat and tears, about to fall off the wagon with a pipe in one hand and a lighter in the other. Pride told me I didn't want none of that.

"Jesus fucking Christ, Winnie, what the fuck are you doing?"

The smoke lingered in the glass pipe, then slowly dissolved into nothing. "I didn't think you'd pop in all of a sudden like that. I didn't know what else to do but offer you some. Scurrying to hide seemed stupid." She carefully emptied the pipe into a tiny square of tin foil.

"You're so dumb," I said. "Didn't you learn your lesson?" My disgust focused on myself after saying that: who was I to talk? I kept going anyway. "Well, while you were here drugging out, Mom was filling me in on how the Rapozo brothers are looking for you."

"What they want?"

"You lose your mind, asking me that?" She was high, and I was rubbing it in.

"Jesus, can you just stop for a second? Let me get my head on straight."

"Let me ask you this. When you fuck up, do you ever think about how it affects everyone else, how you pull other people into your shit?" There was no stopping me now. I was launching into the drug speech heard daily across the world. It probably looked like I was the one charged up on ice. "They know Mom, Winnie. You know, Mom, one of the thousands you stole from, including me, in round one of this shit? Now you are starting round two one day out of jail? What the fuck? B hook you up with that shit?"

She started to laugh. "Calm down, Dad. No worry, beef curry. It's all under control." She clasped her hands together and shook them. "It is certain."

The Magic Eight Ball thing was getting beyond stale. "This ain't funny. I let you stay here even after you stole shit from me. And now you're doing it again? Fuckin' mean, fuckin' cherry. Plus, you got the twins looking for you now, threatening Mom and Mario. You're thirty-four, and one day out of jail. Where's your pride?"

"Pride is a deadly sin."

"Where's your guilt then?"

"Never had it. Listen, if you have a problem with me staying here, seeing as you got so much to steal, let me know right now. As for the twins, let me worry about that. I never planned on staying here long anyway. But like you said, I'm thirty-four, and just like when I was ten, I'm not going to sit here and listen to this shit. Am I a fuckup? No doubt."

"I bet the last time you were one step away from being a crack ho."

"I was a crack ho, but you wouldn't know anything about it. You weren't there."

"You left—with my wallet cleaned out I might add."

I forgot about the CDs and was about to bring them up when she said, "You would've killed yourself if I stayed."

"It was the most fucked-up thing I've ever done, but I dunno about killing myself, please." I wanted some aspirin bad.

She shifted and lay down on her stomach. She rested her chin on her folded hands and looked up at me with dilated eyes and a smiling white face. Her knees were bent and her ankles crossed, covering a homemade cross tattoo on her ankle. Her feet swung back and forth. She was keeping a good beat. Her teeth came out over her bottom lip. "Then you ain't seen nothing. Let me ask you this. If I fuck you again, will it make it all better?"

I walked out and decided I needed that air-conditioned drive around the island after all. The mainland was probably a lot better for driving. If you lived in, say, California, you could drive to the mountains or to Vegas. Hell, you could drive to New York if you wanted to. In Hawai'i, you always went in a circle and ended up back home. But I suppose it was all small, so everyone, everywhere ended up back home anyway. It reminded me of that movie Contact, that space-travel one with Jodie Foster. The movie didn't do jack for me except for the very first scene, where it looked like the camera moved from earth to the outer planets to right out of the solar system, passing stars and all sorts of big-ass colorful and gaseous masses. It was like the scene was saying, "What you are about to see don't mean jack shit in the grand scheme of things, so carry on." But I wanted to think that all this shit with Winnie and the drugs and now the twins meant something, the same twins I used to see around in the old days at clubs, pummeling the shit out of guys, sometimes the guys they even came with, and being asked very, very carefully to leave afterwards. But it all didn't mean jack, I supposed. The Power of Indifference was all about knowing this and taking advantage of it. Maybe I didn't have that power. Winnie seemed to, though. You had to hand it to her in a way.

After I took the drive, side-eyeing the beaches and watching the colors turn as I moved from south to west to north and back south again, like the minute hand of a watch, I came back to the apartment. Winnie was gone, along with all of her new stuff from yesterday. She did leave one thing. A wad of money dangled from my homeless Christmas tree. It was seven thousand dollars. I knew that if the twins were looking for her because of the money, giving me some meant that she wasn't planning on returning it. I didn't know if those twins were killers, but I supposed they had to be, along with their friends. What they did for a living was never clear; you couldn't just call them drug dealers or thieves or loan sharks. They had their hands in all sorts of honey jars, and I believed the rumors about them being part of Hawaiʻi's version of the mafia. They looked mafia-ish, if that was even a word.

After I pulled the money off the antennae, I took off my shirt and crawled into my sleeping bag. I slept for about five hours, waking up only to pee and call in sick to work, which I'd have to scrounge up a doctor's note for. Otherwise, I'd get a demerit on my record. It rained all day, and by nightfall the air had changed from humid to cool. It got so windy that I had to close the windows. I swore I saw a bat fly by, but it was probably just some bird. Anything flying out in that wind didn't stand a chance, but where else did flying things go when there was nowhere to land at night?

Bolohead Row

1

I WASN'T SURE WHERE the term had come from, but I'd first heard it from one of Mom's old clients when I was a kid. He'd said, "I took my kid to da movie and was so crowded, we had for sit Bolohead Row."

For him, that was the first row of seats in a movie theater, the one right in front of the screen. It was called Bolohead Row because everyone seated there had to lean their heads back to watch the movie; old, nearsighted men exposed their "boloheads," or bald heads, to the rest of the audience. When my friends and I would go to the movies, sure enough Bolohead Row would be there, and if there were enough bald men sitting side by side, we would point and laugh before the lights dimmed.

It wasn't until my late teens that I heard the term in another context. The principle was the same—the tilt of the head to look at the action above, exposing the empty nest of hair—only this time the action was onstage at strip bars all over Kapiolani Boulevard and Keeaumoku Street. During my strip bar days,

Bolohead Row was a seat at the stage, a sweaty wad of ones in one hand and a sweaty bottle of beer in the other, where we'd look up and see naked bodies dancing shamelessly in the half-light, bodies that resembled, but didn't look quite the same as, the ones we threw ourselves on in high school. That was before teenage plastic surgery and tanning beds; you could only see bodies like this at strip bars. It was the days before they carded at the door; the days before metal detectors and neonlighted plexiglass poles with water and bubble machines in them. I'd been sixteen the first time I sat at this Bolohead Row, and I'd felt half-dazed and half-sick looking up at tits and crotches, not being able to get away from the thought that this was all wrong, that staring so closely at a naked body was a sin, even if I wasn't religious. The first few times, I had a hard time looking at the faces of the strippers.

By the time Taks and I were in our twenties, we were jaded to the point where the fun of it all was looking for gross flaws like gargantuan areolas, tampon strings, and hemorrhoids and we began calling the entire bar district Bolohead Row. "What you wanna do tonight?"

"Bolohead Row, I guess."

And we'd hit the bars, not only strip bars, but hostess bars as well, and comment on the price of beer and point out the imperfections: the bodies of the strippers when the lights came on at two, the accents of the Korean hostesses, the ridiculous names of the bars, the gaudiness of the décor, the age of the furniture, the pathetic old men, the bad karaoke singing, the bad sound systems in general. We stopped looking up at Bolohead Row and started looking down. We went anyway, though, not because it was still exciting anymore, but because everything else seemed even more boring. By the time I was about twenty-three, there were no new stories. As with Hawaiian music, everything was a remake of an oldie-but-goodie.

So after Winnie was gone and I had slept all day, Taks called me and asked, "You wanna do something tonight?"

And I said, "Maybe, like what?"

And he said, "I dunno, Bolohead Row."

I went because of the alternatives. I could have played with my TV, fighting for airwaves, bending wires and crumpling foil into a big airwave web; I could have read a book—yeah, right. It got me thinking of another context "bolohead" was used in. When you got "bolo'ed," it meant that you'd lost as badly as anyone could lose. In trumps, it meant you didn't even win one pack; in betting on football, it meant that you lost on every single play; getting bolo'ed was getting scalped of every hair on your head. It meant you were left with nothing except fallen follicles and a dumb look on your face, asking, "What the fuck just happened?"

But Taks threw me a curve ball when he picked me up, which he did from time to time, but there was never too much break on the ball to deal with. I agreed to hit Ginger's instead. There was a big firefighter auction that night, so Taks figured that there'd be chicks.

Ginger's was one of those nightclubs that tried its damnedest to look like a mainland club. There was a line at the door, but it was one of those pathetic ones that were held off just so that from the outside the club looked like the place to be. Taks never stopped clubbing, so he knew the new crop of bouncers, the big guys wearing looks of self-importance and not knowing that several years from now eight bucks an hour wouldn't cut it. He shook hands with them, and we walked right in. It had probably been the only part of clubbing that I had missed.

It seemed that every year clubs made the music louder, but that wasn't the case, of course. Oddly enough, the songs didn't change much. Dance songs have impressive longevity in clubs, and when we walked in, the bar staff was in the midst of doing their "Grease Lightning" dance on the stainless-steel bars. Fourteen years earlier, when I was eighteen, the bars had been polished wood.

Taks led us to the nearest bar, and we waited for the bartender to finish her dance. When the song ended, the DJ started "Too Close" by Next, to change the pace. What a talent, what a genius, I thought, and Taks ordered two Bud Lights. "What's the DJ's name again?" I asked.

"Dante. Just Dante."

God, Dante.

We squeezed through people, looking for a place to stand. The dance floor was crowded, but not so crowded that people couldn't just sway back and forth in time to the rhythm and look like they knew what they were doing. As usual, most of the guys looked bad dancing, just as I would have, and a lot of the girls as well. It hadn't been until I was about twenty-five that I realized most chicks didn't know what the fuck they were doing on the dance floor either. The big exceptions were the two professionals wearing black fishnet stockings and dancing on black boxes about three feet wide.

Ginger's was the geriatric club. There were young girls, but it looked like the average age was probably about twenty-five. There weren't too many hoochie mamas—girls dressed in revealing or skintight clothes—so the scene was sort of disappointing. Some of the older crowd consisted of the after-work, nine-to-fivers, so there were people my age dressed in middle-management duds—aloha shirts, business skirts, and

button-down long-sleeved shirts rolled up to the elbows—
looking too old to be there. Feeling the same way, I lit a cigarette
and thought that maybe listening to pundits go on and on about
a pending war in Iraq would have been a better way to spend the
night. At least I controlled the volume of what I didn't want to
listen to at home.

"I'm supposed to meet these chicks here," Taks yelled.

"Man, I gotta work early tomorrow. I called in sick today, so
I have to go home early."

"I need my wing man, bro."

I couldn't decide if references to Top Gun at thirty-two was
pathetic or gay, or both. Taks was moving unconsciously to the
music. He'd always been a dancer, going to those kiddie dances
they used to have back then, the event always named after some
dance song of the time, like Salt and Pepa's "Push It." He didn't
have to think while doing it, which was probably the key to not
looking like a jackass.

Ginger's had once been called Club Plumeria, making me
think that it was a requirement in the lease to name the business
after a Hawaiian flower. Coming here reminded me of Winnie:
she'd been the one who got me past the door in the old days,
when she was into the whole clubbing scene. Back then was also
the first time I'd heard of the Rapozo family, one of the families
who supposedly ran organized crime on the island. The twins,
Ula and Keo, used to go to Plumeria with a few of their other
gigantic friends, who were about my height but much, much
wider. The twins didn't look much like twins, except for their
height and weight; one was white, and one was brown. They
seemed proud that they were twins, like it meant you'd always
have to contest with two guys instead of one. We used to call
them the fortress: they'd be talking to some pretty girl, and it

was like climbing over the Koolau Mountains to get to her. Not that you wanted to with them there, because sometimes they'd pull a guy into the fortress and when they spread back out, like a lion pride done munching on its latest kill, there would be one jacked-up dude in fetal on the ground.

But the fortress wasn't into clubbing anymore, which was probably smart. The song ended, and Dante told us that next month there'd be a big Mardi Gras gala at Ginger's. "I bet it'll be just like New Orleans," I told Taks.

"Stop trying to bring me down, man, with all this negative energy. Look," he said, pointing at the door, "here they come."

Three girls waved at Taks and walked toward us. They looked younger than us, but not by much, which meant they were at the age of desperate husband-hunting. Girls were always husband-hunting and denying it, but these girls were approaching thirty, so they were in high gear. All of them probably thought they'd be walking that aisle at twenty-two. Guys always talked about how so-and-so settled beneath himself, but I suspected that women settled beneath themselves a lot more than guys did. How else would some of these dummies ever get hitched? I had no clue how my beach-bum father had managed it, and not once but twice.

All three were cute, though it was difficult to be cute at thirty. All three wore black clothes and heavy makeup and were Asian or part-Asian. "Hey girls," Taks said, "this is my buddy, Charlie. Charlie, this is Wendy, Marie, and Sloane. Sloane Petersen?" It was a Ferris Bueller joke. Taks was on a roll with movies from 1986. I was sure I'd forget all of their names by the end of the night.

"I haven't heard that one before," Sloane said.

I liked the name, but was convinced that the Johns, Janes, and Jennifers of the world would be snuffed out by the Jordans, Ariels, and Sloanes in another thirty years. These fad names had arrived with piercings and tattoos in the nineties. This Sloane was a bit old to be part of the movement, so I forgave her parents immediately.

"Nice meeting you all. What do you guys want to drink?" I asked, flagging down the waitress, who held a round tray full of drinks over her head. Her right arm was bigger than her left, like a lobster claw. Wendy asked for a Long Island Iced Tea, which was the two-dollar mixed-drink special, Marie wanted a Bud Light, and Sloane ordered a Vodka Martini, which was impressive but pretentious at the same time. "Martini?" I asked. "I feel like Frank Sinatra and Dean Martin are gonna walk in any minute or something."

She laughed. "Nah, I'm just showing my age. Beer makes you full before you get drunk, and the other 'fufu' drinks make me feel like I'm drinking juice, until the morning when the wicked 'fufu' drink hammerheads me."

Hammerhead. I liked Sloane right away.

We had a good time at Ginger's. Taks, Wendy, and Marie danced and took shots while Sloane kept me company. She seemed to want to talk current events, the Middle East and North Korea, brainy shit like that. I didn't mind, though. At least it was something different. When she asked me if I thought we should go to war, I told her the truth. "I don't know much about it, and hardly think about it, but I guess I'm glad there's almost no chance in hell that I'd be drafted at my age." It was a lame and selfish thing to say, but it was the truth.

Sloane frowned. "Are you a Democrat or Republican?"

"I dunno. I never voted."

"Wow, really?"

The conversation was beginning to make me feel on the dumb side, so I tried to think of something smart to say. "Politicians are politicians, I figure. They just help whoever is giving them the money. Since I got no money, I got no reason to worry about who's in office."

"I work at the state capitol. For Senator Yoza."

I wasn't sure which one Yoza was; in fact, the only politician I could think of namewise was the one who'd spent a bunch of his contributors' cash on ice and strip bars in Bolohead Row and then got busted for it. I thought about lighting a cigarette, but smoking was one of those things a lot of girls hated, so I had to hold off and see if she was one of them. "I work at ABC Store," I said. "What does Senator Yoza propose to do about the time anomaly at ABC #64, where time moves slower than anywhere else?"

She laughed. "I will speak to him about it first thing in the morning. In your opinion, will this anomaly spread?"

"It may already have. Anytime I go to the grocery store or the mall or to a movie with Meryl Streep in it, I come in contact with it. I think it comes with some kind of sleep agent, too. I'm thinking it could be Saddam Hussein's new biological weapon."

"Wow, this thing could go way over my boss's head. I just hope Bin Laden or the North Koreans don't get a hold of it. Sounds like something straight from the Axis of Evil."

"I dunno. It smells American to me, probably the CIA. They're just framing the Axis of Evil. It all comes down to the Kennedy assassination."

"Why the Kennedy assassination?"

"I dunno, but it's all about the Kennedy assassination. The first one, I mean."

"You're Hawaiian, yeah?"

"Yeah."

"You're probably a Republican then. The majority of Hawaiians are Republicans, not like the mainland Republicans, but Republicans. My boss is a Democrat, which makes me a Democrat, I guess."

"Like fight? You no-good Democrats."

"Bastard Republicans."

The music cut, and the firefighter auction was about to begin. Taks walked by to let me know it was the best night he'd ever seen at Ginger's in terms of the girls-to-guys ratio. For Taks, Ginger's had a best night at least several times a year. It must've been cherry being Taks. I waited for him to point out a random girl and say, "How's that chick, yo?" Hearing that for the millionth time would have made my night complete. Instead he asked if Sloane and I needed a drink.

The first contestant was a hapa guy—half Japanese and half Haole—who, according to DJ Dante, loved to surf and play basketball and planned on taking his date to the zoo—because he loved animals, too—then a romantic dinner for two, hopefully followed by a moonlight walk on the beach. He took off his shirt, showing off his six-pack abs. He ended up selling for six hundred dollars. The crowd went wild. Taks and I had to give the girls the blow-by-blow because they weren't tall enough to see over all the people. By the second contestant, they got impatient and tried to squeeze into the front row.

Taks and I headed for the bar. "I should become a firefighter," he said.

"It's a good job. We're probably too old, though."

"Speak for yourself. I'll never be too old to play volleyball all day long."

"You have to wash trucks, too, though."

"Cook, too."

"Need to relearn how to take naps, like when we were in kindergarten."

"Need to be able to rent good movies for the station."

"Ten days a month. It's damn rough."

"9/11, though," Taks said.

"Once in a lifetime. Besides, this isn't New York. You get stationed out in Kailua or something, where there's so much rain fires don't stand a chance except on New Year's. I don't think Uncle Pono's house is high on the terrorist hit list."

It was one of those jobs that I'd never thought about until I was thirty, when I was just too old to go through that basic-training shit. If I ever had kids, it would be the job I'd rave about. I wouldn't lay this doctor, lawyer jazz on them. I'd be realistic. "Be a firefighter, son," I'd say. "Make Daddy proud." It was another job not offered in the stack of Life career cards, but I'd fill him in.

"So what happened with Winnie?" Taks asked.

"She left."

"Haha, after one day. Smoking ice again?"

"Yeah. Walked through the door, and there she was: the Little Engine Who Could Give a Rat's Ass."

Taks shook his head. "Let her go, man. Crazy bitch just take you down with her."

"She's let go. I told you about the Rapozo brothers coming into Mom's bar and looking for her?"

"Fuck, no way."

"Yeah."

"She's fucked."

"Yeah."

Taks grabbed my arm. "Seriously, man, let it go. Mixing it up with guys like that, you aren't up for that. Shit, you ever even been in a fight?"

"Nope. Don't plan on getting into one either."

"Well, I got your back, bro."

"It's nothing, man. It's done. Look, here come the girls."

Sloane and the other two came back cheering. "Oh my God, Marie bid like four hundred bucks for one!" Sloane said.

"It's for charity!" Marie yelled.

"You guys wanna come with me and Charlie for a swim?" Taks asked.

"I dunno, we all have to work in the morning," Sloane said.

We ended up having more drinks at the bar. Taks took the three girls to the dance floor a few times while I got bounced around like a pinball by passersbys wearing tough guy faces and looking to kick car doors. The waitresses were slow, so I ordered two beers at a time. When I went to the bathroom, I remember-ed why I'd stopped coming to this place. There was something humiliating about waiting in line just to pee, and when I finally got to a stall, I stood in a puddle of puke, aiming for the hole in the middle of the piss-covered toilet seat. After I was done, I paid the attendant a dollar for that experience. He was an old man in a white tux shirt. I thought about the game of Life and added his career card to the deck.

By closing, Taks wouldn't take no for an answer from any of us, so we ended up driving to Black Point and walking on lava rocks in the dark to get to the ocean swimming pool behind the million-dollar oceanfront homes. "Man, get a load of these houses," Taks said.

I smiled. "Millionaire Estates."

The girls shushed us, probably afraid that some old haole lady wearing hair curlers made of 24-karat gold would come out and shoo us away.

Jagged, black rocks spread in front of us, hiding in the dark. Walking on sharp objects we couldn't see was cherry. The sound of the waves crashing against the shore got louder. I almost stepped on a bird nestled in between rocks. Curious, I stopped and nudged it with my foot. It didn't move; no squawk, no nothing. "What kind of retard birds are these?"

Taks hopped from rock to rock with ease and had to wait for us every ten feet or so. My ankles and knees wobbled with every misstep, so this nature walk wasn't my idea of fun. With their platform shoes, the poor girls were even slower than me. It was a cool, breezy night, though, and there was something about drunkenness combined with wind that always got me going.

When we finally got to the gate, Taks winked at us and opened the door with a key. "Thank God, I thought I'd have to climb the fence," Marie or Wendy said. They were behind me in the dark, and their voices sounded alike. I agreed with whichever one had said it. "How'd you swing that?" I asked.

Taks smiled. "A couple of people I met once rented a cottage here. We made a shitload of copies right before they moved out."

The pool was a paved square, like a normal swimming pool, except the water came from the surf crashing on the rocks. Gallons of white wash splashed into the pool every several seconds. The girls carefully avoided the splash while Taks took off his shirt and jeans, leaving on just a pair of tighty-whities, and threw his skinny ass right in. He yelled as his head broke the surface, something incoherent to let us know that he was alive and happy. "Get your drunk asses in here!" he said.

Marie and Wendy shrugged at each other and stripped to their bras and thongs. The light from a quarter moon revealed the dimples on Wendy's ass. They both jumped in quickly, probably feeling more comfortable in neck-high water. Sloane and I sat at two pool chairs and watched Taks go under, grabbing ass and making Wendy and Marie squeal in delight. I lit a cigarette, because it was just the thing to top off the drunkenness, wind, and two almost-naked girls in the pool.

"They never act like this," Sloane said. "Or at least not since college."

"Yeah, it's a Taks thing. He's got a way of bringing out the kid in people."

"You aren't gonna swim?"

"Nah, I'll spare you flab fest two thousand three."

"Well, I'll spare you, too, then," she said smiling.

"Pfft. You look in great shape."

"Boy, that water really comes in hard there, huh?"

"Yeah. The pool is probably never calm. The water just keeps on crashing in. Force of nature, blah, blah, blah. Couldn't keep that water out if you tried."

"You like the ocean?"

"Haha, not really. I'm more of a townie. Not really into finding my roots and shit."

"Me either. World seems too big anyway. I'd rather fly than dig."

"I like to sit and watch. I'm lazy that way."

"You like to sit and talk." She smiled.

"Not always. Like you said, the world is too big. Sometimes, I hear myself say something, and I swear that shit must've come out of a million mouths before mine."

"Yeah, probably. Try working in politics. There isn't anything out there that hasn't been said before."

"So why are you into it?"

"Never said I was into it; just said it's what I did."

I threw the cigarette in a puddle of water. My lips tasted salty. "Amen," I said.

Taks was trying to teach the girls how to shoot a stream of water from clasped hands. Marie shot herself in the face and laughed and laughed. "This place is a trip. I'm just waiting for some rich haole lady to call the cops on us," Sloane said. "I take it this is where Taks inspects the merchandise?"

"Haha, yeah, not all the time, though. When it gets too quiet, he'll launch into his lava-rock stories, about tourists taking home rocks and having their houses fall on them and shit, like The Brady Bunch tiki."

Sloane laughed. "I remember reading something about people sending rocks back from the mainland to the Postmaster General. Supposedly there's a room somewhere full of lava rocks."

"That's funny. What's even funnier is, isn't it all lava rocks? I mean isn't land everywhere just a shitload of lava rocks?"

"When I was a kid, my science teacher made us put wax and water in these metal pans and boil them together. When the wax melted, he said that's what the earth was like a long time ago. Then when we let it cool, the wax rose to the top, getting hard, and stuff, he said that's what the earth is like now. So I guess it's all lava rocks, yeah."

"Shit, and I thought it was all made when Pele got pissed about something. Screw it, let's swim."

We took off our clothes and jumped in the water. I caught a glimpse of the acne scars running down the middle of Sloane's back. They looked like dozens of tiny leopard spots. It made me sad, but in a good way. I felt like she was real.

The shock of the cold water sent me to the surface with teeth chattering. The faces around me were no longer painted, and all were beaming. The three girls looked pretty, splashing and smiling like children, squinting every time a new load of white wash splashed in, but I didn't join them. I took a deep breath and dove to the bottom. The crashing waves sounded like muffled thunder. The bottom was grainy but flat like the surface of a regular swimming pool. I tried to grip the bottom with my hands, and it felt as if I were getting close, the grains digging in my palm, working like Velcro. But every time I was getting close to a grip, the saltwater gently pushed me back up.

2

At work the next day, I thought about rocks and how everything was gas, liquid, or solid, and how ice was an example of that. Ice came in rock form, then you heated it, then it turned to gas, then it filled your lungs, then it moved through your blood and then your brain; I didn't know what happened to it after that. But my old science teachers always said that mass could neither be created nor destroyed, so I knew it had to move from the brain to somewhere else. Maybe it turned into energy or action, and the most stupid-ass actions at that. After it hit your brain, it stole your mom's money and jewelry, then it got you kicked out of your mom's house, then it threw you into the arms of the other homeless or soon-to-be homeless, into a platoon that stole from others and each other. Then the next thing you knew, you were in jail, and when you got out, the Rapozo twins were looking for you because you'd stolen from the wrong people. But it seemed to me a little bit of it always stayed in an addict's brain, just to remind him that it wanted company or that it was fading quickly and needed replenishment soon. Most likely, though, you just pissed it out. So the sewers were filled with it, and it flowed right under our feet.

I was surprised to see B walk into the store that day, and any leftover good feelings about my night at Black Point turned from rock to gas the second I saw him over the cereal and Pop Tart shelf. He was wearing old Army fatigue pants and a yellow T-shirt that had a faded picture of a buck on it. The word Moloka'i was printed above its horns. When he went to the check-out counter and said a few words, my clerk pointed at me. B looked pissed as ever, like a boxer right before a fight, so when he walked toward me, I didn't know if he was going to shake my hand or punch me in the face. He shook my hand. "Hey man."

"Hey man, what's up?"

He had a hickie on his neck, black-and-blue with a ring of jaundice. "Took me awhile to find you. This is like the twelfth ABC I walked into."

"That's pretty lucky. There's maybe seventy stores."

"I guess so. Hey, can we take a quick one, bud? You got a break coming?"

"Yeah, I'll take a smoke break. Step into my office."

We walked to the sidewalk, parting a group of young Japanese tourist girls, all carrying shopping bags. It was an overcast day, and the cars and buses sputtered out smoke just a little darker than the sky. I lit a cigarette, then scratched the stubble on the top of my head. It looked like B was letting his bald head go. "You quit shaving?" I asked.

"I don't shave it. This is my haircut, then I just let it grow out and get it cut again. You see your sister around?"

"Last time I saw her was yesterday."

"Yeah, same here."

"Mom told me she got a couple of guys looking for her."

"Yeah, I heard."

"I dunno what to say, man."

"Me either. I guess I'm kind of worried, though."

"Not to sound like an ass, but why? Who is she to you?"

A Japanese couple walked into the store. Their legs were pink from the sun. B put his hands on his head, rubbing the stubble. He cracked his knuckles against his skull. "A friend," he said.

"A druggie friend, who, by the looks of things, will end up right back in jail before long. Shit happens all the time."

"True dat. I got a bad feeling, though."

"Can't do shit, I guess."

"We could look for her."

"I wouldn't even know where to start. Besides, it's only been a day."

"True."

"I don't know why I'm telling you this, but a part of me don't ever want to see her again."

"Yeah."

"Not to sound like a dick, but it sure would make life and shit easier."

B smiled. "Yeah, it would."

"Inside joke?"

"Winnie told me that you preached the power of indifference."

"It's sort of true."

"It's fuckin'-a true. Giving a shit is big-time tougher than not giving a shit."

"Yeah."

A tour bus passed us. A group of haole guys with baggy basketball shorts and caps worn backwards drove by on rented mopeds. They slalomed through the white dashes in the middle of the road. "Hey, how about this. What are you doing tonight?"

B shrugged. "Had no plans."

"Wanna have beers tonight?"

"Sounds good. Where?"

"I can pick you up, no problem. I guess Mom's bar is cool."

"That works."

I put out my cigarette, flicking it in the middle of the street so I wouldn't feel like I had to sweep it up later. "So what you up to now?"

"I'm gonna walk around some. I haven't been in this shithole in ages."

"Waikīkī?"

"Yeah."

"Same ol' shit."

"Yeah. Winnie told me that you're Hawaiian. This place must be hell on earth for you."

I wasn't sure what he meant by that, but it pissed me off. Sometimes, it was strange shit being Hawaiian because people kept hinting at what you should and shouldn't like, and most of these Hawaiian Affairs advisors weren't even Hawaiian. Did I hate Waikīkī? Yeah, but not for the reasons people wanted me to hate it. I just hated the job. I didn't give a rat's ass about the tourists or "aina" or any of that shit. It was like people wanted me to go ape-shit over race and become a fucking terrorist or sniper. I wasn't sure if they wanted me to go off because they thought it would help fix shit or they wanted me to snap just to confirm something they felt.

"The job sucks," I said, "but it's a job and sure as hell beats living on the beach or something. Better than jail, I bet."

He laughed, but I could see the "What kind of Hawaiian are you?" look. The answer was simple. I was the kind of Hawaiian who lived in America in the twenty-first fucking century, who liked the comfort and ease that money and technology provided, who wasn't interested in history—or school in general, for that matter. I was the kind of Hawaiian who would rather veg out in front of the TV or go have a few beers with friends instead of surf, lay net, hunt pig, or hold a protest sign in front of the capitol over some land shit. I wanted to ask B if he thought all Japanese people were into trimming bonsai trees, raking sand in a Zen garden, going to bon dances, or acting in a local kabuki theater.

"I gotta get back to work, man, on the clock. I'll swing by and pick you up at about eight. I gotta work early tomorrow."

"Me too. Sounds good," he said.

I went back to making sure ABC #64 had enough frosted strawberry Pop Tarts and Fruit Loops, while also asking myself what it was this guy wanted from me. Winnie was a thirty-four-year-old woman who took my helpings of help and slid the plate back to me from across the table, like a child does with a plate of lima beans. She knows it's good for you, but won't eat it anyway. I told the cashier to take a break and then manned the register.

The pink-legged Japanese couple put the shopping basket on the counter. I rang up one bottle of green Aloe Vera Gel, two bottles of Evian water, and a coconut piggy bank carved in the shape of a monkey. The man pulled out a small map of Waikīkī and spread it in front of me. I pointed to where they were, and he bowed and thanked me. He paid me with a hundred-dollar bill. I gave him change, and as they walked off, I thought about how weird it was that this pink-legged guy was Japanese like the guys I knew. I wondered if a new race was evolving in Hawai'i, if maybe centuries from now, there would be a million copper-skinned Asians who considered themselves natives. I didn't know jack about Hawaiian history, but I figured that the current natives also came from somewhere else and that their looks had probably changed over the generations.

A haole family came in. The son, a teenager wearing an Arizona Diamondbacks cap, didn't look happy to be there despite the fact that he was probably missing school for this trip. They bought a packet of plumeria seeds, a how-to-hula kit, a kukui nut choker, a box of Hawaiian Host Macadamia Nuts, and a beach towel with a picture of cartoon dolphins underwater. They must've been gift shopping. They got five presents for about forty bucks. The wife asked me if plumerias would grow in Arizona. I told her I figured they would, but the package reminded me of those ads for sea monkeys on the back of comic books. I finished the shift wanting a beer something fierce.

The get-together at Mom's turned out to be bigger than I planned. After I picked up B, the cell phone spam started. Taks called me to see what I was up to, reporting that a college basketball game had gone his way and he had cash to burn. Mark called me to say that our old friend, Robert Olivera, whom we called Ollie for short, was back from Thailand and wanted to have some beers. Sloane called me and asked what I was up to. I told them all to meet me at Mom's. It looked like the night was going my way, because I wasn't really up to having a one-on-one conversation about the trials and tribulations of Winnie and what an assistant manager at ABC and an ex-con curry-stirrer could do about them. The answer would've come down to "nothing" anyway, which seemed like the answer to a lot of problems. Do the calculations all you want, zero times any number was still zero.

B came out dressed up, at least what dressed up was maybe ten years ago. He was wearing a shiny, metallic-looking black-and-silver shirt with black acid-washed jeans cuffed at the bottom. He had on British Knight shoes, which I wasn't sure were even made anymore, and a thin, gold rope chain around his thick neck. I hadn't seen one of those since the early nineties. When he jumped into my truck, I said, "Sheesh, styling, huh?"

He touched his necklace. His hands seemed unusually small compared to his thick wrists and veiny forearms. "Not to sound like a chick, but I was in the mood."

I wondered where he'd kept his Superfly gear while he was in jail. But then I thought of my own closet; before I'd moved out of Sheila's, I'd had a leather jacket, hanging right next to my puffy, MC Hammer pants. I supposed B's stuff never had a chance to be pushed to the back.

"This is a nice truck," he said. "Ever take it four-wheeling at Kaena Point or Allen Davis?"

"Nah, not really." I added, "I just use it sometimes to move stuff."

"Cool," he said.

"So some of my friends are coming tonight, too, and my brother. They all called me after I talked to you today. I figured we'd give Mom some business."

"Cool," he said.

"So Winnie told me that the Feds flew you to California the day after you got arrested."

"Yup, Humboldt County. A hundred guys, one phone. Fifty-thousand-dollars bail. Finally got in touch with my lawyer, made bail, came back here to a halfway house. A thousand in rent for that shit. It's pretty funny."

"Don't sound too funny to me."

"The whole thing was a trip. From the day those deputized local cops profiled me for the Feds, to prison itself. It was a year before I actually went to jail. The Feds take their time. You ain't going anywhere."

"Sheesh."

"I'll give you one story. The very first day I get to prison, some guy got shanked by the only other tall and skinny Asian guy in there because a game of horseshoes went wrong. So the warden calls both of us in. I'm sitting there, don't know what the fuck is going on, and the warden tells us how this guy is in a coma. I didn't even say it wasn't me, didn't defend myself, because I was only there for five hours and didn't know anyone. Finally, the warden finds out it wasn't me, and before he sends me out, he says, 'Not here one day, Ching, and you're already fucking up.'"

"Harsh."

"It's a trip."

When we got to the bar, the usual happy-hour crowd was there. Mom's friend, Eddie, was talking Mario's ear off, and the old haole man was staring up at CNN in the same beat-up, paint-stained jeans and T-shirt. Mom stood behind the bar, filling the sink with ice so she could chill warm beers fast. Momo was hooked up to the video poker machine and playing Run 21, quickly pressing her index finger against the glass to match up the cards that needed to equal twenty-one for her to discard them. B and I sat at the bar. I banged my fist against it to get Mom's attention. "I need some service, miss!" I said.

Mom turned around and slapped me on the arm. "He think he one comedian, dis one," she said to B. Then she cracked open two Bud Lights and put them in front of us. "On me," she said.

B thanked her. I lit a cigarette. I wasn't sure how to ask it, so I was just straight with her. "Mom, you hear from Winnie today?"

"What you mean, she staying with you."

"Not anymore. She split."

Mom sighed and shook her head. She told B, "You know, dat girl, one friggin' headache from day one. Cry, no sleep, cry, no

sleep. Den when she could crawl, she used to go around da
house, trying for stick her finger in electrical sockets. I pull her
away, and she would cry and cry. Would give me da horrors.
Den, when she first seen matches, was all ova. She wanted for
light everything on fire."

B laughed. "I tink so all kids laddat."

"True, but not like her. Mark used to, but you just pull him
away, he go look for something else for stick in his mouth.
Winnie, once she wanted dat one ting, dat was it. Charlie told
you about da guys looking for her?"

B nodded.

"What dey like?" she asked.

"I dunno," B said.

I shrugged. Mom was drunk already, which meant she'd
probably started drinking when she opened at two. That meant
over six hours of drinking, and it would be another six before
she would turn out the lights. I was hoping she'd go home and
let Mario close. I wasn't sure if her false-eyelash glue could hold
up that long. I leaned over to Momo and asked, "You get high
score yet?"

In front of her, a ten-dollar roll of quarters was spilt in two.
"No, some ass with the name, 'Bolo' has like the top three spots.
The scores are like impossible. When I saw it, I was like, 'How
the hell?'"

I laughed. "Bolo is my brother Mark. The worst thing, too, is
that he probably just came here one night and put it up in thirty
minutes. I'll show you a secret," I said. Then I squatted under
her, unplugged the machine, and plugged it back in again.

Her eyes widened. "I can't believe you just did that."

"It's just a game."

"He won't be mad?"

"Probably, but I'll just tell him you did it."

She punched me on the arm with a girl punch, dropping her fist like a hammer. What a peach, I thought. "Hey, Mom, remember Ollie? He's back. He's coming tonight."

"Which one is dat? Da Filipino one?"

"Yeah, the Filipino-Hawaiian." I turned toward B. "Ollie went to high school with me and Taks. After we graduated, he got this job selling pharmaceuticals. Didn't go to college. Friggin' guy made so much money from the job and the stock market when it was hot, he retired at thirty and moved to Thailand. He comes back for vacation sometimes. Can you imagine that? His whole life is a vacation, so he's taking a vacation from vacation."

"Cool," B said.

We went to a booth to sit. I didn't know what to talk about, so I asked him if he wanted to play darts. "Nah," he said.

"So how do you know Winnie?" I asked.

"From back in the day."

"You guys going out or something?"

"Nah. Friends."

"She said you visited her in jail and stuff."

"Yeah. Friends."

"So you know her good?" I was beginning to sound like a reporter.

He cracked his knuckles and kept his fingers locked behind his head. "Nah, not really. I knew her back in the day, but we wasn't buddy-buddy. We talked more from jail, writing letters and stuff. She was in there with another girl I knew, and that one showed her letters to Winnie, and Winnie said she knew me, so she started writing, too. I remembered her name, and it was a good letter, so I wrote back."

"Ah."

B smiled. "I was like captain pen pal there in the mainland. At one point I was writing to about twelve people, and most of them I hardly knew. Jail is friggin' boring."

"The movies make it look exciting, in a bad way, though."

"There's some of that, but it's mostly boring—boring and noisy—so worse than just plain boring. Kamehameha Day was cool. Us Hawai'i guys could cook Hawaiian food, called it a religious holiday, told the chaplain what stuff we needed. Had some fights, mostly over the phones. The phone is the only damn thing to the world you got."

"Where do you think Winnie went?"

"Not sure. Could be anywhere, I guess, but I'm thinking she went someplace involuntarily. You know what I mean?"

"She had about sixteen grand. Left me seven of it."

Momo came by and asked if we were ready for another round. I ordered two more Bud Lights.

"Shouldn't go around talking about that," B said.

Momo came back and dropped off the beers. I left the change on the table, figuring we'd just kitty for the drinks when everyone got here.

"Think she stole from the twins?" I asked.

"I know she did."

"Damn."

"Yeah."

"Call the cops?"

"I dunno," B said. "Thing is, she's on parole. You call the cops, a shitload of questions are gonna be asked. I was thinking we look for her, and try to get her square with the twins. I used to know them."

"No shit? When?"

"Back in the day."

"Can it be squared?"

"I dunno, depends what the whole story is. Probably can't be completely squared. I mean, it's gonna cost more than she stole. But it's better than her ending up in the pineapple fields."

I wasn't fully convinced. A part of me thought that it might be better for everyone if she ended up buried out in the middle of nowhere. That was what they would've told me at the Power of Indifference seminar. "I don't get why you're all into this."

"I don't really get it either, to tell you the truth. The first time I visited her, it felt weird. But I like her. Could be I'm just looking for something to think about, like a project or something. It's like I gotta change the beat my life is playing to. Tired of the same ol' song and dance. Know what I mean?"

"Yeah, pretty much," I said.

"Well, let's look for her then."

"We can do that, maybe tomorrow night. But where do we start?"

"With the twins, man."

"Man."

"If it don't pan out," B said, "we gotta start digging. Know anyone that she was in jail with? Time moves so damn slow in there, you talk about almost anything."

"Yeah, actually, my aunt is there."

"Twins don't pan out, check her out."

"Can do."

Mark and Ollie walked in. I hadn't seen Ollie in what seemed like ages, but in reality it had only been a few months. Taks had been the best man at my wedding, but a part of me always thought it should have been Ollie. Taks was one of those guys, though, who would have taken offense at not being chosen. He never would have forgiven me.

Ollie, on the other hand, didn't care who was best man as long as there was a good bachelor party. I imagined he was probably everyone's secret best friend, the guy people would call if they needed to be bailed out of jail for driving drunk, but also the guy they'd call when they'd just gotten dumped by some chick. He'd heard all of my dirt, even the Winnie stuff, and he had this funny way of teasing you about it. He was never into giving you advice you had given yourself. Instead, he'd gently and sarcastically insult you about the stupid-ass thing you'd done:

"I slept with my sister."

"That ice is good stuff, yeah?"

For some reason, it was just what I wanted to hear whenever I found myself in a stupid situation. I wanted confirmation that I was a dummy, but it wasn't the end of the world. This five-six Filipino-Hawaiian, who always dressed like he was going yachting, who was the only guy I knew who said he was going to make a ton of money and get the hell out of Hawai'i and who actually did it, was best friend to all of us: me and Taks and Mark. In fact, once I was married, whenever Ollie came back to check on the properties he owned, the other two saw him more than I did.

"So I'm getting married," I'd said.

"Not to Winnie, right?"

"Fuck you."

"Marriage or Thailand, marriage or Thailand; that's pretty funny."

"That's pretty funny" was his favorite phrase. He'd wanted me to move to Thailand with him, but didn't push it since I was serious with Sheila at the time. I was also flat broke, as usual, and moving from Hawai'i's Bolohead Row to the ultimate

Bolohead Row on the face of the earth seemed like moving from the belly of the beast straight to its ass. I'd needed normalcy, I'd felt, not partying squared. That said, I was damn glad to see my friend walk into Mom's bar.

"B, you remember my brother, Mark? This is our friend Ollie."

B shook hands and then stepped out of the booth to let someone else sit next to the wall. He was one of those guys who probably couldn't stand not having immediate access to the aisle. Ollie sat down, and I slid in to make room for Mark.

"Ollie lives in Thailand," I said. "He's trying to repopulate the Hawaiian race over there."

"Yeah, you told me," B said.

Momo came to take our orders. When she walked away, Ollie raised an eyebrow. "So which one of you guys chasing that? You or Taks?"

"Neither. I got someone else coming," I said. "Just met her last night with Taks. Cool chick. So give us some damn stories before she gets here."

Ollie gave us the rundown of his days in Thailand. He'd told us his routine the last time he was here, and he seemed proud of it. Wake up whenever, watch some TV, go out and eat lunch for about two bucks, go to Blockbuster and rent a movie, come home and watch it, then wait for the night, go out and get laid, not always by a professional, depending on his mood. According to him, the girl-to-guy ratio there was about five-to-one, and a lot of the guys either were gay or treated women shitty. It was as easy as pie. He talked about joining a 24-Hour Fitness over there, and feeling like Dorian Yates, clanging around two-quarter on the bench while most of the other guys struggled with one-thirty-five. "Mark would be a celebrity over there," he said.

He confided to us that he took little nibbles of vitamin V before sex because of the demands of daily sex on a thirty-two-year-old body, and he talked about how much of a joke it was to get prescription drugs in general. Then he said, "Mark told me Winnie got out, but is looking like she's going right back in."

I nodded. "B here is her friend."

"Ah," Ollie said. " You should see how they handle drugs in Thailand. Did you know the cops can just shoot you if they find enough drugs on you?"

"No shit?" Mark said.

"You better watch that Viagra shit then," I said to Ollie.

"No, real drugs, fool."

I'd never taken "fake" drugs before, but ice could certainly make you go all night long. Then again, I'd never heard about someone hopped up on Viagra stealing cars.

"Yeah, it's crazy. You see it in the paper, too. Drug dealers just capped in the street. Sometimes, they'll shut down a club, lock it down, and make everyone take a piss test."

"Jesus," Mark said.

"And I'm talking clubs with like a few thousand people in them. Takes friggin' forever."

"Can they shoot you for testing positive?" I asked.

"They can do whatever they want. But mostly, they either just take you to jail unless you bribe them. It costs like three hundred dollars to get out of it if you're from there—a thousand if you're American."

"Sheesh," I said.

"That's a fuckin' bargain," B said. "There's something to be said for that Thailand policy. Figure, you get busted by the Feds here, it's more like mental torture. You get busted illegally—only it's not illegal because the Hawai'i Constitution does not apply to deputized DEA guys—you get flown to a strange place so you can't get a lawyer, you finally get back home, which costs you fifty grand, then they make you pay rent for a piece-of-shit halfway house."

Ollie laughed. "That's funny."

B put his hand up. He was getting mad. "I'm not done. So you're drug-free at this halfway house, and your lawyer is owning in court, so what do they do? They investigate him and catch him bopping some fifteen-year-old chick and smoking ice with her. He goes down to a judge who brags about sentencing over one million years, and says he's only at least halfway done. Now you got to get another lawyer, which takes time. What are the Feds doing during this time? Pretty routine stuff like apologizing for misconduct, the profiling, the illegal detaining at the airport, apologizing before a complaint can be submitted, so then it's too late to submit a formal complaint. Then, this is the kicker. You get to trial with your new lawyer, and they tell you that if you testify on your own behalf and are found guilty, they'll tack on another fifty percent of your sentence by charging you with obstruction of justice. You can't even defend yourself unless you can somehow, singlehandedly, guarantee to talk yourself to innocent."

He stopped to take a swig of beer. Veins rose on his temples as if he was biting on something hard. "There are a lot of guys there who copped to crimes they didn't even commit because if they testified, it could have meant another twenty years for them. Then there's the whole prison mind-fuck: eight toilets, four showers, two microwaves, and four phones for two hundred and forty guys. People hiding contraband in your crap, like the ten-dollar hits of black-tar heroin, but you aren't a rat, though people always think you are every time they pull you out to give testimony to a related case. Using canned chicken for money. Some of those cans are like ten years old, fucking nasty when they leak. I like the Thailand plan. Give me that fucking bullet in the back of the head and be done with it. I'll tell you this: those fuckers owe me."

"I'm surprised people don't just stop messing with drugs," Mark said.

"They don't stop," Ollie said.

I lit a cigarette. I was feeling hot. My face was pulsing. B was a hothead, and I was catching it like a virus, but it wasn't the same strain as his. I nudged Mark to move him out, so I could go to the bathroom. I waited for dart traffic, then went in to splash some water on my face and take a look at myself in the mirror. This wasn't an unfamiliar feeling; it happened often if I was drinking nearly every night. By about night four, I'd have one of those Asian reactions to alcohol. My face would turn red, and my face and neck splotchy. There were faint patches of red and white all over my head, face, and neck. I wasn't too worried; people tended to notice only if I pointed it out to them, and I never got sick or anything if I kept drinking. But it always made me a bit scared because I knew it meant that my body was saying, "Nuff already." I'd listen by taking a night off. The next day.

I took my first race-horse piss of the night, splashed water on my face again, and went back outside. Mario was playing cricket and was about to close the bull in round four. He paused and put his arm around my shoulder. "You OK, braddah?"

He had the true old-man bolohead: the shiny top with hair brushed back on the sides of his head.

"Yeah, getting splotchy a little," I said.

"Drink water," he said, which was his solution for everything. He never boozed without a glass of ice water on the side. "Mama, get Charlie boy a glass ice water."

Mom looked up from her conversation with Eddie. "You OK, Charlie?"

Mariah Carey was singing about turning into a butterfly. "Yeah, I'm OK. Give me four Bud Lights while I'm up. By the way, Mom, why do you listen to this radio station? I think Momo is the only one under thirty here."

"I thought you kids like this station."

"Yeah, when we were in high school."

She shrugged. "No make you feel young?"

"Makes me feel old, actually."

"Pfft, you still young boy."

I gave up, thinking that maybe she secretly liked hip-hop, imagining her at a DMX concert, wearing a Vince Carter jersey and a cap turned sideways on her head, and throwing her hands in the air and waving them like she just didn't care, was good for a quick laugh. I was wondering at what age you stopped being young to old people.

Eddie turned to me and said, "You singing tonight, braddah?"

"Nah, tired tonight." I walked away, embarrassed about copping a superstar attitude. The shitty thing was that the real reason I didn't want to sing was that I was damn tired of hearing my own voice.

When I got back, Ollie was still going on about Thailand. Mark moved in, and I sat down. It seemed like Ollie was trying to sell living there to Mark. "They got the Internet in Thailand, you know," Ollie said.

Surprisingly, B didn't look bored at all. He was just sitting there, listening and grinning, and the perpetual pissed-off look on his face was gone. The music changed, and "Love and Honesty" came on. I turned toward the bar, and Mom beamed a smile at me: red lightning squeezed by charcoal eyelids.

But when she changed it to the Hawaiian station, I wanted to ring her neck. "Dammit," I said. "I tell her enough with the Mariah Carey, and she gives me 'Love and Honesty.'"

Ollie and Mark laughed. "Ever meet a Hawaiian who hates Hawaiian music?" Mark asked B.

"Well, I don't hate it," I said.

"Whatever," Mark said.

"I don't either," Ollie said. "Granted, I barely got enough Hawaiian blood to fill my little toe. I don't love it, but I don't hate it." Most people forgot that Ollie was part Hawaiian. I wasn't sure if it was because of his height or the way he dressed. He actually owned a blue blazer with a crest on the pocket.

"It's just too damn nostalgic," I said. "Beaches and flower leis and surfing and shit. Pop songs from the seventies, remade with the power-ukulele solos. Eddie Van Halen wannabes need to learn to play the guitar."

"Ever listen to real Hawaiian music, the kind where the words are actually Hawaiian?" B said.

"Yeah, whenever I fly. They always play it on the airplane. I hear it in banks, too."

B shrugged. "Give me a genre of music that doesn't have its hacks. Not everyone can be the Pahinuis or Makaha Sons or Iz."

"I like Motown."

"Well, you'd have to make a damn strong case to argue that Marvin Gaye and Tammi Terrel's 'Ain't No Mountain High Enough' got more substance than 'Love and Honesty.'"

Surprised, I shrugged and said, "It just sounds better." I said.

He took a swig of beer. "That's just taste, man." He pointed at his bottle. "Why is this your favorite beer? Most critics would tell you that the ales and lagers of the world got more taste, flavor, character, and body—or whatever terms they use—than Bud Light."

"You into haole beers?" Mark asked.

B scratched off his label and stuck it to the black table. "Me? No. But if some haole came up to me while I was drinking a Bud Light and told me that it sucked, I'd just shrug and tell him it tastes better to me. If he made more noise, I'd shove this bottle of crappy beer straight up his ass."

We laughed, then I said, "I just don't like the music, man. I guess you could say I'm like the black guy who hates rap but likes jazz or something. I mean, how many versions of 'Ulupalakua' I gotta listen to?"

Ollie smiled. "But you don't even like jazz. You're more like the black guy who hates rap and jazz, but likes Mozart."

"And there's nothing wrong with that," B said, "unless you look down on people who like what you don't like. That's when it ain't right." He peeled the label off the table, grabbed the small glass filled with paper and stubby pencils used for karaoke song requests, and put the label on the glass. He was very careful about it, scratching out air bubbles with the tip of his fingernail.

A few minutes later, Taks and Sloane walked in together. There wasn't any room in our booth, so after saying hi, they sat in the one next to us. I got out of our booth and slid in next to Sloane. Momo came, and they ordered their drinks. I stopped Momo and put in a karaoke song. "Ready to sing?" I asked Sloane. "I put in a duet to prove a point."

"I can't sing." She laughed. "What song?"

"Ain't No Mountain High Enough."

"How does that one go?"

"You'll recognize it when you hear it."

Momo gave us the mics. She paused before walking away, her mouth slightly open, and I was afraid that she was going to say something, make some kind of comment about our trying to sing. But she wasn't looking at us; she was looking toward the door. Then I saw the twins walking with another shorter guy. They walked in single file, their hands inches away from running against the booths and tables on the sides of them. The twins wore T-shirts and jeans, and the shorter guy a wifebeater tank top and sweat pants. All three had on black high tops. The twins looked a lot older than when I'd seen them last, like guys who should be at home with their wives and kids. They were still huge, though, and just looking at them made me feel weak. It was weird to realize that we were all the same species. One of the bowling-pin forearms of the guy in the tank top, who wasn't as big as the twins, but looked in better shape, brushed against a table. A series of triangular tattoos ran from his wrist to shoulder, and a band was tattooed on his upper arm. That one was solid black, like he'd had something there that he wanted to obliterate. All three of them looked like versions of Bolo Badcow, Mark's ogre warrior in EQ. I wondered if Mark was getting off on that.

The music started, and it struck me as stupid to sing now. B looked at me and stood up. I sighed and followed. The guy in the tank top was leaning against the bar and facing us while the twins talked to Mom. Tank Top nudged the white twin with his elbow. Both twins turned around.

It was like a scene from The Bad News Bears. I felt like one of those little blond kids, the sniffling one with allergies. Even B seemed bigger than me, though I was pretty sure I was taller than any of them. "Wassup?" B said.

"Small island," the brown twin said. Except for their size, there was nothing flashy about either twin. I couldn't see any tattoos or jewelry, and their black T-shirts had the Honolulu Police union logo on them. Both had short, basic haircuts, like they'd just gotten Fantastic Sams ten-dollar special; I couldn't get over how much they looked like dads, like they should be on the sidelines of a Pop Warner football game.

B shook their hands one by one. "Wassup, Preschool," he said to the guy in the tank top, the only one with flash. Besides his tattoos, he had long hair that was slicked back into a ponytail. I didn't know if "Preschool" was the guy's name or if B was insulting him.

B pointed to me. "This is Winnie's brother, Charlie."

Now they all shook my hand. My hands were bigger, but bodywise, I felt like a freshman standing next to a bunch of seniors. The brown twin said, "He no look like her. You Hawaiian?"

"Stepsister," I said.

"So what, where is she?" the other twin asked me. He wasn't really that white. It was his dark brother who made him look pale.

"No clue." I shrugged.

Everyone in the bar was quiet, even old man Eddie. The music for "Ain't No Mountain High Enough" was still playing on the karaoke machine, words bleeding from white to neon pink. I started to laugh. Everyone looked at me like I'd lost my mind.

"Sorry, I dunno why I'm laughing," I said.

I think I knew why, though. The whole scene seemed stupid, like a melodramatic showdown in some movie. It stopped being silly when the guy in the tank top hit me in the face so hard that I swear I heard a bottle fall and crash behind the bar.

I didn't see much after that except feet moving all around me. Sometimes the feet would stop dancing and kicks would come flying at my head. All three of these guys had some pretty nice shoes. I stayed on the ground while Mom's screams went off like sirens. I wanted her to shut up, then I heard her scream, "Stop it, you killing him!"

Aside from the occasional kick to the head, I was OK—well, as OK as I could be—so I knew she wasn't talking about me. I turned over and looked toward the booths. Taks, Sloane, Mark, and Ollie were still sitting there, hands folded, looking down at the table like children on the receiving end of a stern lecture. I stood up, and a punch landed on the back of my head. It didn't hurt, so I turned around because it suddenly became important that I see everything. Eddie and Mario were standing by the dart boards, trying not to watch. I turned again, not able to help myself, and a big forearm snaked itself around my neck, and thick, black hair scratched at my chin. I couldn't breathe, but I still kept trying to turn my head to see what was going on. I got lightheaded fast, and a water stain under the AC was the last thing I remember seeing.

When I came to, I was surprised at how clean the floor was. There were no broken bottles or overturned bar stools or tables. B was flat on his back, taking short, quick breaths. His head and face were covered with so much blood that I couldn't tell where it was all coming from. Despite that, it looked like he was smiling. Taks pulled me up. "Fuck! You OK, man?"

I felt OK. I'd always imagined that getting into a fight would be slower. But I was shocked at how fast it went down. Then again, I suppose it wasn't really a fight. It was more of a slaughter. I'd just gotten bolo'ed.

Mom made me sit down in a booth. Momo was patting B's head with a wet towel. Ollie and Mark stood over me, looking worried. "We gotta take you guys hospital," Mom said. "Mario, call da cops, too."

Sloane walked toward me with a wet towel. B struggled to pull himself up. The veins on his forehead were popping out, and all the blood that Momo had wiped off was replaced with a new coat. "I can't breathe" was all he said in between short, rapid gasps of air, but he managed to get up and walk out the door. He looked as stiff as a mummy walking out of its sarcophagus. "We need to take him to the hospital," I said.

Taks drove my truck. In the back, B was lying down, eyes closed. I told Taks to pull over. I opened the door and threw up. "Shit, you probably have a concussion," Taks said.

It would be a first, I thought. "Thanks for all the fuckin' help," I said. "Main thing is that you got my back."

"Why did you laugh, man?"

"Why didn't you jump in?"

"Fuck, I'm sorry, man. I froze."

We didn't talk for the rest of the drive to Queen's Hospital.

All in all, the beating wasn't too bad. I did have a concussion, and there were little bumps all over the top of my head—a bunch of little boloheads—making me wish I had hair. But the doctor wrote me a note so I could stay home the rest of the week, and I was told I was fine to go home.

Before I left, I checked on B. He was in worse shape. He had a collapsed lung, and some cuts on his head had been stapled. One of his eyes was so red that it was hard to see a pupil. The other eye was swollen shut. A tube ran into his ribs, but he was awake. "You OK, man?" I asked.

His voice sounded tired and shallow. "Yeah, but I gotta stay here for at least a night. Do me a favor: start looking for your fuckin' sister tomorrow."

"I'll head over to the prison tomorrow."

"Good."

"I guess there's no squaring shit with the twins, huh?"

"Oh, I'm gonna square shit."

"We should let it go, man. I'm not going to be doing any crazy shit."

"Go find your sister. I'll take care of it. How bad is my face?"

"Pretty bad. Fluorescent lights don't help."

"I fuckin' hate hospitals."

"I don't think anybody really likes them."

When I walked out the sliding doors, Taks, Sloane, Mark, Ollie, and Mom were all waiting for me with worried, guilty looks on their faces. Too little, too late, I thought. That was the thing with help: it always seemed to come too late. I wasn't sure what I expected them to do, but something would have been nice. I felt like someone had strolled into our house and beat my ass while the rest of the family watched, as if it was an episode of Walker, Texas Ranger. I asked Taks for my keys. "I can drive," I said.

"When I told the doctor that B got up and walked to the truck, and then walked by himself into the hospital, he didn't believe me," Ollie said. "Who is that guy?"

"Winnie's friend," Mark said.

Taks handed me the keys and kept quiet. Mom came up to me and said, "You stay wit' me tonight."

We all headed over to the truck in twos, like we were in a wedding party. Mark and Mom were in front, Sloane and Taks were next, and Ollie and I trailed behind. A car rolled up next to my truck. A woman was pulling a baby out of the back. "Winnie needs to be dropped," Ollie said. "You should come to Thailand with me. Maybe you could hook up with a job teaching English or something. I'd spot you till then."

The woman walked by quickly, holding the baby in her arms. It was wrapped in a white blanket with pink rocking horses on it. The woman, wearing an oversized T-shirt and jeans, didn't even look at us. Her hair was messy, like she'd just woken up.

"The funny thing is, I don't even know where she is. I didn't do shit," I said.

"Guilt by association," Ollie said.

"I guess."

"That guy B was awake when you saw him?"

"Yeah."

"That's a real great friend you picked up there."

"Well, he isn't even related to Winnie and he's trying to help her. I feel bad."

"Can't help those who can't be helped, man."

I turned around. "I wonder what's wrong with that lady's kid."

She'd already passed the ambulance out front and was through the sliding glass doors. We all got into the truck, and Sloane slid in next to me in the front. We didn't talk for the whole drive back to the bar. When we got there, Mario was standing out in front of the closed doors, waiting. Everyone told me they'd call in the morning, and I told Mom I was going to my own place. I popped open the glove compartment and took out some aspirin. I didn't know if the headache was from the punches, the concussion, or the beer, but it was coming on strong, and for the first time, the thought of crashing on the sleeping bag in my apartment was a welcome one. I felt so bad that I didn't even smoke a cigarette on the way home.

3

I don't know why I set up a visit with my aunt the next day. I felt horrible, the top of my head looked like the bottom of an egg carton, and I was at the point of never wanting to see Winnie for the rest of my life. But I called WCCC, set it up, and drove off to Kailua with a cap squeezing the bumps on the sides of my head. The sky was clear, and what little clouds there were coasted on the move. I still didn't feel like smoking, and played with the idea of taking this opportunity to quit as I drove past Punchbowl and headed for Pali Highway.

It was a strange feeling, me doing what I knew was dumb. It was dumb to keep moving toward a bad ending. Unfortunately, that is where I seemed to be heading again. I thought about what my old high-school physics teacher tried to tell us when me and Taks were busy in the back row, throwing tiny pieces of paper into the frizzy hair of Shelley Matsugawa, who sat in front of us. He was talking about inertia and how a body in motion stays in motion. It made sense to me. Seemed that in high school a guy could learn just about everything he needed to know. Too bad I wasn't really listening most of the time. As I drove up the Pali, went through the tunnels and started down the mountain, I was thinking that I couldn't seem to stop myself from wanting to see how all this turned out, even though I figured it could only turn out one way: badly. Maybe I was doing it more for B than for Winnie, because I felt bad about him getting his ass kicked. This seemed even dumber because I didn't even really know the guy. Maybe it wasn't inertia at all; I felt more like a pinball than an object moving in a vacuum.

When I got to the prison, I signed in at the gate, then moved through a series of buzzing gates and doors to the rec area. As I walked up the hill, I felt like I should be carrying a folder and a book the way I did back in intermediate school. From the other side of the fence, an innate sang to me "Who's That Guy" from Grease II. She had a good voice, but looked nothing like

Michelle Pfeiffer. I swear that every time I went there, the ladies, most of them Hawaiian, smelled the townie on me.

The rec area was an asphalt square with a tattered volleyball net in the middle. Two basketball hoops faced each other across the hard, black surface, both lacking nets. The square was framed with dark pink, orange, blue, and turquoise doors set in cream-colored walls. There were also turquoise benches, each with a rusting, empty coffee can for cigarette butts. I couldn't see the fence capped with coils of razor wire, which was good, so I made myself comfortable at one of the benches, lit a cigarette, and waited for my aunt.

Aunty Kaula Keaweaimoku walked through a buzzing door and smiled when she spotted me at the bench. Her look screamed "dyke," mullet hairstyle and all. I imagined her clothes outside of prison didn't vary much from what she was wearing: red T-shirt over a dirt-stained, white long-sleeved shirt; blue work pants; and slippers. Maybe she'd pick up a blue flannel shirt when she got out. Because she was my father's older sister, I figured she must be up there in years, but her brown skin was relatively unwrinkled and her curly hair was jet black. The scary thing was that I pretty much had the same Hawaiian mullet in high school. The spongy texture of her hair reminded me of my own.

I stood up, and she gave me a big hug. "Wow, didn't expect to see you here, braddah."

With both arms on my shoulders, she held me out in front of her for inspection. She wasn't much shorter than me. She took off my cap and gently rubbed the bumps on my head. "What da hell happened to you?"

We both sat down. "NALO" was tattooed on her left hand, each letter on a finger, below the knuckles. I wondered if she'd done it herself, because the letters were right-side-up from her perspective. "Hmm, dunno what else to say except I got my ass kicked. Want a smoke?"

She took a cigarette, and I lit it for her. She left it dangling from her lips while she talked. I'd seen her do this the first time I met her, and I wondered why, since her hands were free. She squinted at me, her straight eyelashes filtering smoke. "You one big boy. Must've been one big braddah."

"Was braddahs, and it was the first time in my adult life I ever felt small."

"Winnie?"

"Yeah, sorta, I guess."

She took the cigarette out of her mouth and sighed. "You gotta cut dat one loose I tink so."

"Would be smart. She's in pretty deep shit. But she pulled a disappearing act, so I'd like to find her just to make sure she's alive and all."

"Dat's like letting one fish go, den trying fo' fish da same spot so you catch um again."

"Any idea where she'd go?"

"Not really. She told me all da stories, but you stay here as long as me, you start for mix um all togetta."

Kaula had been there for over ten years for trafficking. Because of her bad record, she'd gotten two hundred and five months of prison for selling about seven grams to an undercover. Probably a week's supply for Winnie, it was about fifteen hundred dollars' worth. From what I knew, someone like B was looking at that kind of time, if not more, if he ever got busted again for anything. "Aunty," I said, feeling comfortable about it because it's what most people call older women anyway, "why do you smoke like that?"

She squinted, eyes aimed over my shoulder. "Habit. Me and your fadda used to lay net, and dis how we had for smoke when we worked da net."

"He was a good fisherman?"

"Da best pretty much. Das all he did befo' you was born. Neva drink nothing until your madda died giving birth to you. He went suck um up afta dat."

"Well, from what I remember, he made up for the non-alcoholic years just fine."

"Ae, like I said, suck um up."

"So can't you tell me anything about Winnie?"

She thought for a second. "You sure you like hear? Some-times, when you hear one story about someone, you tink dey funny kind afta."

"Knew her pretty much all my life. Doubt you could shock me."

What she told me did shock me, though. She told me that when Winnie got to prison, she was quiet and skinny to the point where it looked like you could grab her collarbone like handle bars. A rail-thin noob who kept to herself wasn't an odd site in prison, but Winnie had always been noisy and vain. Kaula said they became friends when they worked in the cafeteria together, which was tough work but made time go faster. I thought of the time warp in ABC Store when she said this, and I imagined that the warp was way worse here.

Working in the cafeteria put pounds on Winnie fast. Then they took a writing class together, and their assignment was to write a personal essay on what had landed them there. Kaula felt that the teacher, some muumuu-wearing haole lady from the university, thought that going to prison like a movie drama. What she wanted in these essays was action, because every time a girl would tell the teacher straight up what got her there—

stealing a car, drugs, whatever—the teacher launched into a speech about the importance of description and details: how did you steal the car; how much drugs; what did it feel like when the cuffs were locked around your wrists? "It was like she wanted for watch movie, not read."

One girl said, "Felt shitty, what you tink?" The class laughed and laughed, and the teacher all but gave up. She told them to write in class, then she read a book, making Kaula remember high school. The next week, Winnie came in with a composition book with a marbled black-and-white cover and about fifty pages of writing. The teacher wanted her to read it out loud, but Winnie refused, so the teacher offered to read it herself. Winnie shrugged. The entire session was spent listening to Winnie's story, and it was a good story. "Was what she wanted: like one movie," Kaula said.

The essay covered the couple years of her life before she went to jail. She talked about how she was so bent on ice, a full-on chronic, that she'd do anything for money to get some. First she did the normal stuff, like stealing from relatives and stealing cars and motorcycles and driving them into chop shops that were disguised as broken-down repair shops. During that time, she flirted and slept with dealers and dealt herself, off and on; but she always ended up in trouble, beaten badly, because she would smoke most of what she had to sell. She told the class about the time she found out she was pregnant and decided to quit drugs: she'd walked into the father's house, and before she could tell him, he kicked her in the stomach because she'd ripped him off a few days before.

In three years, she got pregnant five times, and each time, she lost the baby, sometimes willingly, sometimes not. By the end of year two, she was sleeping on cardboard in downtown, had one change of clothes and no Magic Eight Ball, and sucked dicks for twenty bucks a pop. The teacher made a sad face when she read that, but Kaula suspected she got off on it. The teacher was especially captivated when Winnie wrote that one night a potential customer punched her in the face when he got close and claimed to smell latex on her breath. "You trying fo' give me AIDS!" the man screamed as he sped away.

Winnie was pulled out of downtown by a guy who collected money from the half-assed dealers there. Saying she was too pretty to be living on the street, he hooked her up with a job at a hostess bar he had part ownership in. He fed her, clothed her, and didn't seem to imagine that she'd steal from him. She guessed it was because he was up there and thought that no one would be stupid enough to steal from him, especially considering how he looked. She described him as looking like the scariest ACO at OCCC, which was all the girls needed to hear to understand what she meant. But the guy was out of touch, off the streets too long, and failed to remember that an addict would steal from you if your name was Bush and you lived in the Goddamned White House.

She liked the bar and got the taste for alcohol again, saying it reminded her of her family. She stayed off ice for a couple of weeks, until she met a guy at the bar, a nice guy who was into it casually and turned her on out back one night. Stuffed in heels a half size too small, her feet had been killing her, and she told herself that a hit or two would take the edge off the pain. Sure enough, she held the pipe, the guy lit her up, and her feet felt brand new.

It was on again, and she did both: drink and smoke ice. It worked for a while too, until she came in so loaded one night that, when an older guy told her to sit in his lap, she grabbed a plate full of kimchee and threw it like a Frisbee at his face. It was like all of the men in her life, most of them strangers, were saying the same thing to her all at once, and she lost it. She was fired the next day, but before she left, she stole the mama's Mercedes. She didn't even have to hotwire it; she just took her keys, drove it to the beach, and set it on fire. The next thing she knew, she was arrested. The guy who bailed her out was the one who'd taken her off the street.

She took a beating and was forced to work in a massage parlor to pay back the mama. She lasted two nights before she stole the guy's Lexus, this time calling one of her brothers to pick her up at the beach before she set the car on fire. While she waited, she decided to check the trunk but found nothing. When she saw her brother's car coming, she poured the gasoline she'd bought on the way over the top of the car and lit it on fire. Her brother yelled, "Holy shit, what the fuck!" She told him to take her to their mom's house so that she could say goodbye and then to drop her off at the nearest police station. All her brother could say was, "Man, that was a nice car."

The lady from the university thought the essay could be published, but Winnie declined, saying it wasn't anything she was proud of. "But it's a great story that people would love to read," the teacher said.

"Sounded like a pretty shitty story to me," Winnie said.

The girls laughed. The lady walked out of the class without a copy of Winnie's essay. Winnie took the book with her to the cafeteria and threw it in the oven on pizza day.

After Aunty Kaula told me all this, I could easily fill in the gaps. Mark was the brother who'd picked her up, and the trunk wasn't empty: there was twenty grand in it. I wasn't sure which of the three guys had pulled her out of downtown, but I suspected it was the one B called Preschool; just couldn't imagine either of the twins going solo. I almost laughed at the part where she'd set not one, but two cars on fire, remembering what she'd done to Millionaire Estates when she was fourteen. Winnie was one of those people who argued endlessly with anyone who thought that fireworks should be banned in Hawai'i. "She's screwed," I said.

Aunty Kaula nodded. "Who she ripped off?"

"Ever hear of the Rapozo brothers?"

She laughed. "Dat our cousins! We all from Waimanalo side."

For a moment it seemed all of my problems were solved, then I thought the better of it. "Small island. What if I told you they lost the cars, plus some money?"

Aunty Kaula didn't even ask how much. "She fucked. Just da car, she fucked. Cut her loose, braddah. You cannot do nothing but get yourself into trouble."

"Yeah, it looks like. Was my dad into all the stuff the twins are into?"

"Nope, dat was our cousins. Da only crime dat your fadda ever committed dat I can rememba is living on da beach just because he thought he should be able to. He was into politics, all of dat. Da family had one house."

"I don't remember the house. Just his long, white hair and him talking pidgin all the time, except that he slurred like Ozzy Osbourne. Why did he work at Ala Moana?"

"He wanted fo' live in town 'cause he thought maybe get betta schools for you. He told me one time, 'I no care if da kid turn out like me, but I like give um options.'"

"I dunno if he'd like the way I turned out."

"You went college, right? You all worried about your sista, right? Besides, you still young. Da game not ova yet."

"You didn't tell me the town stuff the first time I came."

"I gave you too much credit. Thought you knew."

I laughed. "Well, I'd like to come back. I like talking to you."

"I'm here. Maybe next time you come I tell you where you can dig up some of your cousins, not da ones chasing around Winnie trying for kill her."

I kissed her on the cheek. "Sounds good."

"Not too late for you, Hawaiian."

"I thought Hawaiian is in the heart."

"Dat's what the haoles and Japanese in town tell you, but Hawaiian is in da blood. But no matta. No get any Hawaiians left in da world."

I sat back down. "People still into the ocean, fishing, hula, and stuff like that. Must still have Hawaiians. There's a Hawaiian-studies program at UH even."

"Dat's just people remembering what one Hawaiian was. All dat stuff dey did back in da day was necessary. You fish, hunt, grow taro 'cause you need food. You dance hula 'cause you celebrate da land and gods. Need um. Needed da land for live and da gods for make da world make sense, but no need all dat now. I tink so your fadda went see dis. He went try live on da beach to try prove can go back, but no can. Even if you try for real, no can."

"So why do you study it?"

She thought for a second. "To rememba, I guess. Make sure dat even no more Hawaiians, still get Hawaiian."

"I'll remember that," I said.

"Remember dis, too, braddah. You going find out dat get only one rule most people live by: dey only give a shit about demselves."

I thought about the night before, when none of my friends had helped me. There was no such thing as the power of indifference. No sane person could be indifferent about himself. I pressed the button. The door buzzed, and I pulled on it. It was heavy, but easy enough to get through.

As I drove up the Pali, I thought about how I put people who went to jail on some kind of pedestal. Winnie, B, Aunty Kaula—they'd say something, and I'd listen like they had some kind of wisdom to share. Who were these people? One was evidently a crack ho, and the others two-bit dealers. I was thinking that I'd gone through my whole life meeting people who thought they could teach me something. When I was a kid, my dad tried to teach me things about the ocean, about land and life—things I could easily go through land and life without. My teachers in school taught me the basic survival tools I'd need: my ABCs and 123s. Mom never tried to teach me much; she took the learn-on-your-own approach. My high-school and college teachers tried to teach me about how the world worked: in the past with history; in the present with political science; in nature with science; and in society with literature. But I slept through most of that because, quite frankly, I could move through land and life without those things as well, doing no worse than some of these teachers. One could just look at the cars in a faculty parking lot to see that their knowledge wasn't getting them far.

I guess they were trying to teach me to be smug like them. Yeah, I might drive a crappy '89 Toyota Corolla, but I've got all this knowledge in my head. Yeah, I might work as a janitor at Ala Moana, but I can tell you about tides and fish and stuff. Yeah, I might be sitting in jail, but I can tell you what being Hawaiian is all about. I passed through the Pali tunnels as the sunlight dimmed, and when I saw the opening on the other side, I thought that maybe owning a Lexus or Mercedes isn't the answer to life, but it sure as hell might make the ride smoother. The way I figured it, the only sure thing about life was that there was an end, whether it be at Millionaire Estates, Countryside Acres, a hospital, an old-folks home, prison, or facedown in the gutter; no matter what, there was an end, and it was the ride that was important. The ride was short, too, so no reason to take the road with a drag-race mentality. Maybe driving to and from work, home, and Bolohead Row in a decent car was not a bad life at all. It was sure better than what Winnie was doing: blitzing through traffic just to hit a wall at the end. She was going through that windshield again, and there wasn't a thing I could do about it because she was the one at the wheel.

Guys like Taks, Mark, and Ollie had it right. Jumping into the fight the night before would've been stupid. They were enjoying their rides, so there was no reason to pull over to help a buddy out of a burning car. It was too dangerous. Just as I was thinking all of this, B called me on my cell phone. "How'd it go?" he asked.

"Learned a lot."

"They're discharging me. Could I bum a ride from the hospital?"

"Yeah. You up to checking some places out?"

"Yeah, no problem. I just need to hit home first to change and stuff."

"That works. Some of the places I wanna look at are close to your place. Besides, we have time to kill. Can't really go to these places in daylight."

"I think I lost my job," he said.

"I got the money from Winnie. I'll give you some to tide you over."

"Nah, it's hers."

"It's not, though."

"True."

I thought we'd take a look at some of these places Winnie had been at, figuring that she would be at none of them, and then I could say that I'd given it a shot, pay off B to forget he'd ever met me, and resume my life. I was thinking that maybe I'd quit work, move back in with Mom, and go back to school to get my MBA. I could find some nighttime job, maybe back at the restaurant I'd worked at, and maybe throw in some of this Winnie money with Taks and see where the gambling would go. Winnie was done, and B was probably going to be taking her drag-race route to the wall any day now. I think I understood that smile he had on his face while lying on the dirty carpet of the bar with a bloody face and a collapsed lung. It was the same type of smile Winnie would have when she said, "No worry, beef curry."

I imagined her having the same smile when she'd set the cars on fire.

When I picked B up from the hospital, he was sporting a hat and cheap sunglasses: the Unabomber look. He walked slowly, as if moving too suddenly might tear the skin off his body. His shiny shirt was gone, and instead he wore a Queen's Medical Center T-shirt. He must have hit the gift shop. I pulled up to the sliding doors, and he stepped into the truck carefully, pausing before he committed his ass to the seat. The skin under his left eye was yellow. "Nice cap," he said.

I drove him to his place. It was two in the afternoon, and school traffic was about to jam the streets. "You sure you up to walking around tonight?" I asked.

"No choice really. Need to move on this fast."

I wasn't wondering much about what to do if we didn't find her, but I was puzzled by what we'd do if by some miracle we did. I wondered if B had any answers. "So what happens if we find her?"

"I don't have a grand plan or anything. I figure we cross that bridge when we come to it."

"We don't see her tonight or hear something, I'm done, by the way." Mark would've said BTW.

"Yeah, I might be, too. I gotta fish me up another job. That shit we went through last night comes with a police report. I'm just hoping some lazy ass gets it tossed to him—or one of the twin's friends."

"She's a big girl, I guess."

"Yeah." He stepped carefully out of the truck and walked up to his hovel. I planned on bringing some of the money with me that night to give to him. The counter in front of his building was open, so I decided to get a three-dollar pack of cigarettes. The woman behind the counter was so old that her skin hung on her face, like the old photos of Indians you see in history textbooks. She was Filipino and had the worse teeth I've ever seen—what was left of them anyway. When she smiled, it looked like she'd been drinking coffee and eating Oreo cookies all day. I asked her for a box of Marlboro Lights, and she slid the box across the counter with a book of matches on top. Her hands were covered with liver spots, and her fingernails were so worn down that they had no white tips. I wondered what she'd looked like when she was young, what she'd done, and how she'd ended up there. It was another ending to Life that the game didn't provide.

I had been a little too slow to miss the traffic and got stuck in it the moment I left B's. There was road construction going on downtown, as usual, and one lane was closed. I passed Chinatown in heavy traffic, looking at the store windows filled with birds and pigs roasting on skewers and heated by light bulbs. I wondered how long the merchants kept that food up before throwing it away.

The sidewalks were relatively empty, except for a few business people and students of Hawai'i Pacific University, the downtown college, muling backpacks and briefcases and walking around with head-down determination to get wherever they were heading. It reminded me of Mark's Plaatmuule, the drone programmed to make him platinum pieces day in, day out. It also reminded me of my notion to go back to school to get my MBA. It was strange being thirty-two, stuck in downtown traffic and thinking about a career. The only job I remember actually dreaming about as a kid was being an archaeologist like Indiana Jones. But that wasn't a Life career card either. As I stopped at a light and the students and business people crossed the street, I looked at both and decided I didn't want to be either. One man, a good twenty years older than me, towered over the others, but his walk was the same. I could imagine the thoughts rolling through his head like a stock-market ticker: "Hit the gym, go home, check the kids' homework, eat dinner, watch TV, maybe catch some of that Wild On stuff on E! Entertainment after the kids are down, catch a few glimpses of the 'Girls Gone Wild' infomercial, take a shower, set the alarm, and kiss the wife good night to remind myself that she's there." I picked up my cell phone and called ABC. One of my cashers answered. "It's Charlie. Do me a favor and take this message down for Gary. Ready?"

"Yep."

"I quit."

I hung up. It was a dumb move, especially with my doctor's note sitting in my pocket. Quitting like that wouldn't do much for my resume and would cost me some references when I went to look for another job but it was the only way I knew how to quit a thing: cold turkey.

I went to Mom's bar instead of home. Momo was there by herself. Promotion to bartender meant you had to do the first shift from two p.m. to eight or nine, and it seemed Momo was moving up in the world. Normally, Mom or Mario bartended, except for the few nights a week when the old Japanese bartender staggered in; so it probably meant that Mom had found a new girl to sit at the bottom of the totem pole. It was a bit early for the old haole man, Rudy, so the bar was empty except for Momo, who sat behind the counter, hugging her knee, and working on a newspaper crossword puzzle. Being there that early made me feel like a kid again, coming home from elementary school. Momo glanced up. "What's the nickname of NFL legend Ed Jones?"

"Too Tall."

She wrote it down. Her top was white today, the usual spaghetti-strap style, and the bar was empty and cold. The air conditioning caused nipple protrusion. "Cold, huh?" I said.

She shrugged and asked me if I wanted a beer. Her naiveté was cute. "So how's your head?" she asked.

"Feels pretty neat. Here..." I took her hand and passed it under my hat. It felt good to be petted like a dog sometimes.

"After you left last night, I was telling your Mom that I was thinking about quitting. I don't want to be around if those guys come back."

"Ah, so you got promoted instead?"

"Yeah. Is it always this slow during the day?"

"Pretty much. Rudy should come in at about four, and some of the old guys might show up at five or six. Other than that, it's pretty slow."

"I want the night shift."

She was being a bit distant, making me think I'd missed that boat. I knew a couple of things about getting women, but of course nothing about keeping them. The getting part was all about returning the interest they were showing and trying to get close fast. With enough time to think about it, any girl would pretty much decide against a guy like me. And women, for the most part, took sex more seriously than men did. They were so worried about being sluts that when they slept with a guy, they'd stick with him for a bit just so it wouldn't look like they were only out for sex. So the idea was to get them in bed as fast as possible. It seemed I'd missed the boat with Momo, and the clock was ticking on Sloane. Besides, Taks might have gotten to Sloane already. I wasn't thinking about all this because I cared one way or another; it was more out of habit.

By four o'clock, I was drunk. The alcohol seemed more potent when I drank it alone—less talking, I suppose. Aside from the few dart games I'd played with Momo, my hands were never without a bottle. My face was hot, and the splotches were probably back. I decided to keep on drinking, not only this night, but for the next few as well, just to see where the splotches took me. Staying drunk: it sounded like a neat science experiment.

When Mom came in at five, I was in front of the video machine playing "Photo Hunt." Looking at two matching pictures of a naked girl on a motorcycle, I was trying to find the small difference between the two: garter, no garter; piece of hair over shoulder, piece of hair behind shoulder. I was toasted. Mom walked in, and I had to close one eye so I wouldn't see two of her. I laughed, thinking, What if the twins came back? I'd see four Rapozos, two brown, two not as brown, eight feet kicking my head. Mom stepped behind the bar without greeting me. "Bust out Life," I said.

Mom pulled out the board game, and Momo joined is on the condition that she get the red car. I spun the highest number and got to move first. I chose to start off at college, as usual, got my $40,000 loan, made the dean's list, and graduated.

It was an exciting life overall. I had a skiing accident, which cost me five grand, and a wedding reception that cost me ten, but after that, I managed to pay off my student loan, won the lottery, bought a Victorian house from Blithering Heights Realty, had a baby girl, paid twenty grand for fifty-yard-line seats at the big game, had a tree fall on my house, but I was insured, ran for mayor, learned CPR, wrote a bestseller, paid five grand for my daughter's summer-school tuition, learned sign language, had a tornado hit my house, but I was insured, and went through a midlife crisis. I turned in my stethoscope for paintbrush and became an artist, helped the homeless, paid for my daughter's college tuition, went fishing, planted a tree, and spun again. At the end of my life, I collected my pension before pulling my car into the crater that was supposed to be Millionaire Estates. It was a cherry life. I counted my money. I had won. "Winnie is screwed, Mom," I said.

"Yeah," Mom said. Starting to cry, she walked to the bathroom.

Momo began putting the stuff back in the box. Over the course of the game, a customer had come in: the same guy I'd seen six nights before. He was wearing the same sweater hood. After Momo got all the stuff in the box, I picked it up and put it in the trash. I walked out of the bar and made it to my truck. I opened the tailgate, crawled in, and rolled on my back. My face was pulsing, and my splotchy skin was itchy. The sky was darkening, like blue cloth soaking up water. I passed out.

When I woke up, my face wasn't itchy, but my mouth was dry and my head was pounding. It was night, but the sky wasn't black. It occurred to me that night was never completely black. You couldn't completely turn off something like the sun. My cell phone was beeping. Mark and B had called while I was sleeping. I sat up, lit a cigarette, and called them back. I was surprised my neck wasn't sweaty.

Mark, Ollie, Taks, and Sloane were at a bar called Mama Koi's, which was right down the road. Koi's was a karaoke/dart bar like Mom's, but ten times bigger. There were seven dart boards instead of two, five video poker machines instead of one, three pool tables, one foosball table, a jukebox, a pinball machine, and an arcade-style basketball machine. All of the waitresses were Momo-like, except two had boob jobs, and on any given night four of them were working. I called B and told him I'd pick him up in a couple of hours, since downtown didn't get interesting till late at night. Then I decided to go check out the others at Koi's, figuring it wasn't every day I got to see Ollie. I drove to my apartment first to grab the money Winnie had left me, fighting the urge to plop down on my sleeping bag and pass out. I took the wad out of the envelope and stuffed all seven thousand in my pocket.

It took a bit of willpower to get to Koi's, and when I did, I wondered if I was going to remember the drive the next day. Some people didn't like to hear that I forgot drives to and from bars, but I wasn't convinced that alcohol had anything to do with it: I rarely remembered a drive to and from work either.

As usual, Koi's was crowded. Dart players rotated from tables to boards, filling their mugs with pitchers every time they went back to their tables, then going back for their turns. Everybody looked as if they had magnets under their feet. I did a double-take at a guy who looked as if he was throwing his darts fletching first: each time he threw, the dart seemed to pinwheel toward the board. I walked past the boards and the pool tables—all taken—and stood at the counter to order a beer. The bartender, a girl in a low-cut top, was displaying her implants proudly, like they were a pair of two-karat diamond earrings. She asked if I wanted to pay cash or run a tab. I gave her a hundred from my pocket. While I waited for change, I scanned the booths for Taks and the rest. They were sitting over by the restrooms. On one side of the booth, Taks was sitting with Sloane and had his hand around her; on the other side were Ollie and Mark. After I got my change and left a dollar tip, I pulled a small stool up to the head of the table. My head was still pounding, and I wondered how the beer would take. I figured I'd either puke or lose the headache. Either was fine with me.

Taks pulled his arm off of Sloane to shake my hand. He was wearing a knitted hat, which he took off and tossed to me. "Wear this, man. You look goofy."

I shrugged and put it on. I had the gangsta look going now. I shook hands with all of them and leaned over to kiss Sloane on the cheek. She was careful with the kiss, as if she didn't want to get makeup on me. "When did you start drinking?" she asked.

"About two," I said. I took a sip of beer and gagged on it, but I kept it down. The sips became easier after that.

"So how's your head?" Ollie asked.

"Good, except I feel a hangover coming on. Jesus, Mark, I keep seeing you out! Won't your EQ kingdom crumble?"

"Nah, all the East Coasters are sleeping already."

Taks and Sloane were whispering in each other's ear and laughing. I wondered if they were talking about me. "I'm going back in two days," Ollie said.

"I thought you were staying for a week," Mark said.

"I pushed up the flight."

I finished the beer in one gulp, then reached out and touched the elbow of a waitress passing by. "Could I get another one?"

She asked everyone else if they wanted another. "Shots?" I asked, and they nodded. "Get me five shots of Crown," I said.

"On a mission?" Ollie asked.

I looked around the table. My thoughts went back to the night I met B. I remembered thinking about the toy in the doctor's office and the mind's tendency to look at a person and decide if he fit in where he was at. Taks was like the king of Bolohead Row. There was no question that he fit in. Mark, Ollie, and Sloane seemed to fit, too. I looked around the bar. I could see at least eight or nine other people just like them: Japanese, Filipino, some with a haole-blood mix; most of them short and skinny. It was as if Taks, Mark, Ollie, and Sloane had split and multiplied. It must have been a trip opening this bar and seeing your patrons split like amoebas as the night wore on. As with the Photohunt game, I began to look for slight differences among them. I was glad when the shots finally came. I needed something to clear my head. I paid and lifted my glass. "To Winnie," I said.

They tapped their glasses against mine. We drank. Sloane excused herself to go to the bathroom.

"What you think?" Taks asked, leaving the question up for anyone to answer.

"She seems cool," Ollie said.

"Which is why I don't know what she's doing with you," Mark joked.

"She's got major acne," I said.

They all looked puzzled. "Yeah, I saw her at the Black Point swimming pool. She got major acne on her back."

"Shut the fuck up," Taks said.

I took a gulp of beer and laughed. "It's pretty gross, though."

Ollie and Mark were quiet. I shrugged. Someone put an AC/DC song on the jukebox for some eighties' nostalgia. I went into radar mode, trying to overhear any of the dozens of conversations around me. All I heard was mumble/laugh, mumble/laugh. "I'll try to give her face a good look when she gets back. It's probably all under her makeup," I said.

Taks shook his head. I wanted to reach across the table and wring his skinny neck. In fact, when I looked at Ollie and Mark, I wanted to do the same with them. I hated all of them. Sloane came back and sat down. I stared at her face. Sure enough, I saw tiny bumps here and there, as well as a couple of small marks on her left cheek that could have been faint bruises. "So you hooking up with Taks now?"

"Well, I don't know about hooking up. We've been hanging out."

Ollie was shaking his head. Mark stood up and said that he was going to look at songs on the jukebox. "You better watch out for Taks here. He will play you and dump you."

"Shut up," Taks said.

A waitress walked out, carrying a platter of sizzling steak. To my mind, there wasn't much that beat the smell of sizzling beef and onions. "Remember the old days, man: the game we used to play sometimes? We'd tell each other's date that the other guy was poison for her, and sure enough, sex would soon follow? I'm helping you out, man," I said.

"You're being an ass."

"Hear, hear," Sloane said.

"Mark my words: because of what I'm doing for you right now, Sloane here will have those legs spread within the next five hours. Look, I even bought the shots for lubrication."

Ollie put his little face in his little hands, and Sloane stood up and walked away. "When you get those clothes off, you'll see I was right about the acne," I said loud enough for her to hear. Taks stood up and followed her.

"That's pretty funny," Ollie said.

I finished my beer and stood up. "I'm outta here."

I wanted out of Bolohead Row. The bars and the stories were all the same. It was the first time I'd ever felt out of place there, and I figured Taks could have it: Sloane, Momo, and all. I walked past what I hoped would be my last karaoke machine, dart board, and little Japanese waitress. She had hair colored with red streaks. I called B and told him that I was picking him up.

The only thing that scared me was the thought that maybe it was all Bolohead Row. What if life was all just sitting close to something, looking up at it, and getting stuck there, your neck turning stiff and what was once neat turning ugly, while your hair keeps falling off the top of your head?

Six-Five

1

ASIDE FROM PATRONIZING small, illegal casinos, I'd never really walked the streets of downtown late at night, and it got me to thinking that there were a lot of places on the island I'd never been to despite the fact that I'd lived here all my life. I'd never been hiking in the mountains, hadn't stepped foot on most beaches, and never walked into many dark pockets downtown.

The people I saw that night were like roaches that had crawled out from the cracks of sidewalks in front of the old two-story buildings and the new bank high-rises.

I parked about a block from the police station and waited for B to peel himself from the truck. He was wearing a hospital gown over jeans, and he had brought a cane with him, a simple black one with a curved handle. We had to go slowly, so I saw more than I would have walking alone. We passed a woman sitting in front of the Honolulu magazine building in a portable nest of crumpled newspaper. We passed two transvestite hookers standing by a traffic light, one a dark Hawaiian with lines coming down from her mouth that made her look like a ventriloquist's doll. In Chinatown, a man was pushing a shopping cart filled with crushed cans and wearing these pants that weren't jeans, slacks, sweatpants, or khakis; they were just brown, straight-legged pants that looked homemade. Or maybe they were corduroys so worn down that the ridges had disappeared. Nearby, a woman in a soiled muumuu was mumbling something about God.

It seemed like every third person I passed asked me for a cigarette or five bucks. One guy stopped us and told us that his car had run out of gas. He was even holding a plastic red container to support his story. He asked to borrow money, then gave us a place of employment and a phone number. I was beginning to believe him and was about to pull out my phone to check out the number when B took off his shades, raised his cane and rested it on his shoulder, and said, "How about I knock you out, fill up your gas can, then come back and light your ass on fire?"

The guy started to say something, but he stopped himself and walked away. One of B's eyeballs was still completely red, the other was swollen shut, and there were patches of purple on his cheeks. The guy must have been tempted to take a shot at him, but B also had the look of the walking dead. Besides, it was two against one.

I wondered if B could even see; I was having a hard time myself. I was blind drunk and couldn't quite focus on the faces we passed, which made me think I could walk past Winnie right now and not even seen her. There was an open bar across the street. "Let's take a look in there," I said.

When I sat down and put my arm on the table, I had to peel it back off. The place was empty, except for a couple of bums sitting at the bar. The bar smelled like the walls were painted with stale beer and wasn't air-conditioned. "Nice place," B said.

I waited for a waitress for about a couple of minutes, then realized that was a bad idea. I walked to the bar and ordered a couple of beers. The bartender gave me two warm cans of Bud Light. When I got back to the table, B said, "I don't think Winnie would be here."

"I don't think she's downtown period," I said. "This is where you come when you don't have money. She got money."

B cracked open a beer and sipped the foam. "That's what I meant."

"Why'd we come here then?"

"I dunno. It was your idea."

I thought about that. It had indeed been my idea. I wondered why. "This is pretty senseless. She's probably sipping margaritas in Mexico or something."

Rudy, the haole guy from Mom's bar, came staggering in. He nodded at me as he passed. I was surprised to see him; I'd always imagined he went home after drinking at Mom's. It was probably just stop one on his route. He shook hands with the bartender and sat at a stool. The bar didn't even have music. "I've drunk in garages more fancy than this," I said.

"Yeah."

"How you feeling, by the way?"

"Not bad. Well, except I can't see out of one eye very good."

"Which would that be?"

B didn't smile. "You're slurring," he said. He turned his head, looking at each person in the bar. He looked at his can of beer, then started all over again. He looked like he was checking to see if he'd missed something. I wasn't sure which was dirtier: the bar or the customers. A pupu menu was scribbled right on the wall and was so faded it seemed written in crayon. Pupus—yeah, right, I thought. Images of giant tuxedo-wearing roaches holding silver platters danced in my head.

I pulled the wad of money from my pocket and counted out two grand. "Take this, man."

He put the money in his pocket. He touched his face lightly with his fingertips, either checking to see if it was still there or pushing it up because it was about to sag and fall off. His closed eye was oozing yellow. "Sorry about what happened, man," I said.

"Was my fault. He hit you, then I hit Keo. Both twins were on me after that. Was dumb. Stupid hands of mine sometimes move without thinking, you know? Smart thing would've been to wait and see if you were going to catch another crack before doing anything. Thing is that they were outnumbered, too. Wasn't thinking about where I was at."

"Which one is Keo?"

"The white one: keo, white; ula, brown. Hawaiian, man."

"Creative."

"Yeah."

"What'd you want to be when you grew up?"

I could see that it struck him as a weird question, but he tried to answer. "Not sure. To tell you the truth, never remember thinking about that. I guess football player. Used to play in high school. Maybe kickboxer." He laughed. "That's what guys like me are: failed teenage athletes. A hunter, I liked hunting pig. Take a pack of dogs and a knife up the mountains. No such thing as a professional hunter, I guess. Ever been?"

"Nope, never fired a gun. I played basketball in high school, though. Me, Taks, and Ollie. Wasn't that great." The way he'd described hunting, it seemed he didn't even use a gun. It figured.

B went to the bathroom, and I finished my beer and headed to the bar for another one. The bottom of my shoes made a crackling-sticky sound each time I lifted a foot. I wondered if this floor had ever seen a mop. I ordered three beers, including one for Rudy, who was sitting at the bar. He raised a can to me. I went back to the table, then B returned. "After this beer, let's go," I said. "This Winnie thing is pretty hopeless. She shows, she shows. Can't really look for her."

"Yeah."

"I'm pretty much done, by the way."

"I understand," he said. "Get out of this, and that other bar scene, man. What'd you call it: Bolohead Row?"

"Yeah."

"Won't find anything there, I figure."

"Yeah. Kills time, though."

"Killing time suggests you're waiting for something good."

"True."

B looked around the bar, making sure no one was listening. "Life, it's all about the six-five, man. You're always betting, and when you win, it's all good; you win what you expected to win. But when you lose, you lose a little bit more. I'm not sure what that little bit more is, but the extra ten percent stings like a bitch."

"Winnie said it a different way."

"Yeah, she never did quite get it. Look at you, man. You just left your wife, right?"

"Yeah."

"Tired of it all, thinking maybe there's something better out there, something new."

"Pretty much."

"If you find something, everything is cool, you won on your gamble. You got what you expected. But if you lose, and it don't look like you're winning, there is gonna be that sting because what you had was worth more than what you bet. You thought you were placing a fifty-dollar bet, but you're actually betting sixty. Six-five."

"Life is a game, blah, blah, blah, right? Not a new concept."

B slapped the table. "Exactly. It's the ideas that have been around forever that are usually true." He looked prideful, like he'd just unraveled the human genome, then he looked at his hand and tried to wipe the stickiness off on his jeans. "When I was in federal holding, we used to use a treadmill to bench. We used to make saimin with pork rinds. One guy was about to lose his girl, so he made her a jewelry box out of Doritos wrappers. Fuckin' sad. I'm not going back to that."

"Not gambling anymore then?"

B smiled. "All this talk is getting me going. This is probably a bad idea, but what the fuck. I know a crap game around here. Wanna check it out? We can call this our last night out or something."

We finished our beers and headed out. I'd forgotten where I'd parked the truck. It was weird, but I didn't feel like I was walking; it felt more like I was stepping over stuff. The bow on the back of B's gown was unraveling.

He was moving faster now. He put his cane over his shoulder, and I followed. Every time a car passed, he turned to look at it. He turned fast when a loud motorcycle passed, but didn't stop walking. He bumped into a homeless man, knocking him down. The homeless man pulled himself up, swearing, then looked at B and said, "I don't got no money." He jogged away from us, and his bare feet went over a broken bottle without breaking stride. "What was that all about?" I asked.

"Chronic-paranoid fucker," he said.

"You ever do ice?"

B rubbed his head. "No."

A couple of cop cars passed us. They were the only cops I'd seen all night. When we got to the truck, a woman was leaning against the passenger window, her hands on the sides of her face, trying to look through the tint. She looked like a fortuneteller gazing into a crystal ball. B tapped her on the shoulder with his cane. She ran off, stopped about a block away, flipped us off, and then ran again. It made me think of Winnie and her Magic Eight Ball.

The crap game was only a quarter mile outside Chinatown. It was in one of the warehouses about a block away from B's place. We drove by the gate and parked out front by the door. Two guys stopped us. They were mini versions of the Rapozo twins: short, compact, with solid-looking bellies hanging over their belts. It took both of them a couple of seconds to recognize B. "Holy shit," one of them said, "what da fuck happened to you, braddah?"

"I slipped in the shower," B said. "This is Charlie."

I shook their hands. B was using his cane again. "You aren't a gambling addict, yeah?" I asked.

"Nah, I do security for these guys sometimes. You're slurring again, by the way."

"I thought you stirred curry?"

"It's all stirring curry: mixing up your beef, carrots, potatoes, onions, your stew on a low simmer. You don't keep an eye on all of it, keep mixing your shit, it all sticks to the bottom of the pot."

It hadn't even dawned on me that stirring curry was a euphemism for something else, or a bunch of something elses. "So what'd you get fired from?"

"A thing I had going with the twins. Who do you think I went down for in federal holding?"

"Ah."

The warehouse was your basic warehouse: wood pallets, forklifts, storage racks, and some big machines. I didn't know what most of them were for. The cement was neatly swept, and there were about fifteen guys standing around a crap table. There was another table close by. This one had aluminum platters of food and a clock radio on it. Hawaiian music. The guys were chatting away. They all seemed to know each other.

B limped in and introduced me. It was quite a mix: the oldest guy looked like he might have kids my age; the youngest guys were younger than me. Japanese, Filipino, Chinese, Korean, Hawaiian—it was like I was at a crap game in the old plantation days, except that these guys had money. A couple of them had big wads of hundred-dollar bills in their hands. It was surprising how friendly the game was. Everyone kidded with each other.

B grabbed a couple of beers out of the cooler. I cracked mine open and took a long swig. The pulsing was in full force now. I scratched at the splotches on my cheeks, hoping the fluorescent lights wouldn't draw eyes. B jumped in on the action. I was no stranger to craps, but I wanted to wait, have a couple of beers first. They were all asking what had happened to B. He told the same fell-in-the-shower joke, then one of them said he'd heard Preschool and the twins had done it to him. B shrugged and said, "It took all three."

The game got quiet after that. The sound of Kealii Reichel crooning some song that I didn't understand the Hawaiian words to made me anxious. I finished my beer fast, then went to the cooler to grab another. When I got back to the table, I asked, "Anyone know what he's singing about?"

"Who? Oh, the radio."

Most of them shrugged, concentrating on the game. A Hawaiian guy, tall and thin, and good-looking, like those guys you'd see in Kramer's clothing commercials years before, said as he was rolling, "He's singing about a flower. It's growing at the base of a cliff. Woot, seven, baby."

Another flower song, I thought. But after seeing downtown at night, I figured there wasn't much wrong with a song about flowers. "The whole thing is about flowers?" I asked.

"Just one flower, yeah, but the whole song. Woot, seven again." The guy was on a roll. I pulled the remaining five thousand dollars out of my pocket. It wasn't the biggest wad in the room.

B bled out his money pretty fast, betting on long odds, silly stuff like boxcars, a square pair, and any number the hard way. He was playing like a first-timer fascinated with all the different crap you could bet on when playing on a real table. By the time the dice got to me, I was up a little. B shrugged and told me he was going to step out for some air. He left his beer on the table and snailed out.

It was a monster roll. I forgot all about my bumps and splotches while I held the dice for at least twenty minutes. It made sense to me, too. The entire week had been fucked up, so there was a certain balance in me being on a roll. By the time I'd hit about minute ten, I would have been shocked if I'd crapped out. I could hit all my numbers—the easy way, the hard way, it didn't matter. The guys were grumbling and ribbing me, but they kept betting more and more against me, waiting for my luck to crumble. Two of them finally stepped away to grab beers. I wasn't sure what my wad was up to, but it became the biggest in the room. All of the excitement made me forget about B, so when he came walking in and everyone took a step back from the table, I turned around to ask him where he'd gone. I couldn't see him very well, so I shut one eye. His cane looked different. It took me a couple of seconds to realize it wasn't a cane anymore; it was a shotgun.

All of the guys around the table seemed calm about what was going on. They all just stepped back and shook their heads. A couple said, "Fuck it, I was losing my ass anyway."

B threw a backpack on the table. Without being asked, everyone began stuffing it with what was left of their wads. I held mine and just stared at him. "You too, Charlie," he said. "By the way, open your other eye. You look like a fuckin' dumb ass."

I opened my other eye, but didn't move toward the bag. The stock of the shotgun hit me on the side of the head. "Ow," I said, feeling ridiculous after the sound came out of my mouth. I put the wad in the bag. The Hawaiian who'd told me about the Kealii Reichel song shook his head. "My cousin is going to fuckin' kill you, braddah."

"Tell Preschool this is for my hospital bill." B laughed. "Tell those mutha-fuckas they need to start giving medical benefits. Tell him the next time he sees me, he better fuckin' kill me, because I see him, he's fuckin' dead. Keys, too, Charlie. I ain't even fucking playing."

I put my car keys in the bag. "Cell phones too, guys." Everyone threw his phone in. I suddenly felt perfectly clear headed and sober. One of the guys joked, "Preschool got some State Farm shit on this game?"

They all laughed. B was making it easy for them to be relaxed. There was no muzzle pointing. After the last cell phone was in the bag, he told me to hand the bag to him. Iz's "Hawaiian Suppa Man" came on. "I like this song," I said. I was on a roll when it came to saying dumb things.

B walked out with the backpack. After he was out of sight, everyone looked at each other, not quite sure what to do. "Should we stick around?" one guy asked.

Preschool's cousin, the tall, model-looking Hawaiian, said, "Nah, you guys can go. Charlie, right? Charlie, you should stick around."

My throat was dry. I walked to the cooler and grabbed a beer. "Too bad can't call the cops," one of the guys said. Most of them laughed and then grabbed a beer for the road before walking out. None of them looked at me. Preschool's cousin went to the office and got on the phone. If there was ever a time to bolt, it would have been then, but at a carless, flabby two fifty, I figured running was a bad idea. I sat down and tried to estimate how much I'd been up. I'd had maybe twenty grand in my hand when B came walking in with that shotgun. He'd played me good. Threw me in the pot and stirred me just right. I'd been doing things he wanted me to do without him even suggesting it, like losing my cool with my friends and bringing the money with me. For the second night in a row, I'd been boloed, and there was some crazy-looking guy named Preschool, which shouldn't have sounded tough but did, probably driving toward me right now. It seemed sort of ironic that "Hawaiian Suppa Man" was playing while I was thinking about all of this. A Hawaiian god who squeezed Alae's throat for the secret of fire I was not—whoever Alae was. When Preschool's cousin came out of the office, I asked, "Who's alae?"

"Not who—what. It's a bird," he said. "Like a duck."

I wondered if an alae was what I'd nudged at Black Point the other night. Damn bird didn't make one sound. "Hawai'i got ducks?"

"Yeah, more than one kind. Hawai'i got a hawk, a crow, a bat, and a seal, too."

I thought about the bat I thought I'd seen earlier in the week. "I never seen any of those."

"Me either," he said.

I was getting something from listening to Iz, though. It dawned on me that what made music good to me was if the artist was singing to God. Maybe that was why I liked Motown: the gospel roots and all. Singing to God was what Iz was doing, and the fact that God didn't exist didn't stop him.

Preschool's cousin pulled a glass pipe out of one pocket of his leather jacket and a small plastic bag out of his other pocket. The bag was one of those little ones that people put jewelry in. After loading the pipe, he heated the bottom with a pink Bic lighter. "Stole it from my chick," he said, embarrassed. I wasn't sure if he meant the ice or the lighter. "Wanna hit?" he asked.

"Yeah, what the hell," I said. We leaned against the crap table, and after he took a hit, he passed me the pipe. I had a hit but couldn't find the apple Jolly Rancher taste. It did wonders for my hangover and drunkenness, though. My head started to clear up, and I had to blink a couple of times to make sure the double images were gone. I felt like I'd been handed a pair of glasses. "Preschool gets pissed at me when I smoke," the cousin said. "Don't say nothing."

We took a few more hits each. He put his stuff away, then grabbed a can of passion-orange juice from the cooler. "Want one?" he asked.

"Sure."

He handed me a can, and I drank it while thinking that every car I heard pass was Preschool's. It reminded me of B looking at every car that had passed us downtown. "Shit, he's on ice," I said.

"B? Would be easy enough. He deals out of that crap building he lives in. Pretty much owns it. You see him wearing that hospital gown? Crazy bastard."

"Motherfucker."

"You didn't know?"

"I don't know shit."

He smiled. "Somehow, I believe you."

Finding out these things all of a sudden, I felt like hopping up and down. Since I couldn't, I rocked on my feet, rolling back and forth from my toes to my heels.

A car pulled up out front. Preschool was wearing the same things he'd had on at Mom's bar: white wifebeater top, shiny sweatpants, and pair of black Nike high tops. His hair wasn't slicked back, though. It was a puffball. He looked like one of those cannibals on Gilligan's Island except he had a mustache and goatee. I saw something else: one of his ears was cauliflowered—fluffed up and bumpy. It was what I'd imagine an ear with cancer would look like, if there were such a thing. "Keoni, go outside and untie your fuckin' cousins," Preschool said.

"I was gonna leave them there—you know, teach them a lesson. I'll let them go now."

As Keoni passed him, Preschool grabbed his arm. His bicep got hard, and a squiggly vein rose from it. He pulled Keoni's face up to his. "You been smoking, dawg?"

"No way, man," Keoni said, acting like he was mad that Preschool asked.

"Go get your fuckin' cousins."

Keoni strutted outside, his walk cocky to make it look like Preschool had asked him instead of ordered. It was a casual, runway walk. I wondered if he was pouting his lips. "Charlie, right?" Preschool said.

I nodded. I was revving up now. I looked for a gun on him, but it didn't look like he had one. I wanted to hit him to see what would happen. Fantasies of kicking his ass began popping inside my head. The images were popping so fast, I felt like my head was a bag of microwaving popcorn at minute three.

"I heard you were up," he said.

"Twenty grand at least."

"Damn, too bad," he said. "Well, let's get outta here."

"Where we going?"

"Heard you got your car jacked, too. I'll take you home."

The sky was a flat early-morning blue. There weren't any beams of sunlight, but I saw the clouds clearly. They were on the move, and the wind sprayed my skin, making it tingle. Preschool stepped into his Lexus SUV. It looked like the same model that Mark had and was even the same pearl color. Keoni was cutting gray electrical tape off the two guards. Preschool rolled down his window. "Close up," he said. He turned to me. "Where you live?"

"High rise across the street from Punahou."

"Good, I thought you were gonna say Waialua or something."

I looked in the backseat: no gun, no knife. "Nice car," I said.

He shook his head. "Toyota makes some solid cars. I had another one just like it, but it got burnt up. Heard about that?"

"Yeah," I said.

"So was my cousin bullshitting me back there? He hit the pipe?"

I thought about how I should answer this. "Yeah," I said. Making like a rat was probably a good thing at this point.

I wanted to smoke a cigarette, but with the gym get-up, muscles, and all, Preschool looked like the anti-smoking type.

"Fuckin' chronics," he said. "Up to my fuckin' elbows in chronics. Sometimes I think I should move to the Big Island and start a taro farm or something, you know? Get in touch with da aina, you know what I mean?"

I did know. It sounded pretty good to me, all except for waking up at dawn and farming. "Yeah," I said.

"You seem like a good guy," he said. "Real calm and shit. Sorry about the other night, man. Business and shit. We took it easy on you, dawg."

He'd been the first one to hit me. "I understand," I said. "I went to visit my aunty the next day. She told me the twins are my cousins."

"No shit? What's your last name. We probably cousins, too. They my cousins."

"Keaweaimoku."

"Sounds familiar. Waimanalo side?"

"Yeah. My dad was a fisherman. His name was Blackie."

"Crazy guy—had white hair when he was like thirty?"

"Yeah."

He smiled. "Fuckin' small island. Shit, I remember him small-kid time. He used to come over to my dad's house, try to rally the Hawaiians to take back the beaches or some shit like that. Whatever happened to him?"

"He drank himself to death."

"Damn," he said. "Fuckin' chronics, I tell you. That's the one thing that pushes the shit out of my buttons. Winnie, she pushed them good. After all I did to help her, she pulls that shit. Might have been the most irritating thing I ever saw."

I agreed with him on the chronic thing, even though I was probably tweaking. "I would've been pissed."

"What's the most irritating thing you ever saw?"

I had to think that one over for a second. "You know when Saturday Night Live guys make movies? You ever see the ones that came out like ten years ago?"

"Eddie Murphy shit?"

"No, like Adam Sandler, Chris Farley. They made those movies where they were spoiled rich kids, dumb as hell, and some guy with a Harvard degree was trying to steal their inheritance or something. So they went to get their GED or sold car shit to prove they could run Daddy's company."

"Yeah, what about those?"

"Those movies pissed me off. I was always cheering for the guy who busted his hump to get the MBA from Harvard, worked his way up in the company, and then wanted to take over. Fuck the spoiled kids. I'd take capitalism over nepotism any day. Those are hours wasted I'll never get back."

"You being a wise-ass?"

"No, no. It's sorta like that, though, you know? The most irritating things are things that take time from you, or something like that, you know?"

"You high?"

"Yeah, I think so. I ain't a chronic, though."

"You watch the news?"

"Not too much."

"You see this Iraq shit? Man, calling for war, no evidence of weapons of mass destruction, shit like that. It's fucked up, dawg."

I wanted to laugh, but remembered what happened the last time I did. "You anti-war?"

"Nah, but I'm a criminal. That no-evidence shit ain't right." He looked at me. "Stop fidgeting, man."

My hands were fluttering on my lap. I stopped them. "All this talking to me—this some sort of benediction?" I liked that word benediction. I heard it in the movie LA Confidential.

"Don't be stupid. I wanna tell you something serious, though. First, imagine your burial."

It was easy to do, considering circumstances. I closed my eyes. I saw a hole in the ground; Mom, Sheila, Mark, Mario, Taks, and Ollie were standing over it. Then they each tossed a single red rose in the hole. It was about all my imagination could muster. "Got it."

"Now picture those people at your funeral ten years after."

Mom was dead, Mario was in the hospital with some terminal illness, Mark was in the apartment with a Moses beard playing a computer game in his boxers, Taks was in Ginger's picking up girls, Ollie was being taxied by boat in Venice, wearing that blue blazer with the crest on the pocket, and Sheila was holding a little girl's hand and telling her to look both ways before crossing the street.

"Life goes on, huh?" Preschool said.

"Yeah."

"Was anyone missing from the burial, anyone important?"

A lot of people were missing: old friends I hadn't seen in years, relatives I'd never met, and ex-girlfriends. B wasn't there, of course. I'd only known him for a few days. Winnie was missing. "Yeah, some are missing, I guess."

"There are two types of people. Those who care about you, but life goes on, and those who don't really give a shit, and your dying won't even amount to a piss in their bowls of Cheerios. I take care of myself first. Know what I'm saying, dawg?"

Sheila was at my funeral. It made me feel like an ass. "Yeah." Great, I was having another unsolicited Dr. Phil moment. I was beginning to wonder if, when people looked at me, they saw someone lost or someone who had lost something; or maybe they just thought they were smarter than I was. Either way, I was sort of grateful for Preschool's advice because maybe it meant he'd let me utilize it.

When we got to my building, he told me to point out my parking spot and then parked there. Fluorescent tubes squiggled on the ceiling, glowing white. This world had an obsession with fluorescent lighting, trying to make everything look like heaven. "I need to call the cops and tell them my car is missing."

"Tell them tomorrow."

"What should I say?"

"Tell them it got stolen from here."

"They won't hassle the security guard?"

"I didn't see any cameras. Security guards need to watch the lobby and shit, too. It'll fly. Got insurance, full coverage?"

"Yeah."

"There you go then: new car." He put his hand on my shoulder. "I need to go up with you."

"OK."

While we were in the elevator, I was thinking about work at ABC. A few weeks ago, the staff had been given a book to read, something called Retail Selling Made Easy, and we got tested on it. The book had a bunch of quotes from Emerson, Thoreau, and Webster, but got real stupid once the author started talking. I aced the test only because most of the stuff in it was memorably stupid, like the saying "When you reach for the stars, make sure you don't get mud on your hands." That made no sense to me. There was no fucking mud between the sky and your hands. The writer had probably fucked up someone else's quote. The book also said, "A person without a goal is like a person without a rudder." That one sounded familiar too, and the author probably changed a couple of words, trying to pass it off as his. Thinking about this book while going up the elevator, I felt so happy I wasn't working at ABC anymore. When the elevator stopped and the doors opened, I was so absorbed that I just stood there. The door bounced back and forth against Preschool's arm.

I let him in. "Damn, she clean you out? Fuckin' chronics, I tell you. It's always the hands that feed them that they bite off first."

"Nah, I just moved here. Getting a divorce."

"That sucks."

"Yeah."

"I'm gonna take a leak."

"OK."

I opened the window and looked out. The wind was blowing nicely. The leaves on the trees were banging against each other, sounding like applause. I thought about the Vanilla Ice–Shug Knight story: how Shug Knight had hung Vanilla Ice over a balcony to get him to sign the rights of "Ice, Ice Baby" over to him. I wondered if the paparazzi chased Shug Knight around. I stepped away from the window as the toilet flushed. The water faucet went on, and the pipes rumbled; my fridge vibrated and hummed. Preschool came out and shook my hand. "Take my number, dawg," he said.

I reached for my cell phone, forgetting I'd put it in B's backpack. I had to scrounge around in my boxes for a pen and piece of paper. I found a pen, but when I tried to scratch the tip on the cardboard box, ink didn't come out. "What's with your TV?" he asked.

I was sitting on the floor, shaking the pen. "No cable."

I looked back in the box and found a calculator, a cheap solar one. I wasn't sure if there was enough light to get it going, but I said, "I'll take it down with this until I can get my pen working."

He gave me his number. The last four digits were all eights; three numbers were easy enough to remember. He shook my hand again. "Call me if you see Winnie or B or both of them, and I'll insure you. You won that money fair and square."

"Cool," I said.

"They're going down sooner or later. Take care of yourself first."

"Why do they call you Preschool?"

"I used to teach preschool. Played football at UH, got a degree and everything."

"What happened?"

"I got wise. Don't regret it, though. Watching a bunch of fuckin' kids all day every day made me one mean motherfucker. Call me if you hear anything."

I nodded. Preschool left. By the time I managed to fall asleep, the sun was beaming through the windows. My heart had been twitching so fast that I thought I'd get a cramp. It wasn't Preschool that made my heart beat like that. It was the ice.

2

I had the mother of all hangovers when I finally woke up: every hangover symptom in the book, squared. My throat was dry, my stomach was queasy, and my head was pounding so hard that I held it with both hands just in case my skull split open. When I coughed, the pounding hurt even more, and I didn't even have the energy to wipe off the globs of mucus that landed on my chin. I coughed again, and my eyes teared. The back of my neck was bathed in sweat, so I forced myself up to take a shower. I felt so bad that I figured there was a fifty-fifty chance I'd drown.

The shower helped. I drank some of the water shooting down, but the water hitting my skin helped more. It was like I was a drooping flower being watered. I played with the idea of writing a song about me being watered like a flower after a drinking marathon and a few hits off the pipe. I thought up a couple of lines of a first verse, but a song about a single flower growing on the side of a lush green cliff it was not. I felt my head. Hair was growing out and the swelling was going down.

After I got dressed and decided to get on with the day, I remembered that I was without phone or car. I sat down, confused. It was a weird feeling not having a car or phone. Then I realized I no longer had a job either. Where was I planning to go, and who was I planning to talk to? I figured I would go and look for a pay phone so that I could report my truck stolen. I had no clue how much a call on a pay phone cost these days. I circled the room once before plopping back down on the sleeping bag—sort of like dogs do before they lie down to sleep. I didn't know what else to do, so I went back to sleep, thinking I had nothing now, but it wasn't so bad.

Someone was knocking on the door. There wasn't much light coming in through the window. It must have been around seven p.m. It made me nervous that someone was knocking on the door, but after the last few days, I felt like nothing could shock me. It could have been Ed McMahon telling me I'd won millions, and I wouldn't have been surprised.

I opened the door. It was Preschool, still in his tank top and sweats. The stretch marks between his chest and shoulders sprawled out on his skin like spider webs. There was too much flesh under that skin of his, especially his ear. It looked like the blood in his ear had boiled and then froze. I wondered why only one of his ears was like that. He looked a lot like his cousin, just swelled up like a corpse, but rock-hard. "I got gifts," he said. He pulled out my keys and cell phone from his pocket. He handed me the keys. "Motherfucker, and your truck didn't get torched."

I took the keys. "Wow, where was it?"

"One of my boys found it parked on the side of the street in Kalihi. The keys were still in the ignition. B probably thought you'd call the cops first, so he dumped it fast, I guess. I'm wondering who picked him up." He handed me the cell phone. "You look like shit. Throw on some workout clothes. We going to the gym."

I had to think if I had clothes like that. I poked around my laundry basket and pulled out a plain white undershirt. I had a bunch of those for work. I found a pair of shorts that I hadn't worn for so long that I was sure zipping them up would cut me in half. I went to the bathroom and changed. The waist on the shorts wasn't too bad, but the legs were cutting off circulation in my thighs. It was like I was wearing khaki spandex.

Preschool wanted me to drive my truck, so he parked his car in my spot, and we headed to the gym. "So if those fuckers would try to get in touch with you, how would they do it?" he asked.

"Hmm, I don't have a house phone, so it'd actually be kind of tough. I suppose they'd call one of my friends, but I don't think they have any of the numbers."

"Turn left here, dawg. You realize you got the big fuck-over from them, right? Like you said, you were up twenty grand, and B fucked you over."

"Yeah, that's why I doubt they'll call. For all I know, both of them flew to the mainland by now."

"Nah, they still around."

"How do you know?"

"Turn left at the next light. It's rare that someone skips when they run from here. Makes it easy for me, but you gotta be a dumb motherfucker to steal from me in the first place. They ain't smart enough to get off the island. You want your money back, right?"

"I could use it."

"Like I said, insurance. B isn't going anywhere, by the way. You know what's funny about your friend?"

"He wasn't really my friend. I only knew him for a few days."

"You saw that piece of shit he lived in? That fucker was pulling in at least five grand a week stirring curry in there."

"No shit?"

"I shit you not. The place was empty when I had it checked out today. He planned this. Living like a fucking monk in that roach trap fucking cracks me up. I got a little payback, though."

"Mind if I smoke?" I asked. I was in my own car.

"Yeah, slide me one."

"You smoke?"

"I sneak one here and there. Wife would kill me." He laughed. "I can't even smoke in my own car, dawg."

It cracked me up watching him light the cigarette. He looked like a defensive lineman lighting up at the bench. "So what'd you do for payback?"

"I took his car to the beach and had a little bonfire. Roasted marshmallows and shit."

"Motherfucker, he had a car?"

"Yeah, he had two: cherry '69 Camara he used to work on, and a Blazer. I got the Blazer."

"Man, he made me pick him up."

"Turn into this parking lot over here," Preschool said. "Yeah, he had a lot of shit, shit he got through me. Pulled a Winnie on me. I'm too fucking nice. Keo and Ula always tell me, too. I gotta cut that shit out. Seems like I spend half my time chasing fucking chronics."

I turned off the ignition. Even drug dealers hated their customers, I guess. "I heard you pulled Winnie out of downtown a few years back."

He laughed. "That wasn't me, that was B. He brought her to me to see if I could hook her up with a job, which I did, by the way."

"I thought he just got out of jail?"

"Fuck that, he's been out for a while now."

"He was in federal, though."

I cracked my knuckles and touched my head for a second. It was a tell. B had been lying to me the whole time. "Fuckin'-a."

He laughed. "You are one gullible motherfucker. I feel for you, dawg. I feel your pain."

We were parked in front of a warehouse in Kaimuki. Fluorescent light streamed through louvers at the top of the walls. "What are we doing?" I asked.

"This is my gym. We gonna work out."

"If they wanted to get in touch with me, they'd call my mom's bar and leave a message probably. What makes you think they're together?"

"You do time with a guy, you find out what that fucker is really about. You know what B's big thing is? He's a nice guy, like knight-in-shining-armor nice. I'd put money on the fact that he's trying to help Winnie, feeling guilty about bringing her in with me and shit, then going to federal, and I'll bet even more that he's gonna try to call you because he feels guilty for fleecing you like he did. Nice guys are fucking predictable, man. I like nice guys."

He stepped out of the car, and I followed him to the warehouse. "I thought you were a nice guy."

"Nice might be the wrong word. I'm gullible—like you, dawg."

"B lies a helluva lot for a nice guy. I think he was icing out last night."

"Don't surprise me. That shit is nasty shit."

We walked into the warehouse. My brain was hurting from thinking about what the hell was really going on. Then again, it could have been the hangover.

I'd passed this building many times. I never knew what it was, never really cared. It looked like an old warehouse from the street, but evidently it was like a thug-training academy.

One of the first things I noticed was that Preschool was the only one wearing a tank top. It almost seemed like it was against the rules to wear a tank top, which must have sucked because there was no AC, just propeller fans in each corner of the gym. There was a boxing ring in the center and each of the four sides had different kinds of equipment. The free weights were against the back walls, the weight-lifting machines were to the right, and there were mats to the left. Eight guys, paired off, were rolling around with each other on the mats. That explained Preschool's cauliflower ear. By the entrance were things to hit: speed bags, heavy bags, and even one of those wooden mannequins with sticks coming out of it, like in a Bruce Lee movie. There wasn't a treadmill, stationary bike, or StairMaster in the place. I was surprised there wasn't a corner where people were dressed like ninjas or practiced espionage. Actually, with these crooks, training would have probably come more in the form of a class on how to purse-snatch or collect money from an addict, basically the opposite of what you'd see in a self-defense course for women. The whole place smelled like leather and sweat.

I followed Preschool to the back. He nodded at people as he walked through, and just about every guy he passed paused what he was doing to give Preschool a nod. Never once did anyone look him in the eyes, though. The clanging of metal grew louder. When we got to the back, I saw the twins. One had on a red T-shirt; the other, darker one, had on a yellow T-shirt. They were benching. They didn't stop for Preschool. After they finished their set, the white one wiped the bench with a towel, then they both came over. They looked him in the eyes without a problem. With five forty-five-pound plates on each end, the bar on the bench was bending. They shook our hands. "Remember Charlie?" Preschool asked.

"Cousin, ah?" Keo looked at me.

I felt embarrassed. They talked like they were trying to make friends, and I didn't even want to know them. "Apparently," I said.

"So what? You gorillas done with the bench?" Preschool asked.

The twins began to unload the bending bar. "Yeah. No act, Preschool, I catching you," Ula said.

"In your dreams, old man."

They headed toward the squat rack. Preschool lay on the bench, lifted his legs and crossed his ankles, and started turning out rapid repetitions with the bar. The bar was going up and down so fast, it was a blur of metal. He racked it. "Warm up."

I lay on the bench. When I lifted the bar, I had to pause to get it balanced. My arms were shaking under forty-five pounds. It was embarrassing, but I slowly brought the bar down to my chest and pressed it up. I did about ten reps before racking it. I stayed on the bench to give my chest time to rest. The burn faded fast, but my elbows were killing me. "So, why are the twins interested in Winnie?"

"They just backing me. Think about it. When us three came, had over five guys at the bar, and it's a small bar. Always bring backup."

I stood up. Preschool put a forty-five pound plate on each end.

"Anyone ever fight back?" I asked.

"Sometimes. Usually ain't a problem, though."

He pumped out reps just as fast as before. He racked the bar, then sat up.

"So my friends aren't complete assholes then?"

"I didn't say that. They did what most people do, though. To tell you the truth, I wanted that skinny fucker Taks to jump in. That would've been nice."

I lay down on the bench. "You know him?"

"I know who he is. Fucking Don Juan wannabe mother-fucker. I got eyes all over the place, dawg." He smiled.

"Small island," I said.

When I took the one hundred and thirty-five pounds off the rack, my arms almost gave out and I felt like I was going to drop it on my chest. Preschool walked behind me and stood over my head. I needed a spot. I squeezed out about eight reps before reracking the bar. The elbow pain wasn't as bad, but my chest felt so stiff, the muscles filled to the brim with blood, that I stood there like a zombie. It was all quite a humiliating experience.

"Man, how much you weigh?" Preschool asked. "You outta shape."

"About two fifty. Never got into lifting, though."

"Ah."

He loaded the bar with two more forty-five-pound plates on each end. He lay on the bench and began pumping the reps out. There was a difference in speed this time, but it was still fast, and he managed to pump out about forty repetitions of two twenty-five with his feet still crossed at the ankles. His shoes didn't touch the ground, and he didn't even strain on the last one. "We'll keep it light. I don't wanna be loading and unloading this friggin' bar," he said.

I lay down under the two twenty-five. I got the bar up, but had to pause for a few seconds before bringing it down. When the bar touched my chest, it felt stuck there. I let it crash on my chest then I jerked up. My ass and one of my shoulders rose off the bench. I managed to get the bar about a third of the way back up, but my body was so crooked that a forty-five-pound plate started to slide off. Preschool grabbed the bar from me and held on to it. Instead of putting it back on the rack, though, he took a couple of quick breaths and curled it up. The veins on his biceps looked like they were going to pop. He held it under his chin and smiled. "Show-off," I said.

"Don't sweat it," he said as he put the bar back. "You got heart. Almost had it up. You got the mana, the lima ikaika."

"I thought it was going to smash me," I said.

"Nah, I had it. Wanna spar or something? Maybe it's more your speed." He pointed to the mats. One guy was having his arms stretched by a leg-lock. He was rapidly tapping the mat.

"With you? Hell no."

He laughed. "Man, you gotta start working out. I'll ask the twins if I can get you membership. Ah, I ain't much into this. Wanna go grab a beer? I gotta call it an early night or the old lady will be all over my ass."

"Where?"

"Your mom's."

We said goodbye to the twins, then left the gym. I was glad to be out of there. The place made me feel too much like the kid being picked last for kickball. We drove toward Bolohead Row. Preschool started to talk. This guy liked talking. "So what happened with you and your wife?"

"Same ol', same ol'. Got married for the wrong reasons, blah, blah, blah. I was a bad husband. It's good we didn't have kids, I guess."

"No, tell me what really happened. What was the last fight?"

It was an embarrassing story, but I told him anyway. "Well, she found my porn collection."

He laughed. "Where'd you keep it?"

It was getting even more embarrassing, but I went on. "Let me first say it's damn-near impossible to find a hiding place when you're married."

"Don't have to tell me that."

"OK, so I built shelves in a stereo speaker and put them in there."

"Jesus, dawg, James Bond shit. What happened?"

"Let me just tell you what a pain in the ass it is to have to bust out a screwdriver to take something out of a wooden box and then put it back."

"I can imagine."

"It worked for awhile, but I lived in a townhouse, right? So I'd be closing windows and doors and checking behind myself. I couldn't catch it all, man. Between the windows, doors, speaker boxes, and screwdriver, it was too much to deal with. Plus that, I find out I'm living with fucking Sherlock Holmes. She suspected something was going on, but waited till she found the source. One day I left particle-board shavings on the carpet from screwing the speaker box closed, and the speaker wasn't placed exactly on the compression in the carpet, so she knew it had been moved. I came home from work, and there she was, standing over an open speaker. She treats me like I'm cheating on her, and after thinking about all the shit I went through to not get caught, it was hard to disagree."

"Man, just take a quick jerk off the Internet or something."

"Well, the thing was, and she explained it to me, not that I had porn—she didn't care so much about that—but that I had porn, and I had her, and I wanted the porn more than her. We weren't really having sex there at the end. Actually, we weren't having much sex in the middle either."

"That's some funny shit."

"She was right. I didn't want her. And I didn't want to work toward wanting her again. So we sort of agreed that it was over, standing there over the X-rated version of Free Willy. I'll tell you, it was some embarrassing shit."

"That's a good story, Hawaiian."

"Someone told me recently that there aren't any Hawaiians left in the world."

Preschool thought about that one before talking. "Damn, that's a harsh thing to say."

"Could be true, though."

"I'm Hawaiian," he said.

And it was the first time I really thought about the consequences of what Aunty Kaula told me in jail. About what it might mean in real life. Maybe it was why I didn't like the music, or most of it anyways. How could there be Hawaiian music if there weren't any Hawaiians left? Just a few days before, I'd heard a Hawaiian version of Firehouse's "Love of a Lifetime." Copying an eighties hair rock band? Wasn't that a sign that the music was dead? Kealii Richel sang about flowers, but not flowers dying, which they were; Iz sang about Maui, but in the context of DC Comics's Superman. Makaha Sons may have expressed something truly Hawaiian with "Hawai'i '78" and the Pahinuis with "Waimanalo Blues," but songs like these were rare, and today there was some young Japanese kid amping his ukulele and hawking cable Internet access. Kealii Richel sang about stuff that was disappearing, Iz was dead, and Japanese kids were trying to be Randy Rhodes on the uke. The only Hawaiian music left was played during the kahiko competition at the Merrie Monarch Festival, and that was only once a year. It was weird, but I think the things that were considered contemporary Hawaiian were the very things that were killing Hawaiians: ice, jail, the ukulele, the Republican Party, and mayonnaise on beef stew. There weren't any real Hawaiians left. I was in the truck with a guy who said he might want to start a taro farm one day, but what he really wanted was his money back, and I was a middle-class guy who didn't know what he wanted. We were only Hawaiians in a technical sense. In terms of what we wanted and how we acted, we were really Americans: money and spoiled indecision taken to excess. It don't get more American than that. I wasn't sure, that there weren't Hawaiians left on Ni'ihau, though.

Thinking about all of this—and about Sheila and the porn—brought me down. Pulling up to Mom's bar didn't help either. I remembered the promise I'd made to myself to stay the hell out of Bolohead Row, but Preschool was dragging me back. I wondered if he was really going to return my money if he found B or Winnie. Both B and Preschool were damn nice guys. It was sort of funny. I'd always imagined that, in general, criminals were assholes, especially if they had the mana, the lima ikaika, as Preschool said, but these two guys seemed to like to do what most people liked to do: laugh, talk, share their theories on life, do people favors—normal stuff. They were different, but not different the way most people thought they were. They weren't crazy guys into anarchy or anything. They fought for their friends and they fought for money, like most people did. Maybe the only difference between a regular dude and a criminal is that the criminal is willing to go all the way. There was something admirable about the fearlessness of it all, the idea that these guys could really commit to a thing to the point of putting their own necks out there, risking the rest of their lives. It was easy to see why Winnie liked them; they were like her in their willingness to commit to a thing, and I supposed it was all well and good until one of them turned on you. I wasn't an expert on violence, but it seemed that when guys like this had it out for you, they committed to their goal with extra fervor. The pride that sat on their shoulders was built up like Preschool's body, pumped, veiny, and ready to cut you in half if you messed with it. These guys were real criminals, not the dumb-fuck purse snatchers, muggers, spouse abusers, or drunk drivers that showed up in the Police Beat column of the newspaper. I'd once read a story in the paper about some guy on a 7-Eleven hold-up spree. Who in fuck's hell never heard that 7-Eleven doesn't keep much cash in its drawers? The guy made out with about forty bucks and a handful of Slim Jims. He was so dumb that he repeatedly robbed the stores. These were dumb fucks. Maybe Winnie wasn't so much like the real criminals after all.

I wanted to see how this thing played out, but I wasn't totally naive about it. I knew that whatever I did, one of them was going to turn on me if he survived, and there was a good chance that I wouldn't even see the end coming. Violence was sudden with these guys, like a bat through the night.

When Preschool and I walked into Mom's, it was surprisingly crowded. The booths were filled with little Japanese guys who shifted in their seats when they saw him. It didn't seem like he noticed it, but I could tell he puffed up a bit with each step. I remembered what he'd said about hating addicts and wondered if it was the clout that he was addicted to. I could see it was a powerful thing, because I was the guy walking beside him. I felt the tingle of it all, and it was a good feeling.

All of the booths were taken, so we went up to the bar. Mom hadn't changed the station. Na Leo, the Hawaiian version of the Supremes, was singing about love and candles. Glasses clinked behind the bar. Mom's back was to us, and when she turned around, and she shot me a dirty look. "Wow. Busy, yeah?" I said.

"Friday. Sometimes Friday busy. You know dat. Mario, come get da bar. I need to talk to Charlie."

Mario looked over from the dart board. He was doing good, about to close out the bull in five rounds, with plastic house darts no less. He turned back to the board and threw his last dart. The machine blared sirens and flashed blinking lights after he hit the bull. Mom walked around to my side and grabbed my arm, leading me outside. Preschool followed us. The fact that it was Friday finally registered with me. It had been one week since I'd come here after packing up the last of my boxes in Kaneʻohe. That night I'd come in and found Mom playing Life with Mario. Tonight, most of the drinkers were kids, and none of the same people were there, not even Momo. Then I saw the guy in the sweater hood and had to amend that assessment. He had a booth to himself. His hood hung over his head, so I couldn't see his face. He looked harmless enough. He was smaller than Ollie. When we got outside, I asked, "Hey, who is that sweater-hood guy in there?"

Mom shrugged. "Quiet boy. Come in all da time."

It was a nice night. I lit a cigarette. The wind blew the smoke away. "Mom, this is, . . . umm . . ."

"Ryan," Preschool said. It was sort of disappointing to learn that he had a normal name.

"You wuz here da last time, yeah?" Mom said. "You one of da ones looking for Winnie?"

"Yeah."

She looked at me while talking. "Why you looking for her? What she did to you?"

"She stole my car, lit it on fire, and stole twenty thousand dollars from me."

Mom sighed. "I no more twenty thousand dollars. Insurance neva cover da car?"

"It did," Preschool said.

"What if you got da money den? You leave her alone?"

"Yeah, it's business, you know? If I get the money, plus interest, it's forgotten."

"How much interest?"

Preschool began to count with his fingers. I stared at his ear, surprised by what he was saying. "Hmm . . . twenty-seven grand with interest."

"OK, you give me time den? Den you leave Winnie alone?"

She was getting into it now. "Mom, you don't got the money. What the hell are you going to do? Winnie got herself into this."

Her eyes turned flat, she closed them, and then opened them again. It was a deadpan look, like we were playing poker against each other. I was surprised that the look didn't hurt me, but I actually felt sort of relieved.

"Shut up, Charlie," she said. " If you don't know why, you don't know nothing."

Preschool smiled at me. "Yeah, shut up, dawg."

I sighed and walked to my truck, propping my elbows on the tailgate, smoking my cigarette. I was still close enough to hear them. "Don't take this on if you can't pay," Preschool said. "How you gonna pay?"

"Like Winnie would. I gonna take my son's car, torch it, get some insurance. Da check might take a while. And you want one bar? I give you da bar."

Preschool sighed. "What kind of car your son got?"

"Lexus SUV."

"And he just gonna give you the money?"

"My son will, yeah."

"I don't know shit about bars."

"You pay me, I run um for you. You no need even come."

"Draw up some papers, and I'll take a look at them. Or my lawyer will look at them. I don't know nothing about running a business."

"Easy, I run um."

"Winnie know about this?"

Mom paused to think for a second. And with that, she basically said, Yeah, Winnie knows. And that meant Mom knew where Winnie was. "Winnie knows," she said.

I turned around and stomped on my cigarette. "Mom, this is fucking stupid. Mark won't give you the money, and how the hell are you going to survive without the bar? Fuck Winnie, Mom. She's just gonna do it all over again."

"Charlie, shut da fuck up. Just shut up. You don't know shit, boy, you know dat? You don't know nothing. Besides, I can always refinance da apartment. You don't know nothing."

"Relax, dawg," Preschool said. Then he turned back to Mom. "This don't cover her friend, by the way. He owes me money, too, and no one gonna bail him out."

"Da Chinese one with all da tattoos? I no care about him, just Winnie."

"Like I said, I'll send my lawyer over to look over the bar deal. I also want to see Winnie."

Mom shook her head. "No, no Winnie."

Preschool thought about it for a while. "OK, no Winnie. If the bar checks out, we can do this deal. But she fucks with me again, she had it. I see her again around Kalihi, she had it. You better keep her nose clean."

"I will."

I threw my hands up in the air. "You can't keep her clean, Mom. There's no fucking way."

Preschool turned to me. He whispered. "Get in da fucking truck and shut da fuck up. I fucking had it listening to you. Get in da fucking truck now."

I got in my truck and lit another cigarette. Cars passed by. I turned on my headlights and played a game in my head, one that I used to play with Winnie when we were little kids. I counted every fifth car and claimed it as mine. I managed to get a Jaguar and a BMW before Preschool got in the truck. I would've beaten Winnie, I was sure, having tagged the nicest cars. "Drop me off at my car," Preschool said.

The ride back to my apartment was quiet. I continued to play the game as we drove. I counted every fifth car that passed. When we got to a traffic light and the King Street cars went by, it was hard to keep up, especially in the dark. I found myself guessing at makes and models based on their headlights. After we passed through the intersection, I said, "That was uncool, man."

"Your Mom was right. You don't know shit."

"I know you lied to her. You can't let that shit go. People will start looking at you different."

"The difference between you and me is I can do whatever the fuck I want. I do shit. You just stand by and watch shit happen."

"I don't steal bars from old ladies."

He smiled. "You getting brave. I got nothing against bravery, but it's just talking shit unless you can back it."

"You aren't Hawaiian, man." I had no idea why I said it, but it was the only thing that popped into my head. It was like I wanted to insult him, but I wanted to be careful about it.

"I'm Hawaiian, and I know it. You're Hawaiian, too, dumb ass. You either got the blood or you don't."

"You like Hawaiian music?"

"That's a stupid fucking question. Don't matter."

"I guess. So you gonna kick my ass when we get to your car?"

"No, but you're cutting it close, dawg."

I lit a cigarette. "Want one?"

"Nah, going home to the wife."

"You got kids?"

"Yeah, three."

I pulled behind his car and stopped. "Damn. They take hula or anything like that?"

"Yeah, both my daughters do. I don't know why I'm letting you in on this, but what the fuck." He dialed his cell phone. "Jimmy, wassup, man," he said. He turned to me and asked, "What's your Mom's last name?"

I told him. He repeated the name on the phone. "Can you get me numbers on who called this lady and who she called the last couple of days?"

I sighed. He hung up the phone. "I won't get the numbers till tomorrow. Now's your chance, Hawaiian. You can act or do nothing. I'm betting on nothing."

He stepped out of my truck. I wanted a beer something fierce, so I stayed in the truck and drove to the liquor store down the street. I was in the mood for something different, though, and I remembered that Sloane drank martinis. I decided to give it a shot. I bought a bottle of gin, vermouth, and a jar of olives, for class. I also bought a liter bottle of Diet Coke just in case. There was a rack of porn mags by the counter, each in clear plastic wrapping. I needed to start budgeting my cash. I hoped this drinking-at-home thing would take.

I didn't have any martini glasses—or glasses of any type, for that matter—so I made a martini in an empty Big Gulp cup. I took a sip and decided martinis weren't for me, so I mixed the gin with Diet Coke. I even put an olive in, which I ate and found out wasn't for me either. The gin was OK, though. I turned on the TV and watched a Friends rerun. I remembered hearing that one of the cast members criticized reality TV in an interview. The fact that he didn't like it made perfect sense to me after I'd watched the first five minutes of the rerun. I added two more wire hangers to the TV.

I wasn't really watching. The sound just made me feel more at home. I started to think about Mom, what she'd put on the line to bail out Winnie, and figured it was about the dumbest bet I'd ever seen. Betting on Winnie wasn't even a six-five bet; it was more like betting on boxcars or Little Joe in craps, which was like one in thirty-six. I wondered if Preschool was going to let Winnie slide. I doubted it. She'd hit his pride, and that was probably unforgivable. I was pretty sure B would end up dead within the week. It was weird how no one ever left Hawai'i when shit hit the fan. Nobody ran away to the mainland. That was why I gave Ollie so much credit; he'd done exactly what he'd planned to do and gotten out of Hawai'i. I didn't know why I didn't leave. It didn't make much sense for a guy who wasn't into the ocean to stick around on this rock.

Drinking by myself was getting me drunk fast. I drank about half the bottle of gin, then turned off the TV and headed downstairs. I drove back to Mom's bar. So much for staying away from Bolohead Row.

When I got to Mom's bar, it was still crowded. It was a young crowd, and the karaoke was going full force. Some Japanese guy wearing baggy jeans and a skate shirt singing was "Iakona." At least it wasn't "Quando Quando Quando." He had a good falsetto. Mario was behind the bar. The hooded-sweater guy was sitting there, talking with him. I guess he'd been asked to move from his booth so that a group of people could sit down. I walked over and listened to them talk. He sounded like he was from the mainland. Mario opened a beer and handed it to me. "Where's Mom?" I said.

"In da beer closet. Man, dat sista of yours." Mario shook his head.

"Yeah, I dunno why Mom's all pissed at me."

"She just stressing, know what I mean? I going see what I can do."

"Yeah."

The guy in the hood glanced up. He looked Mexican or something. He had bad acne and a small mustache. Two tear-drop tattoos dripped from one eye. He was drinking a Budweiser. Still half full, the bottle was no longer sweating. I guessed he wasn't much of a drinker. "Momo working tonight?" I said.

"Nah, she get da early shift now. Today her day off anyway."

Holding my beer, I waited for the dart traffic. One of the guys yelled at his friend for not pushing the button that reset the board after he was done throwing. I walked through and headed to the beer closet.

Mom was sitting on a box of Coronas, drinking a glass of Crown and smoking a cigarette. Boxes of other beers were stacked up around her. The room was lit by a single light bulb, but it was a lot brighter than out in the bar. I moved some boxes and sat across from her. "Tell me where Winnie is," I said.

"What about da guy you came with?"

"He's gonna find her. Guys like that have connections all over. He contacted a friend who is going to trace the numbers you called. That deal was bullshit, Mom. Is B with Winnie?"

"I dunno. Even if you talked to her, what you going do?"

"I dunno. Something, I guess. I'm drunk."

"Me too."

"So where she at?"

Mom sighed. "Not supposed to be like dis, you know?"

"What do you mean?"

"I dunno, but not supposed to be like dis."

"Yeah."

"Winnie and B both stay at home," she said.

"You're kidding."

"Only since last night. My neck kinda sore. I slept on da couch."

"They gonna leave?"

"Was my fault or what? I thinking was my fault Winnie turn out like dat."

"Nah, you was a good mom."

"Good ol' Charlie," she said.

I left the bar, grabbing a beer for the road from Mario, and headed over to the apartment. As I passed the bars and restaurants on Keeaumoku, I wondered if a drama like this was going on in someone else's life. Maybe there was a stripper in one of those bars hooked on ice and blowing off her boss to make a bit more on the side to pay her debt. Maybe there was a bar owner hooked on ice, hair frazzled, eyes dull, handlebar collar bone, watching her bar sink underground. Maybe there was a hooker, or a bunch of hookers, paying off their debts by blowing off anyone who walked through the door: debts ranging from money owed for immigration to money owed for drugs. Someone was blowing someone, I figured, having cock in mouth was about the most degrading picture my mind could conjure.

There was so much money in Bolohead Row. It was strange to think that most people owed. Who'd they owe? I remembered seeing a picture of Bolohead Row, circa 1880 or something like that. The roads were dirt, and instead of bars and restaurants, there were trees—banana trees, I think. An old Hawaiian man had his back to the camera and was walking away. He wore a long-sleeved white shirt, light-colored pants, and boots. With a stick over his shoulder and a hobo sack tied to the end of it, he was walking toward the mountains.

3

Even though they'd only been there for a day, the apartment looked like a hideout. A blanket and pillow were on the sofa, and empty soda cans and pizza boxes covered the table. On the floor by the kitchen were a couple of big duffle bags with a few T-shirts and denim legs peeking out. The TV was on, but no one was in the living room, and the fan oscillated, blowing air over the sofa so that the end of the pillow case flapped every few seconds. I walked by Mark's room. He was on his computers as usual. The boxers were orange this time. I knocked on Mom's door. Winnie opened it.

She sat back down on Mom's bed, wearing a T-shirt, probably Mark's or B's, and surf shorts that were too big for her.

Her clothes were all black, contrasting with the whiteness of her skin. Her hair was rubber-banded on top of her head, stretching her widow's peak. The TV was on in this room, too, and she ignored me, watching it and sitting crossed-legged with a big crystal ashtray filled with ashes and cigarette butts in front of her. A glass pipe was on the hill of ash. "Where's B?" I asked.

She stretched her arms without looking at me. The sleeves of the big T-shirt rose, making her look like she had wings. "In the shower."

"So what, you guys moving in here or something?"

"No, no, just until B straightens out things."

"After that shit he pulled, good luck."

"No worry, beef curry."

B came walking out with a frayed towel around his waist and packing one of those bodies guys dream of having: a body that looks like the one in the poster of the human anatomy. The only fat on him was the bulge on one eye. The swelling had gone down, and the white of the eye peeked out beneath the puffy lid. There were more bruises on his neck and chest—more hickies. He walked past me, probably heading for the duffle bags by the kitchen. Almost losing the towel, he dragged one foot behind him.

"What's with this cold-shoulder shit?" I said.

"Mom told us you came to the bar with Preschool."

"Hold on a second. Let me get this straight. First off, I get my ass beat because you owe some guy money. Then B robs me of truck, cell phone, and cash and hits me with a shotgun. Both of you lie to me all this time. And I get the cold shoulder? What Goddamn Bizarro world do you live in?"

"OK, allow me a rebuttal," Winnie said. "You got your ass beat because you laughed, or else they probably would have left you alone. You got money stolen from you that was never yours in the first place. You got your truck and cell phone back. B said he tapped you with the shotgun to make sure that it looked like you guys weren't in it together, and basically—not that I expected you to do anything else—but the only thing you contributed was bringing Preschool to Mom, making her think fast and dumb, and now she wants to sign over her bar. Why exactly am I supposed to be happy to see you?"

"What about all the bullshit you and him fed me?"

"No one wanted you involved in this. It's easy to not get involved if you don't know nothing. When Preschool talked to you, didn't you look like a jerk who knew nothing? That's how you were supposed to look. Charlie, I know you so well. Doing nothing is what you're best at."

I sat on the bed and lit a cigarette. I could hear B and Mark talking. "Any beer in the fridge?" I asked.

"I don't think so."

"What you watching?"

"Just zoning out pretty much . . . thinking."

"Why is this guy helping you so much?"

"He was trying to help me a little bit when I split. But after he caught that beating, he snapped in the head or something. It shook something in him, I dunno. So now both of us are in the same boat, and we can help each other because we trust each other. We're both in the same boat."

"That was pride that shook him, I guess. So dumb."

"Weren't you just telling me how pride was oh-such-a-wonderful thing? What'd you say? 'You're thirty-four. Where's your pride?'"

"I went to your old house in Kailua: the prison. Kaula told me all that stuff about what happened before you went to jail. All that plate throwing and car burning. Was that pride?"

"Probably. I don't know. Maybe suicide."

"You still smoking?"

She smiled. "Why, you buying?"

"No, just asking."

She leaned down off the bed and pulled out a small duffle bag from under it. She opened the bag and took out something wrapped in plastic. It was about a pound or two of ice. It struck me as funny how ice looked so normal, like something you might come across in a supermarket. Most drugs were like that: coke and heroin looked like powder; weed looked like oregano clumped together; and ice looked like, well, ice, or maybe more like rock salt or rock candy, depending on the color. It didn't look dangerous at all. "Jesus, what are you going to do with that? Bludgeon Preschool?"

"No, sell it, dodo. Break it up and sell it. B's got it all planned out. We both got connections from being in jail and all. It's trippy. When they shipped him to the mainland, it opened up choke connections. He got this from the mainland, from some guys he met in jail there. Jail is so funny. You went to school in business, right? Being in jail is like—what's it called— networking. It's almost like you can't be a successful criminal without going to jail at least once to learn new things and meet new people. That sort of sounds like a poster slogan for the army or something, huh?"

"So B's big plan is to become the Tony Montana of Hawai'i?"

"Sounds like it."

"And he's bringing you in on it? Even with—since you're into using business terms—your employment history and resume?"

"Yeah, he was honest about it, too. He said that once I become a liability, he's just going to keep my connections and dump me. And after this one, he'll never let me handle too much."

It was one of the dumbest plans I'd ever heard: the pipe dreams of two two-bit ex-cons. I supposed a lot of the dumb fucks out there had the same type of dream, thinking that, from some kind of imaginary life in an MTV rap video, they could step into real life. It was like they could look in a mirror, but not see what was there. Winnie and B couldn't see that they were in some small apartment in Makiki hiding out from a big bad Hawaiian at a parent's house. They couldn't see that this was probably the golden age of their hair-brained scheme—the only place where any hair-brained scheme could have a golden age being in the imagination. "Sounds like you guys have it all figured out."

"Yeah, we do."

B and Mark came walking in. Winnie put the ice back in the bag and slid it under the bed. "Mark, Mom said something about burning your car to get some insurance money to help Winnie out. Hear that one?" I felt outnumbered and wanted to get someone on my side.

"Yeah, right," he said. "She isn't going to burn shit."

"She was improvising. No worry, beef curry," Winnie said.

"Well, I'll leave you guys to it then. Any cash left over from what B here stole from me? Preschool tried to lie and tell me he was going to get me some of it back."

"It was never yours, cuz. Besides, we wouldn't do you like that," B said. He was jumpy. Probably took a couple of hits and went straight to the shower.

"OK, I'm outta here then, I guess. Preschool got kids. B, you got any kids?"

"None of your fuckin' business."

"So you don't need anything from me then? OK, I need a beer. I'm outta here."

"We never expected anything!" Winnie said, practically screaming. Her upper lip rose, exposing sharp teeth. I thought she was going to spread her black wings and bite me. Mark walked out with me. "Throw on some clothes, man. Let's grab a beer," I said.

"Nah, I'm OK."

"Do me this favor, come with me."

He paused. "OK, let me shut off my computers. Just a couple beers right?"

"Yeah."

I waited for Mark, turned off the TV and fan in the living room. He came out, and we headed downstairs. "How's Ozzie and Harriet up there?" Mark said, pointing up.

"Stupid. More like Bonnie and Clyde. Ozzie and Harriet is a hard eight in craps. Did you know that? Eight, eight the hard way, a square pair. It's been eight days since I packed up my stuff from Sheila's. Magic Eight Ball. It's weird how life can be symmetrical like that."

In the parking lot, Mark's voice echoed, bouncing off the pillars. "You're talking weird, man. How much you drank?"

"A ton in the last eight days. Maybe eight beers tonight? I think I rolled at least eight hard eight playing craps last night. I must've spun an eight when I played Life the last time. Does the number eight mean anything?"

"You're talking crazy. Sounds like you had more than eight beers."

"I know seven is supposed to be lucky. I guess that makes eight one past lucky."

"I told you, RL is overrated, man. People always dog me about playing a computer game, saying I could be doing something better with my time. What is better? Nothing out there is better. I make money, I have friends, I have fun. It's the wave of the future."

"It's like crack. Evercrack, remember?"

"No—that upstairs is crack."

We got into the truck. I pulled out from the garage for better reception. The number ending with four eights was easy enough to remember. I was waiting for eight rings, but it only rang once. "May I speak to Preschool?" I asked, sounding weird to myself.

"Yeah."

"This Charlie."

"What's up, cuz?"

"Winnie and B are at my mom's apartment."

"Got an address?"

"Yeah. Bring a wooden stake."

I gave him the address. There was an eight in it. I hung up the phone.

"Jesus, man. Why'd you do that?" Mark said.

"Put them out of their misery."

"I hope nothing happens to my computers."

I drove us to the nearest 7-Eleven and bought a pack of cold beer. I wanted to head to Sandy Beach, take the winding road in the dark. Mark didn't say anything as I guzzled beers and tossed the bottles out the window like grenades. "Incoming!"

Doing nothing was what I was best at. I was tired of that shit. While doing the one-handed slalom down the east coast, I imagined Winnie's funeral. She'd look at home in that open casket. We'd all be there—even me, if Mom would let me. I had to do it; it was never going to stop. We'd all get hurt sooner or later, and she'd be the invincible one riding away on the motorcycle. Winnie and cockroaches, man; Winnie and cockroaches—the living undead. As for B, well, I figured I was doing a public service. The last thing Hawai'i needed was another wannabe kingpin. As if he were a part of the conversation, Mark changed the topic. "What was up with you last night? You being a prick to Taks? Not that I minded, but it was embarrassing for that girl."

I'd completely forgotten about Taks, Sloane, and Ollie. It was shocking to hear that it was just a night ago. "Ollie leave yet?"

"He leaves tomorrow. He's spending time with the folks tonight, I think."

"What time is it?"

"It's one thirty. Tomorrow's Saturday. I have a raid tomorrow. East Coasters' weekend, so I have to be on early. Think it's OK to go back?"

"Not worried about Winnie?"

"As far as I'm concerned, you're just accelerating the process, you know? I don't blame you. She's my sister and all, but once she stole from Mom, that was sort of it for me. I held her money for her. It was all I was going to do."

I hurled another grenade, turned out my lights, and pulled into the Sandy Beach parking lot. An old Honda Civic with smoke coming out of the cracks in its windows was next to us. "You were too young, but Winnie used to bring me here with her friends."

"Jesus, memory lane, man?"

"I can't believe you don't care," I said.

"Power of indifference."

"No such thing. There's the power of self-interest, though. Everyone got that in spades. No one needs a seminar in that."

A guy popped out of the Civic, squinting at my windshield.

I got out, walked up to him, and said, "When you reach for the stars, make sure you don't get mud on your hands."

Then I hit him and hit him again. There were two other guys in the car. They just looked down. Mark grabbed me from behind. The guy crawled into his Civic and split. There was something about committing violence that made me feel more like a man. I wasn't trying to grip the bottom of the pool anymore. "I killed her, man."

"Well, want to try and save her?"

The air was salty. I smacked my lips. Mark drove, and we sped back to town. My hands throbbed for the first time in my life. Throbbing hands felt good.

Instead of calling Preschool, I called Sheila first. I knew she was probably sleeping, so I was surprised when she answered. "Hey babe," I said, still breathing hard and smacking my lips.

"Charlie?"

It sounded weird, her calling me by my name. "Yeah, babe. I wanna come home."

It was quiet. I thought maybe we got disconnected. "Babe?" I said.

"Sorry, Charlie. Sleep it off."

"I'm serious."

"This isn't home anymore, Charlie. I have to go."

This time the line did go dead. Too little, too late. I wanted to tell her I would never watch porn again, but I knew that wasn't what mattered. I called Preschool. This time it took several rings for him to answer. It stopped ringing, and the other end of the line was silent. "Preschool?"

The voice on the other end laughed. "Preschool can't come to the phone at the moment. But don't you worry. You'll be seeing him soon, motherfucker. The Magic Eight Ball tells me: outlook not so good."

I hung up. "I think it's OK if you go home now," I told Mark.

"Yeah, that's where we're going, right?" Mark said.

"Nah, I think I'm gonna head to my place."

"OK, man. Don't sweat tonight, man. It's one of those things, you know, that people say they'd never do, but you put them in the situation, who knows? If they're being honest with themselves at least. I don't hold it against you. Seems like you're doing it for Mom."

"Yeah . . . Winnie made it, by the way."

After I dropped Mark off, I spun the truck around in reverse so hard that the front end slid across the asphalt, probably balding my front tires. I ran two red lights and got to my apartment in forty-five seconds. At least I wasn't going to have to pack much. The TV, all of its drippings of aluminum foil and wire hangers could stay. I grabbed my boxes, happy that I'd never made a home of this place, and sped off. I was surprised that B had managed to get the jump on Preschool, but it was his voice on Preschool's phone and I had no doubt he was coming for me. The big problem now was that I had no place to go. I was a man with no plan. I was going to feel much better once the sun came up.

Seven Out

1

I'D HEARD ONCE that red cars get into more accidents than cars of any other color. It made sense, red being the target color and all. Red was bulls-eye. The thought made me feel worse about sleeping in my red truck outside Preschool's gym. I didn't have much of a hangover; I felt more dehydrated than anything else. Then another feeling struck me, one that was unfamiliar: it was the morning, but I wanted to drink. It was a sick feeling, but there was also a crazy sense of pride that came along with it. It was like I'd been called up to the majors.

Whenever the word alcoholism popped up, it seemed to always come with the word denial. This seemed stupid to me. Only a dummy who was an alcoholic could fail to see that he was an alcoholic. I mean, if you found yourself wanting to drink often, you were an alcoholic.

I had big problems, and it seemed alcoholism wasn't tops on that list. I drove to the store and bought myself a forty-ounce beer, thinking that a six-pack was too much because the last beers would be warm when I got to them. I went back to the gym parking lot and waited. I turned on the radio and switched it to the Hawaiian-music station, trying to create a positive mood and all, considering it was the big Hawaiian twins I was hoping would help me out. Every hour or so, I drove to the store to get another forty, figuring I had to recharge the alternator. By hour six, I was having a hard time keeping up. I spent most of my time staring in my rear view mirror, imagining B would come at me like a kamikaze pilot and smash his car into mine. I wondered if Preschool had gotten Winnie before B got him. When it starting raining in the late afternoon and I couldn't see much in the mirror, I was glad I'd downed all those forties. It made me more relaxed.

The twins showed up about four. The rain had stopped, but the sky was still smog-gray, and the wind was gusting so hard that it rocked my truck a couple of times. I jumped out to stop the guys. My tongue got a bit twisted up because I didn't know what to call them. Finally I yelled, "Twins!" They turned around and walked towards me. Like the last time I'd seen them, one had a red T-shirt on, the other one yellow, and both shirts had the Hawai'i state seal on the front. The arms of their shirts were so stretched out that when the white one, Keo, scratched his shoulder and the sleeve moved up, there was an indention from the cloth in his skin. Both shook my hand. "Charlie, right?"

"Yeah."

"Wassup?"

"You guys hear from Preschool?"

"Nope, wassup?"

Both of them were graying at the temples. It was weird how it felt like both of them were answering me at once, like there was a kind of psychic connection between them. Then again, I was drunk. "He found B and Winnie last night and I don't think things swung his way."

"What you mean? Da crack ho and da bolohead guy?"

I told them the story. They were pretty straightfaced, and it occurred to me that it might have sounded like I set Preschool up. They seemed to believe me, but there was no way to be sure. People had been bullshitting me all week, and I couldn't tell they were doing it then, and I couldn't tell if they were doing it now. After I told the story, the only thing the twins said was, "Jesus, what time you wen start drinking?"

"Early. I'm kind of nervous, I guess."

"Keaweaimoku your last name, right?"

"Yeah."

"We remember your fadda. He used to take us fishing. Small island. No worry about B. You drinking in da morning, you putting one foot in da grave anyways."

"You guys aren't worried?"

"We worried about Ryan, yeah," they said, using Preschool's real name. "But dis bolohead guy? We not worried. Every once in a while get one guy think he all nuts, pull dis kind shit. Watch too much fuckin' TV, movies whateva. No worry about us, cuz. You come with us."

Keo grabbed me by the wrist. His hand and forearm were covered with curly black hair. They led me to their car, a black Chevy Tahoe SUV. I felt like a child being walked across the street. I hopped in the back. My head started to pound because no alcohol was coming in. I wanted a beer. "Hurricane watch is up," Ula said. He was driving.

Keo turned around and winked at me. "No worry, Hawaiian. We take you home. Our Mom make da best beef curry. We get one pot at home."

I wasn't very hungry. "I know you guys don't know me. Thanks."

"You family, cuz. No worry."

"Man, what I need is a job. I gotta get me a new place or I'll end up living downtown or on the beach or something."

Ula laughed. "One thing at a time, braddah. First you eat."

"How long do you think it'll take for you guys to find B?"

"Depends. You said he get one chick with him, yeah? One chick and one big chunk ice?"

"Yeah."

"Fast den, real fast. Small island. Maybe if he wen pull da mountain man by himself, take long time. But one chick and ice he gotta dump? Fast."

Keo started dialing numbers on his cell phone. Ula had both hands on the wheel. He was so wide that his shoulders bulged out from both sides of the seat. I wanted to smoke a cigarette. We were going though Kahala, heading toward Hawai'i Kai. When we passed the fancy houses in Hawai'i Kai, I figured they must live in Waimanalo. The rain started up again and slowed traffic. We passed Sandy Beach. The ocean was messy, blown out by the wind. After we passed Sandy's, the land turned green. "Someone told me the other day there aren't any Hawaiians left," I said.

"Sounds like something your fadda would say," Ula said.

"I think so get about a hundred thousand of us left," Keo said. "But I dunno if get any pure-blooded Hawaiians left. We get a little more den one-third, which is more den lots of people."

"One hundred thousand—that's less than ten percent of the population. And like you said, most of those got like less than one-third Hawaiian blood."

Keo was talking on the phone. "Get some in da mainland prolly, but yeah, we didn't say we wasn't a dying race," Ula said.

We turned left and headed toward the mountain. "How many Japanese, Filipino, and haole people got, I wonder." I said.

"A fucking ton," Ula said. "And dat's just in Hawai'i. Get millions and millions worldwide. But we only get maybe one, two hundred thousand worldwide."

My head started to clear up a bit, but my stomach was churning. I didn't know why I was asking all of these questions, as if the twins ran the census bureau. I looked out the window, looked at the green and tried to feel a connection. All I saw were trees, though. We ended up in front of a big single-story house. Parked out front were a pick-up and Honda Accord. A big boat was on the side, sitting on a rusting trailer, and covered by a blue tarp. Every time the wind gusted, the tarp puffed up like a parachute. We got out. Chickens were clucking behind the house. A few wilting plumerias tumbled in front of me. "Only you guys live here?"

"Us, our wives, our kids, and our madda. Only Mom stay home, though. Da kids went beach with their moms even though get hurricane watch."

I expected something else from the guys who supposedly ran stuff in town: some kind of mansion behind a stone wall, cameras hovering over the driveway; maybe half a dozen cars, at least one of them a Lamborgini Diablo; a pair of rottweilers or maybe dobermans, like on Magnum PI, barking at the gate. Basically, I expected Millionaire Estates, but I was looking at Countryside Acres.

The inside was even more of a letdown. Toys were scattered across the carpet. Keo stepped on a GI Joe action figure. "Fuck," he said.

The living room was all toys: half for adults, half for kids. The twins had an impressive audio-visual thing going on. Big-screen TV, Sony stereo with speakers mounted in each corner of the room. On one side of the huge TV was a glass case filled with different kinds of seashells. The other side of the TV made me feel more secure. A tall case was filled with guns—high-caliber rifles and shotguns—even a couple of compound bows. A book with Ted Nugent's picture on it sat on a stack of magazines on the coffee table. Keo moved a basketball out of his way with the tip of his foot. Ula called out, "Mom!"

An old Hawaiian woman walked out from what looked like the kitchen. She was a big lady, probably about as heavy as I was, but shorter. One of her calves was swollen, and tiny veins spread across it. Her hair was stark white, and she wore it up in a ball, a chopstick holding it in place. "Mom, remember Uncle Blackie? Dis his son, Charlie."

The old woman walked to me and kissed me on the cheek. "You come eat," she said, taking my hand and leading me to the kitchen.

She walked to the stove and turned a knob. A big pot was on, pushing down the metal coil beneath it. "You want something to drink?" she asked.

Ula walked in. He was the same color as his mom. The dad must've been the whiter one. "No give him beer," he said. He opened the fridge door, which had a calendar and a magic marker dangling by a string. He pulled out a couple of cans of iced tea and tossed one to me. "Sober up," he said.

"You guys eating, too?" the mom asked.

"Yeah," Ula said. "Da kids, too. We all eating. Dey on their way from da beach. Crazy, going beach on a day like dis."

"I told dem," the mom said.

Ula led me to the dining room, which was decorated with pictures. I sipped on my juice as I looked at all of the photographs. A lot of them were typical: Ula and Keo as little kids, roly-poly, opening presents in front of the Christmas tree; Ula and Keo in football uniforms, posing on one knee; Ula and Keo at a prom, busting the seams of their tuxedos. Some of the pictures were much older. Some were of so-and-so place a hundred years ago. One of the old ones showed three big Hawaiians sitting on the boat that I'd seen outside. The color was faded. One of the guys was my dad. He was holding an ulua over his head of white hair. It was the only picture of him in the room.

We ate dinner about an hour later. The entire family ate at the same table, a shiny koa one with a sheet of glass over it. The kids chattered away, asking for this or that, mostly toys from their dads. The wives looked like haggard ex-prom queens. One was Japanese; the other looked mixed something or other. Both were younger than their husbands. The kids wouldn't stop talking, so I slid outside to smoke a cigarette. The backyard was packed with chicken cages, but the birds were quiet now. It was really quiet in fact, except for the wind whistling something in my ear. I put out the cigarette, but didn't know where to put the butt. I palmed it and took it in the house with me, feeling self-conscious about the smoke smell.

I sat back down at the table. The kids were taking their plates to the kitchen, and the wives were washing dishes. One kid was stranded in a high chair. He threw a mushy piece of carrot at me and laughed. Ula told his wife to take him out of the room. The mom apologized and pulled the baby out of the chair. "You got a college degree, yeah?" Keo asked.

"Yeah. Business—marketing."

He slid a piece of paper to me. "Call dis guy. He might get you one job down at da pier. He one union guy, was my dad's friend."

I picked up the piece of paper and put it in my pocket. "Thanks, man."

"No problem. No worry, it's a legit job."

"You guys have a helluva family here."

"Thanks. Rowdy, but yeah, good family. Family is everything."

"They know what you guys do?"

"What we do?"

"I dunno, you guys aren't gangsters or whatever?"

Ula looked at Keo and laughed. "See, I told you: too much movies. You get one place for crash?"

"Shit."

"What?"

"I left my boxes in the bed of my truck. I forgot about the rain. All my stuff is soaked probably."

"We'll get your truck tonight. You can crash here for a while."

"Thanks. Why you guys being so nice?"

"Mom would kill us if we wasn't. See dat old lady with the gout leg? She da gangster," Ula said.

"Your dad was her cousin. Gotta take care. Ohana, braddah."

A cell phone rang. Keo answered it. He said a couple of words into the phone, stood up, and jotted something down on a ripped envelope. He hung up. "Dey found Ryan," he said.

"Let's go," Ula said, looking at me.

We left before I could sneak a beer out of the fridge.

2

We went further country, into Kahaluu, passed a few Hawaiian hedges—broken cars lined up on front lawns—and drove up to a crime scene on the side of the road. Just like on TV, there were squad cars and yellow plastic tape with "Caution" printed on it, blocking off the area. The twins talked to the cops, who let us in. We crawled through mangroves. My shoes were getting wet. The water had a stagnant smell to it, like soup rotting on a stove. I couldn't see very well because of the dark, but when we got out of the bushes and I looked out, I thought I saw a body facedown in the low tide. I wouldn't have seen it except that the body was wearing something white. It was probably Preschool. While the twins talked to another cop out in the water, I thought about that burial stuff Preschool brought up last night: who would show up and how life went on after. I felt bad about laying that Saturday Night Live stuff on him. Mud gushed into my shoes. My socks were wet, and I decided that I wasn't interested in seeing my first dead body, so I stepped back through the mangroves and stood by the twins' car.

The cops were chatting about a basketball game they'd seen on TV last night. Then they started talking about Preschool. "Seen that big elephant fucker in the water?" one asked.

"Yeah, big steroid fucker. Must've made a good target. How could you miss?"

"No hope in dope."

The other one laughed. "How about these fuckin' twins, man? I'd like to try one of them."

"Nah, they cool."

"Guys like that can't move. Fuckin' dance around them all night."

"Good target."

"Who's this guy?" one said, noticing me.

"Who fuckin' cares."

"What you looking at?"

I turned away. I'd gone to school with a couple of guys who later became cops. It blew my mind that they carried guns now. They were crazy motherfuckers in high school. I wondered what was on that psych test you had to take to become a cop. There was this thing about the popo that most people missed: cops were the biggest, baddest gang on the island—the bad ones anyway.

The twins walked back through the mangroves. They shook hands with the cops. The one who wanted to try one of them was grinning as he shook their hands. We got back into the car and drove further east. The twins were quiet. Ula said, finally, "The fucker scalped him."

We turned off the highway and up a small road. The headlights shone on the dirt and gravel, and the tires spit gravel into the wheel well. We went over a single-lane bridge with white, wooden rails. There was probably a stream underneath, but I didn't hear water. Everything on the sides was green.

Further up, we turned into an even smaller road. California grass slapped the rearview mirrors. We pulled up to an old house. Ula stopped the car in front of a garage made mostly of green corrugated fiberglass. There were cars in the grass, mostly old ones. One truck was so corroded that the tailgate was gone and the bottom of the bed was almost completely rusted. I could see the rear axle clearly. When we got out, two pit bulls came charging toward us, barking like crazy. Keo lifted a foot and kicked one of the dogs in the head. It staggered, then fell. The other dog ran off, yelping. Ula pulled a plastic case out from under his seat—one of those cases that look like a ratchet set—and removed a gun from it. It was a Glock, I think, the black semi-automatic made out of ceramic, or something like that, so it didn't rust. Ula tucked it in his jeans, under his shirt. Light shone from behind the house. The sounds of a ukulele, accompanied by a guitar, came from the direction of the light.

The guys behind the house were singing and playing music. They sat around on unfolded chairs, and most were keeping a can of beer between their feet. The guy playing the guitar had a joint dangling from his lips. One guy, a skinny dark one, lit up a pipe, smoking ice. They were all Hawaiian, but not nearly as big as the twins. I was taller than any of them. The tallest one wasn't even six feet. None of them looked scared when they saw us, but they stopped playing music and the one with the ukulele got up and gave the twins a hug, and shook my hand. He was an older guy, around fifty, skinny as hell, and dark like the one smoking ice. The smoker could pass as his son. No women were there. "Come in da house," the older guy told the twins. He handed me the uke. "Kanikapila with da boys," he said. He led the twins inside.

The others introduced themselves. I went to each one and shook his hand. The one smoking ice held the glass pipe in front of me. "Like one hit?" he asked. I shook my head. "Grab one beer from da cooler den," he said.

I grabbed a beer and sat down. It was windy, but not cold. It was a humid night, probably an hour or so until it would start raining again. The chairs were set up in a circle around a lantern. The guy with the guitar and the joint said, "So what, know how play?"

"I used to." I strummed slowly, doing my Gs, Cs, Ds and my Fs, B-flats, D-minors, and C-7s. Then I tried to pick a thing or two. It was better to stick to the strumming.

"What you like play?"

"I dunno if I remember any songs," I said. Then I started strumming "Moloka'i Slide." It was one of those F, B-flat, Dminor, C-7 songs, easy enough to play. Back in the day, I must've been able to play a good thirty songs with those chords, anything from "You're Still the One" to Richie Valens's "Donna." It took me a while to get going, but it was coming back. My fingers tripped over the strings a couple of times, trying to go too fast, but I didn't stop and start over. I just plowed ahead, shaking my wrist like my hand was on fire.

All of the guys were singing. The guy playing the guitar had a good voice. It was one of those happy-sappy songs that had made me want to quit playing the uke in the first place, but now it was bringing back old feelings. The line "Take me back to da kine" sort of resonated, considering my current circumstances.

"Not bad, can tell you rusty, but not bad," the guy with the guitar told me. The two pit bulls came around, and the one Keo had kicked sniffed my shoe carefully, then licked my hand.

We played a couple of other songs, and when I sang on the last one, the guys were impressed. The kid smoking ice grabbed the uke from me, and they asked me if I remembered the words to "Kawika." It was one of those songs with all-Hawaiian lyrics, but I told them I'd give it a shot. I was glad I didn't have the uke. The words came back to me, and even though I could hear my mistakes, I kept plowing forward. I thought about my revelation the other night: that good music was about trying to sing to a nonexistent God, and I thought maybe a part of it was also hearing your mistakes but going forward anyway. I knew that good singing was about hearing your mistakes. Maybe good living was about the same damn thing.

I managed to do a decent job with it. There was a lot of drama to the song, and I imagined it wasn't about flowers or white beaches or the good old days. But when I asked if anyone knew what the song meant, no one could tell me. I was having a good time anyway and I'd almost forgotten that I hadn't smoked a cigarette in a while, but the taste of beer reminded me.

When the twins came out of the house, I was on my third beer. They motioned to me to come with them. I shook hands with everyone again, and the guitar player shook my hand hard, pressing a little plastic bag into my palm. The bag had a small rock in it. I put it in my pocket, then headed back to the car. The rain was coming down now, and the guys scrambled toward the house, one hustling the cooler in his arms.

Before we got into the car, Ula pulled the gun out from under his shirt and put it back in the case. As we drove off, Keo said, "We taking you back to your truck."

He didn't mention my crashing at their house, but I understood. We took Likelike back to town. The rain poured down harder, and thunder came, sounding like bombs being set off in the mountains. "So, is it safe for me to stay in town?" I asked.

"Should be cool," Ula said. "B stay in Kahaluu supposedly. He trying for dump some batu off on dose guys."

"He smoked with dose guys," Keo said. "He going be up all night."

"They didn't see Winnie?"

"No, was just B, dey said."

The rest of the ride was quiet, except for the rain beating on the windshield. Before we got back to the gym, I said, "Sorry about Preschool. He was a nice guy."

"Yeah, he could be one real prick sometimes, but he was one nice guy," Keo said.

I couldn't have said it better myself. Then Ula said, "Fucka could bench a ton."

And that was the eulogy of Preschool. I thought about his wife and kids and wondered what they'd say to that.

We got back to the gym. The windshield of my truck was shattered, and the hood was ripped off. When I got out to look for the hood, I found it in the bed, bent in half. All of my boxes were gone. I wanted to laugh. Nine days ago, my biggest problems had been Sheila and ABC. I understood the wrecking of my truck, but why had the hood been folded in half, then thrown in the back? Only someone truly demented would do a thing like that. I would look like Buford T. Justice driving around in that thing. The twins got out of their SUV. "That fucka gotta be put to sleep," Ula said. "Come with us."

I got into the SUV, wondering why my truck hadn't been set on fire. It would have been a Winnie thing to do. "Any place we can drop you off?" Ula asked.

I couldn't think of one. A bar would've been good, but I wouldn't have any place to go after that. "I can't think of one."

"You come back with us then," Ula said.

Keo cleared his throat. "I dunno if dat one good idea," he said. "You heard him. He no more no place for go."

"We got stuff for do tomorrow."

"He should come with us for dat, too. Da more, da merrier."

"He good college boy. He shouldn't get involved."

"He stay involved. You seen his truck?"

It was the first time I'd heard the twins disagree. "I can just crash in town someplace. It's cool," I said. I wanted to show that I could take care of myself. What I said didn't come out like assertion, though. It sounded more like a polite shot at getting pity. "Seriously, I can find a place." Pity again.

Keo sighed. I wondered if he was maybe the leader of this duo, the one who got the final word. I doubted it, though. It seemed more like if one refused to back down, the other would comply, no problem. "You even like come with us tomorrow?"

"I could if you need me." I was leaving the ball in someone else's court again. It was like those stupid conversations Sheila and I used to have: Where do you want to eat? Where do you want to eat? Anything is fine, up to you. Nah, up to you. I wanted to break out of it, so I squeezed my hands together and added, "Actually, I want to go. Looking for B, right?"

"Not looking, finding," Ula said.

"I could do that."

"We ain't robbing, by the way," Keo said. "It isn't about money anymore, and even if it was, dat's not your money. Ryan might have said different, but not yours."

He didn't trust me. He figured I'd sold Winnie and B out because of money. Speed up the inevitable and score some money to boot. "It's not about the money," I said. "I can't do anything until this guy B gets off my back. I just wanna move on, you know?"

"OK, you can crash our house den," Keo said.

Ula turned around and faced me. "So what you doing after all dis done?"

I thought about that and figured these last days had done nothing to help me in that department. I still had no clue what I wanted to do, but it seemed I was at least narrowing my options, or my options were narrowing me. I knew Sheila wouldn't take me back, and ABC wouldn't either; not that I really wanted them back. I swore to myself that my Bolohead Days were over, and the possibility of Mom and Taks not liking me much right now made that decision easier. I wasn't even aware of it, until that moment, sitting in the car behind the twins, rain beating on the windshield, that I'd cut my ties with all my old songs, that I was no longer in danger of going through life simply repeating tired habits, and the uncertainty of that was scary. The cut wasn't a clean one, though. It was messy, and it wasn't over yet. "Maybe I'll check out that job you guys were telling me about."

"Get a hobby or something. And not drinking beer. Something to keep you out of trouble," Keo said.

This made me think of Mark, and his Everquest. Maybe he had it right. That game of his kept him out of trouble because he was indifferent to everything else. He had all he needed: friends, fun, challenges, good times and bad—all without risk. He wasn't sitting behind two pissed-off Hawaiians with a dead cousin, and he never would be. EQ was safe. It gave his brain all the stimulation it needed, but more important, it gave him stroke, more mana, more lima ikaika than Mark, the ex-valet, community-college dropout would ever have. And all that power, all that admiration that his alter ego, Bolo Badcow, had come risk-free. More people knew who Bolo Badcow was than who the Rapozo twins were. More people knew who Bolo Badcow was than there were Hawaiians on the face of the earth. The population of EQ junkies, just one of many computer games, exceeded the population of an entire race. Still, playing that game didn't seem like living, whatever living was. "Yeah, I could probably use a hobby."

They took me back to their house in Waimanalo. Everyone was sleeping. The twins tip-toed through the door, but all of that weight on the tips of toes made more noise than me using my whole foot, walking lightly. "Crash on da couch," Ula whispered. "We wake you up tomorrow."

"Can I grab a beer to get me to sleep?" I asked.

Keo shook his head. "Just go sleep."

The couch was one of those big, L-shaped sofas, and after I put the back cushions on the floor, it was actually quite roomy and definitely more comfortable than my sleeping bag. Thinking about the sleeping bag reminded me that I hadn't put it in the back of my truck with the boxes. Instead, I'd put it in the cab of my truck. This meant I still had one thing left, which was comforting. I tried getting to sleep, knowing it'd be a big-time challenge without much alcohol in the system. I tossed and turned, laying on just about every part of that big couch, trying to find the sweet spot that would knock me out. I might have been able to fall asleep except for the noises.

I was used to falling asleep to the sounds of traffic and the periodic airplane, flying overhead, but this place had none of that. The noise from machines could be reassuring. When you heard the wind whistle at night, your mind screamed, "Ghost!" But a whistle followed by the sound of a car downshifting from fourth to third reminded you that there was no such thing as ghosts. When you heard the bushes shake suddenly, it sounded like a big animal was creeping up on you, but a jet flying overhead reminded you that there were no big animals in town, just the occasional crackhead thief, which for some reason was a more comforting thought. None of the reassuring sounds were at this house. When the wind whistled, I heard ghosts; when the bushes shook, I heard giant wild boars. When little feet rattled the ceiling, I wondered how big the rat was and if I'd wake up in the morning with one ear nibbled off. I was in the land of vampires and zombies now. Watching a dull light come through the window was the last thing I remembered, that and the chickens shaking in their cages.

3

There was no rat when I woke up. Instead, a little girl, maybe three years old, was lying on me, smiling. Her face was right above mine, and she was rubbing the top of my head, fascinated with the stubble. When she saw that I was up, she jumped off, falling on the sofa cushions I'd put on the ground the night before. She bounced off the pillows like a stuntman, then went running down the hall. Keo came out to the living room, wearing jeans and an old T-shirt. "You get clothes or what?"

I sat up and rubbed my eyes. "I don't got nothing."

"I'll get you one shirt den. You only little bit taller den me. What's your waist?"

"Thirty-nine," I said, embarrassed.

"Same as mine, I let you borrow jeans. You betta wash um, eh, after."

I went to the bathroom. The linoleum on the floors was new, but there were gaps between some of the tiles, and there was a rotting hole where the pipe went through the ground. The toilet rug was pink, and some towels were olive green and others purple. Nothing matched. I pulled the ice out of my pocket. It was small enough to wash down the sink. I emptied the plastic bag and put on the clothes Keo had loaned me.

Even though he looked a lot bigger than me, wider at least, the clothes fit well. The shirt was worn down from washing so much that the blue material seemed to have a gray haze over it. The jeans fit well, too. As I walked past the mirror by the door, I caught a look at myself and liked what I saw. I looked very local, whatever that meant. The girl who'd been on my stomach earlier peeked from around the corner, held her hand over her mouth, and laughed. She went running off, still looking in my direction, and almost collided with Ula. Ula swept her up with one hand before she hit him. It was a scoop and catch. Her hair was light brown, which led me to believe she was Keo's kid. It was the same color as Winnie's hair. "Dis one is one rascal," Ula said. He put her down, and she ran off towards the bedrooms. "Keo stay out by da truck already. We go."

"Where we going?"

"We going pick up some boys, then head for Kahaluu. We going derby."

"Cock derby?"

"Yeah."

It was another place I'd never been to before, a cock derby. Taks used to go a lot, and there seemed to be one somewhere on the island almost every weekend, but I'd managed to miss them all. I only had about twenty bucks in my wallet, but I guessed we weren't going there to gamble. We headed out to town first. The rain had played itself out, and all that was left was a bright, sun shiny day with light trades, the kind of day you'd see on a postcard or calendar in ABC Store. It was Sunday, and it seemed like a nice day to be outdoors while watching chickens flurry and bleed.

We picked up three other guys. All of them were Hawaiian, but much smaller than the twins. One was Keoni, Preschool's cousin, who'd turned me on after the crap game. He sat by me. The other two guys sat in the back. One of them was a skinny guy who looked especially rough. He had tattoos on his arms that looked like the drawings of a six-year old. One was a really bad picture of a palm tree that was scribbled over with more ink. That was his version of tattoo removal. All three of them carried plastic cases that looked like ratchet sets. It looked like we were heading to shop class, not a derby. Keoni leaned over to me and whispered, "See any of your money back?"

"Nope."

"When we find this guy, let's see what's in his pockets. Need to find which car is his, too."

"OK."

"I heard what happened. You sell out your sister, you should at least get something."

According to my version of morality, which was admittedly very flimsy, I didn't deserve a dime. But I nodded my head at his secret plan as he whispered it in my ear. Keo was on the phone again, and Ula pulled the plastic case out from under the seat while driving. He handed it to Keo. "You ever shoot a gun before?" Keoni asked me.

"I've never even touched one."

"OK, never mind then."

The guy with the tattoos in the back said, "Listen to dis fucka, fucking Billy da Kid. Da only thing you shot was bottles in your backyard."

Keoni turned around. "Well I plan on shooting more than that today."

"Yeah, yeah."

Keo put the phone down, muffling it against his leg. "Shut da fuck up," he said. Then he went back to talking. Ula put in a CD. It was Iz's "Hawaiian Suppa Man." All I could think was, at least these guys didn't get psyched up to Tupac. Then I thought about asking for a gun, too, since it was me B was after, but just looking over at Kaipo playing with his made me squeamish. I felt sick having that thing so close to me. Keo hung up the phone. "Makeloa going meet us there," he said.

"Man, why'd you call him? I hate that fucker. 'Makeloa'—the guy ain't even Hawaiian."

"Mexican is closer to Hawaiian than most," the other guy in the backseat said. "They part Indian, part Spanish. They got Indian."

"Don't start that shit," Keoni said. "Samoans closer to Hawaiian than Mexican and you hate Samoans."

"Yeah, fuck Samoans," the guy in the back said.

Ula looked into the rearview mirror. "Shut da fuck up," he said. I wouldn't have been surprised if he'd reached one hand back at Keoni like a put-out father. Keoni reached into his pocket and pulled out a small bottle of pills. He took a couple out and put one in my hand. He winked. "I didn't know there were Mexicans in Hawai'i," I said.

"More and more everyday," the tattoo guy said. "When they shipped me to the mainland, I met guys up there. Net-working," he laughed.

"B was saying something about that," I said.

"Got choke in Maui," he said. "Crazy fuckas even taught me how for make bombs and shit, like Al-Qaida."

Maui was another place I'd never been to. "There was a Mexican-looking guy in Mom's bar the other night," I said. "Or at least he looked Mexican. Small-ass guy with a couple of tear tattoos on his face, the kind you see in movies."

The tattoo guy laughed again. "That's Makeloa, and those tattoos, the movies didn't make those up and what they mean."

"All immigrants," Keoni said. "Just like the old days, they taking all the jobs. I'm telling you guys, stirring curry and the prisons is all the Hawaiians get left, and we handing it over. Last night, I was at this strip bar, and this little Vietnamese fucker, the owner, was getting all pissed off cause I was touching one of the girls. I told him to fuck off, and this guy kicks me in the fucking chest. Can you believe that?"

"I don't remember that," the tattoo guy said.

"You went home already, was only me and Danny back there."

The other guy in the back seat, Danny, nodded. "Yeah, was funny. He kicked him, and Keoni stood there, all shocked. The kick didn't even make him step back."

"What'd you guys do?" the tattoo guy asked.

"They started swearing at us in Vietnamese and we left," Keoni said. "Shit, they acting like that, they probably get gun behind the bar."

"Pussies," the tattoo guy said. "We go back there tonight."

"Sunday, though," Danny said. "Shitty chicks."

"Fucking shame, you broke-dick motherfuckers," the tattoo guy said.

"What would you have done?" Keoni asked the twins.

Ula looked in the rearview mirror. "What you think?"

Keoni nodded and popped a pill in his mouth. We started rolling down Likelike, heading towards Kane'ohe, then Kahaluu. It was a familiar route, the same route I'd taken coming home from work every day when I'd lived with Sheila. But we passed that turn, and as I looked back, the tattoo guy was looking straight back at me. "Too late to turn around now," he said.

I turned back around. "So how'd you guys get into this?"

"Keo's and Ula's dad was a bad motherfucker back in the day," Keoni said. "You never heard of him?"

"Nope."

"He was big-time. They said he used to be the toughest guy on the island."

Nepotism. I wondered if all of their fathers had done it as half-assed as this back in their day. "He was your uncle, by the way," Keo said.

"Shit, we all related then," Keoni said. "Small island."

"Yeah," everybody said in unison.

After we passed Kane'ohe and drove into Kahaluu, we saw a bunch of picketers on the side of the road. They were holding signs and waving at cars, like they were running for office or

something. One of the signs said, "Kahaluu: Drug Free Zone."
Some of them sat on lawn chairs, drinking bottled water. It was
hot, a bad day for sign-waving. I watched the faces as we passed.
I recognized one of them. It was the ice-smoker from last night.
Keoni busted out laughing. "How's this drug protest? Look at
that guy. I know that fucker. He's one of the biggest dealers
down this side," he said.

The tattooed guy looked out. "Shit, half these guys are
fucking dealers or users."

Keoni slapped his knee. "Fucking clowns, I tell you. Danny,
doesn't that one fucker owe us money?" He pointed out of the
window.

Danny shook his head as we passed the protesters. "Ice: the
other white drug."

Keoni laughed. "Preschool would hate this shit."

The tour-bus mood was sucked out of the car after Keoni
mentioned his cousin. It got real quiet as we passed the
mangroves on the left side of the highway. It seemed like a weird
place to leave a body. It was too close to the road. I wondered if
B had dragged him through the bushes and mud, or if he'd just
marched Preschool out there, then shot him. It was a lot to drag,
but Preschool didn't seem the type to eat that walking-the-plank
stuff. Either way, it seemed like a dumb place to leave a body.
Then it occurred to me that the last time I'd seen Winnie and B,
they had pounds of ice with them. I'd lay a bet that B was
smoking it. Whether or not Winnie was with him, I had no clue.
But I'd learned my lesson about looking for her earlier in the
week, and at this point, I guessed it didn't really matter. It was a
nice day, though, and the water in Kaneʻohe Bay was like glass.
Granted, it was a brackish-brown glass, but I still imagined
myself throwing a rock in that water, wondering how far those

ripples would actually go, as big as the Pacific Ocean was. Not too far, I supposed, considering there were waves somewhere out there, and a ripple against a wave stood no chance.

We followed the coast for another few miles, then turned left towards the mountains. It was the nature of living on an island: every turn was either mauka—inland, or makai—seaward. We drove about a mile or two in, and asphalt turned to dirt and gravel. The bush was so thick that not much sunlight got through. "We almost there," Keo said. The guys all stuffed their guns in their pants, except for the tattoo guy, who had a holster under a flannel shirt he'd put on. "All you guys gonna shoot your nuts off," he said. "Too much fucking movies."

"I got the safety on, no problem," Keoni said.

The gravel road ended and the truck rolled over sandy-colored dirt mined with big chunks of rock. The truck bounced us in all directions, making me feel like a man walking a tightrope in the wind. There were rows of cars on both sides. We stopped at the entrance. Teenage boys stood guard in front of a sign that had a fluorescent pink arrow, pointing left. Keo rolled down his window. Just like going to the nightclubs with people who had clout, no charge. One of the boys, a teenager, saluted, and we parked the truck right there at the arrow and headed out on foot. "The kids make good money," Ula said. "Me and Keo used to do this." Another Life career card missed.

The small road opened up, more rocks, more tall grass. The cars were packed in. It was like a used-car lot except the aisles were filled, too. No one was getting out of here until the cars nearest the entrance were gone. Keo pulled out a piece of paper and told Ula to slow down. We creeped by the cars. Keo was looking for a license plate. Taks's old, orange Porsche was in the line-up. "Guarantee he supposed to be here," Keo said.

Ula said. "What he did, walk?"

I looked up at the mountains. "Could he be up there?" I said.

"Fuck, I hope not," Keoni said. "Maybe he is, though. Pulling the John Rambo or some shit."

"Jeremiah Johnson," I said. "He told me once he likes to hunt. I'll say this, though, if Winnie is with him, no way he's up in those mountains."

"Our dad used to take us prawning up there," Ula said.

"Stop," Keo said. "There it is." He pointed to a black '69 Camaro. The rear was crammed against bushes. B didn't seem to care about his paint job.

"Nice car," Keoni said.

"Danny and Keoni, stay here," Ula said. The rest of us went walking toward the tarps. I almost expected some of the tents to have signs by them saying "Bearded Lady" or "Strongest Man in the World." Instead, each tent housed lawn chairs, picnic tables, coolers, and little boxes with air holes in them. The roosters were crowing, mad at the sun.

The derby did actually remind me of a small carnival. Cars and grey tents were packed in, corralled in by two old bedroom cottages. The smell of pig shit was everywhere. Ladies and gentlemen, children of all ages were walking back and forth between the tents and cars. We passed an old Filipino couple grilling food under a tent. They were selling steak plates for seven bucks—not bad at all. We passed a group of guys all wearing red T-shirts and sitting under a tarp, playing cards. A kid was curled up in a ball, sleeping on a long, white cooler. One red-shirt held a rooster while another wrapped thread around a yellow chicken leg, tying a sickle knife into place. "Charlie, stay with me," Ula said. "Keo and Lono, you guys go dat way. Me and Charlie going check out da action." Lono was the tattoo guy's name.

"We should stay together," Keo said. "He might not be by himself."

"No worry," Ula said.

Keo and Lono disappeared behind a van. Ula turned to me. "Eva seen one chicken fight?" he said.

"Nope."

"We go check um out."

The pit was under the biggest tent. Six rows of aluminum bleachers surrounded it. People were packed into their seats, shoulders squeezed together. A wall of ladders had been set up behind the bleachers, each one occupied by one or two people balancing near the top rung—more tightrope-walking. Just about everyone was yelling "Even, even" or "Jess, jess."

"What are they yelling?" I asked.

"Even is even odds, straight bet, Ula said. "Jess is giving da other guy odds, ten to eight odds. If you bet hundred bucks and you give jess, you get eighty if you win, pay hundred if you lose. I going find us one ladder."

Ula grabbed a kid's belt buckle and gently pulled him off a ladder. The boy fell into his arms like a baby. "Wassup, Ula," the boy said.

He put the kid down. "Let braddah check it out," Ula said. "No forget, keep one eye out for B."

The ladder wobbled as I climbed it. When I got to the top, I had to squeeze my shoulders between an old Filipino man on my right and a woman sharing a ladder with a little girl on my left. The little girl was yelling, "Jess! Jess!" A Japanese guy across the pit pointed at her and raised two fingers. A two-hundred-dollar bet was made. It was Taks. I didn't want to wave, thinking I'd accidentally make a bet. How everyone kept track of all of this was beyond me.

About ten people were in the pit, which was a fifteen-by-fifteen carpet of dirt, and there were two lines in the middle, probably starting points. The entire pit was gated with flimsy wood. I'd seen playpens more durable. I yelled down at Ula, "How do people know which one is supposed to be the favorite?"

"They know," he said.

The pit emptied, leaving two handlers, two birds that looked identical to me, and a guy in the middle, probably a referee. The two handlers cradled their birds, both a shiny brown/black, and let them peck at each other. Both birds were missing their combs. They were brought to the middle of the pit and let go.

The birds spent so little time on the ground, it seemed like the dirt was electrified. The jumps at each other became uneven, like two balls bouncing, one with more air in it than the other. One feigned landing and jumped again just as the other was about to touch dirt. Before the one with less air could get back up there, the other landed on it, yellow feet first. A knife was buried into the bird's chest, and blood spurted out. The crowd burst. That hurt one didn't give up, though. Even toward the end of the fight, it went after the other, feet tucked under, moving across the dirt like it was on wheels, burning out blood. It occurred to me that the poor bird didn't really want to kill; it wanted to live. Only a thing wanting to live bad could wheel itself around like that.

I looked around the bleachers, through the Hawaiian, Filipino, Asian, and mixed-blood faces screaming for blood.

"Ho, you seen da bugga come down!"

"Mean, ah? Stay all bus up, and da bugga still going. Get heart, dat one!"

Pidgin was alive and well at cock derbies. There was no sign of B. The cheers died down while bets were being settled. The hurt bird finally ran out of gas. The winner pecked at it three times, then died himself.

When the next two birds were brought out, people around the pit began betting with each other all over again. One of the birds had a comb and was much smaller than the other. Some guys laughed. No one yelled even. Everyone yelled, "Seven!" Poor bird. I climbed back down the ladder. "Don't see him," I said. "I'm gonna smoke a cigarette. Want the ladder?"

"I'll come with you."

We walked away from the wall of people, passing food stands, beef stew, laulau, following the guys who'd just lost the fight. When we got near the cars, one of the guys threw the dead bird in the bushes without breaking stride. I stopped and lit a cigarette. The winners came soon after and threw the winner in the same bushes. "Boy, this isn't some kind of health hazard?"

"Like da EPA comes here," Ula said, bending down to tie his shoes.

"I don't think he's here," I said.

"His car's here," Ula said, hunched over, his T-shirt stretching across his back.

"Should we go back to the car?"

"Yeah, why not."

The entire lot was like a landfill. Broken and unbroken green bottles, cigarette butts, stiff chicken corpses, a rusted, burnt-out generator, plastic plates and utensils garnished with dried-up grass. The sun pounded down on all of it, putting the valley on simmer. Keoni and Danny were standing by the Camaro. The heat had to be getting to them. Keoni took a couple of swipes at his legs, like he was trying to kill mosquitoes. "I got into a fight the other night, my first one," I said. I aimed my cigarette at a chicken corpse and fired at the stiff feathers. Missed it by a long shot.

"Yeah, how was it?" Ula asked, making me feel like I'd just told him I'd been laid for the first time. Saying either at over thirty was pretty pathetic.

"Natural, I guess. I was wigging, but natural."

"Fighting when you mad is easy."

"Lotta Filipinos here. Lotta Hawaiians, too."

"Lotta country people."

"Maybe I should move out to the country."

"Wake up to crowing roosters and the smell of pig shit every morning."

"Take me back to da kine. Need to brush up on my pidgin."

"You either talk it or you don't."

I was dizzy. It suddenly occurred to me that I wasn't sure if I was talking to Ula or myself. Ula had to hold me up. The sky was damn beautiful. I wanted to get poetic, maybe etch out a lyric or two about the sunny, blue sky, but it just seemed impossible. There just wasn't a blue like it anywhere, whether on cloth, metal, or TV. The only word I could think of was real. It was the original blue, the blue we tried to copy. Even calling it blue seemed stupid. I caught my balance. Ula leaned me against a car. "Da sun with all da alcohol you drank how many days in a row making you sick, I think so."

"Yeah." I was beginning to feel splotchy, and I wasn't even drinking.

"Shit, look, we boxed in. We go wait for Keo, den we go wait for da derby finish and take off. We take da Camaro, too. Fuck with braddah a little bit."

"You no like make sure he no stay?" Keoni asked.

"Keo was asking around. If he was here, Keo going know."

Keo and Lono walked toward us, both with Bud Lights in their hands. I licked my lips. Bastards scored without me. "Nobody seen him," Keo said.

"His car right here," Ula said.

"Yeah."

"We go take um," Ula said.

"Cherry car," Keo said.

It was nice, but not cherry. Erosion framed the windshield, and tiny black paint bubbles freckled the hood. I tapped on the door. The tapping lacked that hollow sound of newer cars. I kicked it. Not even a dent. I imagined this thing going down the wrong way of a one-way street, barreling through Toyotas and Hondas like a rock through paper. Ula frowned at me. "Cut that shit out."

The twins leaned on the car while Keoni, Danny, and Lono went to work. The hood was open, and the engine was running in less than a minute. Keoni stuck his head out the window, "Ho, get AC in here!"

"Woot, shotgun!" Lono said.

The two of them sat in the front. Danny got in the backseat, pushing a complaining Lono toward the dash. I leaned against the door with the twins. One more of us, and the car would've probably rolled over. I thought about Winnie. "Hey, I wonder what's in the trunk? Can any of you guys open it?"

I walked to the back of the car. I carefully stepped over the thorns, trying to sweep the bush off the rear end. A piece of string was holding the trunk together. More string flopped out of the trunk, dental-floss thin, making a trail leading to another set of bushes about ten feet away. The bushes were so thick that the leaves reminded me of the people watching the fights, crammed together on bleachers and ladders. I picked up the string and gently tugged on it. "Hey guys, what's this?"

It was as if the car was tied to the bushes, so I tugged both ways. Neither would give. It was weird how a thin piece of string could seem so strong. I thought of my father, how he and his friends had once gotten together to pull banana trees out of someone's back yard. The roots had been so strong that they'd had to wrap chains around them and pull them out with a truck. I put down the string and looked towards the tents. About fifty yards away, a little guy with a sweater hood was walking towards me. He was looking right at me, then he started running, getting closer fast. I turned the other way. The string was on fire, a little fire man walking the tightrope.

B stepped out of the bushes, wearing fatigues and smiling, giving the little fire man an encouraging pat on the ass to go get 'em. Then it hit me. I felt like Wile E. Coyote. "Uh guys?"

"Pull the string! Rip it out!" The sweater hood guy was sprinting, waving his hands in the air, and tripping over big rocks. It was Makeloa, the Mexican guy. He looked like he was running with fins on. He pulled out a gun and started shooting. Screams. He stumbled toward us, shooting dirt and the sky. I tugged on the string hard, but it was anchored to something in the trunk. I wrapped the string around my hand and pulled as hard as I could. The trunk popped open and a pipe bomb rainbowed through the air, like a bouquet being tossed at a wedding reception. I was betting everyone stopped to watch it, even Makeloa. My palm was burning. I let the string unravel out of my hand. The pipe hit the hood of a car. Bang! And I mean really fucking loud.

I got up fast, and B was already on me. I wasn't fast enough. He was smiling as he jumped and drove something right in my chest. I stood there for a second, looking down at the handle sticking out, noticed a ponytail tied to the hilt, then I looked at B again. As I fell on my ass, he pulled out a gun, but he wasn't looking at me anymore. I tried to grab him for some reason, hands on ankles like I was trying to shatter the necks of beer bottles. He kicked me, and Ula caught me. His face was black. I couldn't breathe, but I could see. B was running toward Makeloa, firing right at him. Makeloa dropped on one knee and fired. Ula put me on the ground. The sky was damn nice. It was color deserved to be copied again and again, even if no one could ever get it right.

Everquest

1

WHEN I'D BEEN into Everquest, my main character was a monk named Kigai Limubai. Like everyone else, I'd had a necromancer before him, but some guy in Mark's guild was quitting, and he gave me the monk character, which was at level 57 at the time. As a monk, I had to pull monsters to the guild one by one so that we could kill them. It was a tricky job, but I was pretty good at it. I never knew why the toon was named Kigai—hell, I didn't even know why I was named Charlie—but I liked him. When I quit and turned him over to Mark, I missed him, missed the game—not so much because the game was fun, because it wasn't at the end, but because everything else was so boring. It was like going to Bolohead Row. It's why I did a lot of things, I supposed.

In the hospital, I thought about Kigai, about how funny it was that I'd done the same thing in what Mark would call "RL." I went to that derby to pull B, to get him single and out in the open so that the others could pounce on him when he came out.

I was the bait. I was also thinking about him because I wanted to start playing EQ again, either that or move to Thailand. Mark was right: RL was overrated. At least my RL was.

After I woke up, and the doctors told me how lucky I was, I thought about the time Winnie had been told the same thing. She'd wanted a cigarette after her coma, but a smoke was the last thing I wanted. What I wanted, more than anything, was the pain to go away. Apparently, the knife had just punctured a lung, and I'd be out of the hospital soon. I tried going back to sleep, but there was an old man in the same room as me, moaning and moaning—the sound of life ending. I was getting mad, but anger made my chest hurt more, so I closed my eyes and shut out the sick old man, thinking about how stupid it was for me to be there. "That's funny," Ollie would say. I tried to laugh, but it hurt too much, and after the pain went away, I fell back asleep. I dreamed of the sky.

When I woke up, I was in a different room. There were people in this one, most of the people I'd imagined would be at my funeral. Mom was sitting in a chair by my bed, Mario standing behind her. Sheila was standing at the window, looking out. Mark and Taks weren't in the room, but I could hear them outside the door. "Was fucking insane what happened at the derby, yo: bombs, guns, everything," Taks said.

"What happened?" Mark asked.

"That guy, Winnie's friend, went nuts," Taks said. "A car blew up, then he was shooting at everybody till he ran out of bullets. He got shot I don't know how many times before he went down. He was probably on ice."

"Sounds like suicide," Mark said.

"Yeah, looked like it, too."

"Anyone else die?"

"Nope, just him. Couple guys got shot, though, so I guess death count is still pending. Cops came in fast, way out there. One cop is waiting to talk to Charlie."

Waiting to talk to me—I could tell him what color the sky was when it had all gone down; and I could tell him how, no matter how bad you know things are going to turn out, the moment when you realize your life resembles Looney Tunes can be damn funny. I could also tell him that getting stabbed ain't so funny, and that there is nothing funny about staying at a hospital, but he didn't need to hear all of that. Waiting can suck, which he knew, doing can suck even harder, which I knew, and that was that. It was something a typical fighting chicken could tell you, and the image of chickens talking combined with the painkillers made me smile. The painkillers had to have something to do with it because it wasn't that funny.

But it sounded like Taks had a new story, finally, and I was happy for him. I opened my eyes, and Mom was sitting there. Saw my eyes open. She got up and walked to the side of the bed, eyes red, probably from a hangover. She licked her upper lip. Her tongue was speckled with white. She leaned down and whispered in my ear. "Winnie stay OK. She wrote me from da mainland."

"That's pretty funny," I managed to say. She waited for me to wake up to tell me that. Cherry.

And I wasn't surprised. It had never occurred to me before, but I realized that the girl was practically unkillable, like the vampires in Anne Rice's novels. Fucking Nosferatu. That would've made B her zombie, poor guy. She knew he was mind-fucked from going to prison and that he had a grudge against Preschool and the twins, the ones he'd refused to testify against.

Charm, ice, and translucent skin—the siren song, the proverbial apple, the bite on the neck. I felt for B. She'd bitten me once or twice, too.

But it was like me and Winnie had agreed that day I picked her up from prison, the air is dangerous, so I had a hard time holding it against her. I'd never talk to her again as long as I'd live, but I had a hard time holding it against her. All anyone was doing was trying to live, and who was I to talk? "No worry, beef curry." She had us all fooled. It was the thing people missed about ice: yes, addiction is like a disease, a contagious one, and some people can carry and spread it, but survive; while others fold to it, like hepatitis or something. It was cool that I'd had it cut out of me before I could pass it on to someone else.

Everyone saw Mom talking to me and approached the bed. Taks and Mark came in. They all looked stumped about what to do next, like they wanted to pat each other on the back, say, "Cool, he's OK," then leave the room and get on with their lives. I didn't hold it against them, though. It was what I wanted to do. Taks pulled out a small slip of paper from his pocket. "Look, you're famous." It was a small newspaper clipping from the Police Beat section. The article was about as big as an obituary. "A cop was hanging around earlier, wants to talk to you," Taks said, putting the clipping in my hand.

I started to say something, but it hurt too much. "Let him rest," Mom said. They all began filing out of the room. Sheila, the last to leave, kissed me on the forehead and brushed my shoulder with a fingertip. She walked out, too.

Everything in the hospital room matched. The beige curtain went with the white walls, the towels were all white, and my light-blue gown matched the white blanket draped over me. The machines I was hooked up to didn't seem out of place in the room, even next to a vase of flowers, and when the nurse came in wearing a carnation-colored outfit, all of the colors were so light that they all seemed to match. All these light colors were supposed to be comforting probably, but they were making me feel sort of sick. I closed my eyes, thinking that these were the same colors you'd find on the board of Life, especially the pink and baby-blue people pegs. The fluorescent light heightened this effect.

I struggled to get the clipping in front of my face. It said:

Windward Oahu
Man Stabbed, Suspect Found Dead at the Scene
A 32-year-old Honolulu man was stabbed yesterday at a farm in Kahaluu. Witnesses say the suspect then removed a gun from his coat and began firing at others on the scene. Two others, a 40-year-old male and a 25-year-old male, were injured. All three victims are in stable condition at Queen's Medical Center. A 30-year-old Arizona native is being held for questioning.

I wasn't sure why the cop wanted to see me. Most of them couldn't find their own assholes without an army of proctologists helping them anyway. Besides, the newspaper got it about right. Maybe it would've gotten more press if it had happened at a golf course. I didn't really want to talk to anyone; talk was just noise, and I had made enough of that kind of noise the past week. Anything that came out of my mouth now would sound like bad karaoke. I still didn't know what living was, but I knew it wasn't a game. I'd had it with flailing around like a roach in a toilet bowl—that Life career card didn't pay enough. I wanted to burn the whole board and live something fierce.